A WORD WITH THE DEAD

A DCI EVAN WARLOW NOVEL

DCI EVAN WARLOW CRIME THRILLER #17

RHYS DYLAN

WYRMWOOD
BOOKS

COPYRIGHT

Print ISBN 978-1-915185-45-7
eBook ISBN 978-1-915185-44-0

Published by Wyrmwood Books.
An imprint of Wyrmwood Media.

EXCLUSIVE OFFER

Please look out for the link near the end of the book for your chance to sign up to the no-spam guaranteed VIP Reader's Club and receive a FREE DCI Warlow novella as well as news of upcoming releases.

Or you can go direct to my website: https://rhysdylan.com and sign up now.
Remember, you can unsubscribe at any time and I promise I won't send you any spam. Ever.

OTHER DCI WARLOW NOVELS

THE ENGINE HOUSE
CAUTION DEATH AT WORK
ICE COLD MALICE
SUFFER THE DEAD
GRAVELY CONCERNED
A MARK OF IMPERFECTION
BURNT ECHO
A BODY OF WATER
LINES OF INQUIRY
NO ONE NEAR
THE LIGHT REMAINS

A MATTER OF EVIDENCE
THE LAST THROW
DRAGON'S BREATH
THE BOWMAN
ONE LESS SNAKE

CHAPTER ONE

GARETH LLEWELLYN SQUINTED against the October sun, tracking the drone's path across the crisp morning sky. His daughter Megan's eyes sparkled, flicking madly between the drone and the controller in her hands.

'Dad! Look how high it's going!'

Gareth grunted, a mix of pride and mild concern tightening his chest.

The air bit cold, carrying the scent of damp earth and decay from a summer long gone.

They were high on Betws Mountain, an autumn patchwork of rust and gold punctuated by the alien white angles of wind turbines whose blades carved lazy arcs through the air. A low hum carried on the breeze.

'Not too high now, *cariad*,' Gareth warned, but Megan's fingers danced over the controls, urging the drone higher.

Not the most expensive on the market, not by a long chalk, but a £300 birthday present it still was. Maybe it didn't have all the bells and whistles, but still it had a good few with it being foldable, lightweight, having a 4k UHD camera and lots of modes, including auto follow and auto return, not to mention a two-mile range. Therefore, it needed a bit of care and attention on this first outing.

The wide-open, undulating sea of grass that was Mynydd

y Gwair—translated into Grass Mountain—made an obvious choice as a venue.

They stood on an observation point, a rise above Amman-ford. The Black Mountains rolled out to the north, dark and hulking, while to the south, Mynydd y Gwair rose more gently into the light. Their target today, the highest point for miles, stood east of them: Penlle'r Castle. Once a thirteenth-century fortress for the Lord of Gower, now just whispers in the dirt. Most days, you'd drive, or cycle, or walk right past it on the mountain road without even noticing.

But not today. Not from the view the Llewellyns were getting.

The drone dipped suddenly, caught in a gust.

Megan yelped, wrestled with the controls.

Gareth's hand twitched, ready to grab the remote, but she steadied it deftly.

'I've got it, Dad,' she said, jaw set. 'I can handle it.'

Pride and worry warred in Gareth's chest. Eleven years old and already so determined. Just like her mother. God help the boys who would fall for her. God help them, too, because they'd need to get past him first.

He grinned at that.

He'd had to face Megan's grandfather. And that had been terrifying enough the first time. But it was always worth fighting for something you loved, he reckoned.

The drone climbed again, a black dot against wisps of cloud.

Megan whooped.

Then, abruptly, she fell silent.

'Dad,' she said, voice small. 'There's something weird.'

Gareth's brows folded down, and he cupped his hand over the tiny screen. 'Weird how, *bach*?'

'Down there.' Megan pointed, her finger trembling slightly. 'In the shadows. Is that…'

The image sharpened as she brought the drone lower.

Gareth's breath caught.

Sprawled in one of the ancient ditches was a shape. A *human* shape lying motionless. Next to it, a bicycle on its side.

'Can I have the controls, *cariad*?' Gareth kept his voice steady with some effort.

Without complaint, Megan handed over the remote.

Though no expert, Gareth knew how to handle the controller from experience with his own drone. The camera quality was astonishing for an entry-level machine. He manoeuvred closer, easily reading the name on the bike.

The drone hummed, a mechanical insect against the morning sky as his fingers twitched on the controls, heart hammering as he guided the machine lower.

Megan's eyes, wide and innocent, fixed on the screen.

'Dad, what's wrong with him?'

Gareth swallowed hard.

The camera's ruthless clarity left no room for doubt.

The cyclist lay sprawled in the ditch, a broken marionette in garish yellow and blue Lycra. Colours meant for life, not… this.

The Ribble bike, top-end and gleaming, lay twisted nearby. An obscene juxtaposition of precision engineering and crumpled flesh.

And the cyclist's chest remained unmoving. No rise, no fall. Just the wind ruffling the surrounding grass.

Bile rose in Gareth's throat, the taste of fear and panic filling his mouth. He tried to push it down, focusing on the task at hand.

The left arm. Christ. Bent at an angle arms were never meant to achieve. White bone glinted through torn skin.

'Dad?' Megan's voice quavered.

Gareth jerked, realising he'd been silent too long. He forced his voice to steady. 'It's alright, *cariad*. We're going to get help.'

But it wasn't alright. The position of the body, the violence written in every broken line—this was no simple tumble.

'Megan,' he managed. 'Bring it back. Now.'

'But shouldn't we—'

He handed back the controls. 'Do it now, Megan. I need to make a phone call.'

The drone whirred home like an anxious bird.

Gareth's fingers fumbled and felt numb as he reached for his phone. Once he'd dialled, he held it to his ear as the drone neared on its automatic return programme. He gripped one of Megan's shoulders, seeking and giving a smidgen of mutual comfort in this moment of shock and uncertainty. The harsh truth of their discovery was sinking in. It made his movements clumsy and his thoughts foggy.

'We're calling for help,' he said, his voice sounding distant even to his own ears. 'Stay close, *cariad.*'

They watched the drone return and settle on the ground a few feet away.

Megan pressed against his side, her small frame trembling slightly. Her next words came out as a whisper.

'Is he just sleeping, Dad?'

The innocence of her question twisted something deep inside Gareth. He swallowed hard, trying to find the right words to shield her from the brutal reality without lying outright.

A flock of crows let out their mocking caws lower down the mountain, where the trees began. Or were they conferring? Chattering out a statement: Mynydd y Gwair, a site of conflict for centuries, once again a theatre of violence.

Gareth waited, praying for a signal. For someone to make this right.

'Emergency. Which service?'

'Police.' His own voice sounded alien in his head. 'We're on the mountains near Ammanford. Betws Mountain, near the lookout point. There's… There's a body.'

The words hung in the air once he'd uttered them.

What had begun as a birthday adventure had become something far darker in a matter of moments.

Penlle'r Castle, visible only as a rising mound of earth, loomed behind them. Men had died protecting it. But now its ancient ditches guarded a new and terrible secret.

'You say a body. Not breathing?'

'We've spotted it on a drone,' Gareth explained. 'Should we get closer? I have my eleven-year-old daughter with me.

There is no one else around. I can't tell if it's breathing. We're a good mile away.'

'Okay. Stay where you are. A response vehicle is already on the way. Can I take your name, sir?'

He gave it to them.

Megan picked up the landed drone and sat at a picnic table, looking a little morose and anxious.

Gareth unslung a backpack.

'Let's have a cup of tea while we wait, eh?'

He took out a thermos and some cups and fished around for some biscuits.

'Is the drone going to find things like this every time we fly it, Dad?' Megan asked.

Her dad let out a sympathetic exhalation. 'No, *cariad*. It isn't. Here, have a Kit-Kat.'

He smiled at her, oozing reassurance as he spoke, burying the thought that her suggestion had triggered in his head.

A drone that somehow always found the dead and injured? Now that would make a great Stephen King novel.

Megan accepted the biscuit and the tea.

Within a couple of bites, chocolate had woven its spell to make both father and daughter feel a little better about their day out. They were on Kit-Kat number two when the flashing blue lights rounded a bend in the road on its way to them.

CHAPTER TWO

DETECTIVE CHIEF INSPECTOR Evan Warlow sat in a café in Narberth waiting for his partner, Detective Inspector Jess Allanby, to join him for a cup of tea. He'd already had a small pot to himself, which had yielded two small cups' worth, but he'd refrained, with admirable restraint, from buying a cake. His eyes kept straying towards the brownies, carrot cake, and tasty flapjacks, but it was getting late in the day, and he didn't need it.

Temptation was a terrible thing.

By way of distraction, he turned his attention to his phone.

Leo, his Australian grandson, had brought home some play school art, which he'd proudly posed with. Of course, having been praised for his efforts, he'd wanted to do some colouring at home, and Reba, his mother, had sent a video from Perth. A classic of its kind where everything had started off rosy, but descended quickly into chaos when baby Eva, who'd been having her tea at the time of her brother's colouring in, lobbed a lump of squishy avocado onto the masterpiece Leo had been working on, triggering a toddler tantrum from him and giggles from the baby. Leo only stopped wailing when Reba brought out a frozen yoghurt on a stick to placate him.

It worked a treat.

Warlow had watched it eight times. He'd laughed at every showing.

They'd left work a little earlier than usual for Jess to find some gifts for an old friend. The obvious choice had been Narberth, the old Pembrokeshire county seat with a history as long as his arm, full of galleries and independent shops and eating places.

Through the window of the café, across the street, sat Fire and Ice. A shop that sold spirits and wine and artisan ice cream with not a dragon in sight.

George R.R. Martin, eat your Winter-is-coming heart out.

In fact, it would likely be a toss-up between tea and an ice cream for Jess since she was a self-confessed gelatoholic.

Warlow wondered if he ought to call in and get a bottle of his favourite Jin Talog, since they were running low and this was one place that stocked the small batch gin. Regrettably, the company had ceased production so these remaining bottles were a rare treat.

Jess might even leverage the ice cream as a celebratory one since today the builders had begun work on the property she'd finally, officially bought with money from the sale of the house she'd shared with her ex in Manchester.

Cloddfa, an old Welsh word for quarry, was a proposed three-bedroom barn conversion in Rosebush, which, at the moment, was a few unfinished walls and no roof. Luckily, she'd bought the plot and ruin from the same builder employed to carry out the renovation work. After a busy summer, the contractors were at last free to get on with the job.

Warlow knew the boys, a two-man team with subcontracted trades added as they went along, and he and Jess had planned to visit on the way back to Nevern to see how they were getting on.

At 3.20pm, he got a text from Jess:

All done. Meet me at the ice cream place.

> Now there's a surprise: Goggle-eyed smiley emoji.

Warlow paid for his tea and grinned as he crossed the street.

————

NOT THE INCIDENT Room at Dyfed Powys HQ in Carmarthen. Not this time. Instead, an open-plan office with desks where the detectives could do their paperwork.

Reports. Spreadsheets. Online courses. Diversity training. Professional development. Always something to do.

Detective Constable Rhys Harries leaned against a desk, his brow furrowed as he stared at the bulletin board.

Sergeant Catrin Peters, recently returned from maternity leave, and already almost back to her pre-pregnancy weight and figure, approached with two steaming mugs.

'Penny for them?' she asked, looking up at him.

At six foot four, he towered over her. Towered over most people.

He managed a weak smile. 'Just thinking about next steps regarding promotion.'

'Yes. The honeymoon period after the written exam doesn't last long, does it?'

Rhys sighed. 'It's not only the prep for the interview. It's the responsibility. Being in charge, making the big decisions.'

'You've already proven you can do that as an acting sergeant,' Catrin pointed out.

'True, but it's not the same as making it official. Permanent.'

Catrin placed a hand on his arm. 'Rhys, I've seen you in action. You've got good instincts, and you care about the job. That's half the battle right there.'

He proffered a strained smile. 'I appreciate the vote of confidence. But what the hell am I supposed to do next?'

Catrin held his gaze. 'I know many people who've passed the exam and then sat back. For all kinds of reasons. Shift work, family, the job. Before they know it, they're five years further on and have to re-qualify for the Board.'

'That would not be my plan.'

'Right, if you're serious, I can help. I've got the T-shirt. It's all about competencies and evidence for the same, and interview technique. There are some very good online resources. But the first thing is to know yourself that you really want to do it.'

'I do.'

'And Gina's on board? Because it will eat into your time together.'

Rhys nodded. 'It's all a part of the plan.'

Catrin raised an eyebrow. 'Okay. I'll send you details of the online support and workshops. There are loads of videos. Some free. Some you'll have to pay for.'

'Okay,' Rhys said, unusually serious.

'Anytime. And remember, we've all got your back. Gina's in your corner, and so am I.'

As if on cue, DC Gina Mellings appeared, files in hand. 'There you are,' she said to Rhys. 'I've been looking for you. I wanted to ask you about this report.'

Catrin stood. 'I'll leave you to it. Think about what I said, Rhys.'

As she walked away, Gina threw him a glance. 'What was that about?'

'Sergeant stuff,' he replied. 'Catrin was giving me some advice.'

Gina's face lit up. 'So, you're going for it?'

Rhys chewed his lip. 'I'm thinking about it. I could wait it out. They're talking about scrapping the exam system and going over to SIPP.'

'You'd better explain that.'

'Sergeants and Inspectors Promotion and Progress. No exams. Natural progression. Bit like snakes and ladders. But that's not likely to come in until 2027.'

'Then you should listen to Catrin. Get as ready as you can.'

He smiled at her enthusiasm. 'Maybe. It's a big step. I'll have to prove myself.'

'So, prove yourself,' Gina said. 'The Wolf thinks you're ready.'

Before he could respond, Sergeant Gil Jones sauntered over, a mischievous glint in his eye.

'Ready for what?' he asked.

'Just getting some advice on promotion.'

Gil nodded. 'Things have changed. It was all stone tablets and chisels when I took the written.'

Gina rolled her eyes. 'Here we go.'

'No, really,' Gil continued, undeterred. 'We had to carve our answers into granite. Like the Ten Commandments. Thou shalt not commit overtime without prior approval. All that malarkey.'

Despite his anxiety, Rhys grinned.

'Did you get it first time?' He wisely did not add, 'like me.' The implication was there, though.

Gil tilted his head. 'Third time lucky for me. And I'd be very careful who you ask that question of. People are so easily triggered these days.'

Gina shook her head. 'No, I think only you would be triggered by that, sarge.'

'All I'm saying is you have to tread lightly. Exams and promotion are traumatic and discussing them brings back uncomfortable memories.' He feigned a serious expression. A big feat for Gil. 'We have to be aware of our individual sensitivities, people.'

He let the statement hover in the air for a while, knowing that everyone in that room had read the recent critique splashed all over the media of how much the Service, and indeed all Police Service, had spent on workplace wellbeing and other consultation fees and online courses, whilst at the same time targeted with saving a percentage of the budget on actual policing. 'I expect you've heard the new version of that old Dolly Parton number, *D.E.I.V.O.R.C.E.* It's the follow-up to *I wanna hold your handcuffs.*'

In light of the groans he got, Gil simply said, 'All true.'

Catrin looked across. 'Those are terrible.'

'Okay, come on,' Gil said. 'Welsh karaoke songbook. That's the challenge. I'll start us off…'

He paused, looking pleased with himself, and continued, 'A Bacharach classic as sung by Dusty, *The Leek of Love*.'

Catrin dropped her lids to half-mast.

The door opened, and a man, almost as tall as Rhys, stepped through the door into the office. Detective Superintendent Sion Buchannan walked with a permanent stoop but, nevertheless, stood an imposing figure. He scanned the room before wrinkling his nose.

'No Evan?'

'Personal time, sir,' Catrin said.

'Right. I'm about to rain on his parade. I suggest you get the Incident Room set up. They've found a body on the mountain near Ammanford. I expect he will want to get over there this afternoon, no matter where he is now. We have an ID. A missing cyclist called Russell Milburn. Can I leave it to you to contact him?'

Buchannan ducked out.

'Ammanford. Isn't that Mr Warlow's neck of the woods?' Gina asked.

'He's Swansea Valley by birth, but the Black Mountain's a next-door neighbour,' Gil explained.

'Very much the industrial side of our patch,' Catrin added. 'At least, it used to be.'

Gil picked up the phone. The others watched and waited while he filled in the boss.

At this stage, there were few details. They would come.

When Gil ended the call, he turned to the expectant faces. 'He wants Catrin to run the office with Gina helping on the days she isn't here.'

'Good idea.' Catrin smiled at Gina.

The newest member of the team smiled back. 'I'm looking forward to it.'

'So, that leaves us as shock troops.' Gil threw Rhys a wary glance.

'Back on the road, sarge,' Rhys said with a grin.

It would be the first time that Gil had been in the field since being shot by an arrow on the case before last.

They gathered up their things and decanted to the Incident Room.

Nothing special. Nothing but a large room. One recently used for a domestic violence refresher course. But soon, the desks and monitors and chairs would fill up with CID, indexers, secretaries, and uniformed officers co-opted onto the team. But, as Gil dumped his belongings on a desk, the space was eerily quiet.

'Tidy. We'd better be there first,' Gil said.

'Am I driving, or you?' Rhys asked.

'I quite fancy being chauffeured in the job Audi.'

Rhys grinned his agreement.

Catrin was already pushing two large boards on castors into position. One a whiteboard that would become the Gallery, the other beige, covered in corkboard affectionately known as the Job Centre for posting images and actions.

'Here we all are, back together again,' Rhys said, hands on hips like the Jolly Green Giant waiting for Gil to gather his coat.

As he followed Gil out, he heard the disembodied voice of Detective Sergeant Catrin Peters née Richards.

'*Don't go Brecon my heart,*' she shouted.

A look of surprised amusement crossed Rhys's face. 'She's back.'

Gil nodded his approval. 'Not bad at all as a first attempt, much as I hate to admit it.'

CHAPTER THREE

THEY WERE GETTING into the Jeep, Jess with two scoops of ice cream on a cone and Warlow finishing a one-scoop cup, when he took the call from Gil.

The wordless glance he threw Jess told her all she needed to know.

He finished the call, buckled up, and pointed the Jeep east.

'Where?' Jess asked.

'About as far east as we can go. Another border case on the mountain above Ammanford. Strictly speaking, it's not in our jurisdiction, though only by a couple of miles. But it's a cyclist who's gone missing from our side of the line.'

'Name?'

'Russell Milburn. Catrin should be sending through what intel we have.'

It took five minutes for Jess to finish her cone. The remains of Warlow's ice cream melted slowly in the cup in the centre console.

Jess's phone chimed a notification, as did Warlow's, but it was the DI who opened the information from Catrin and read it out loud.

'Russell Milburn, aged forty-four. Reported missing by his

partner last night when he did not return her calls after a meeting at the Black Mountain Community Hospital...'

She read on in silence, her brows folding as she did. 'Chief Executive of the Dyfed University Health Board.'

She looked up at him then.

'Shit,' hissed Warlow.

No one deserved an untimely death. When it occurred, especially when it arose from unnatural causes, fallout resulted. The dead person wronged, partners, families, sometimes whole communities torn apart. But when they involved high-profile individuals, added layers of complexity got thrown into the lumpy mix, whether political or otherwise.

Warlow felt a familiar tightening in his stomach on hearing this news. Not that he was a stranger to having a spotlight on him and the team. That came with the territory, and he prided himself on knowing that they applied the same rigour to every case. Whether the dead person had been a homeless substance misuser or a fallen-from-grace politician.

Jess noted the clenching of Warlow's jaw muscle. 'Did you know him?'

'Knew *of* him. Tom has some connection down here. Medics he was in school with who ended up back here. Surgeons in the same field. It's a small world. I'm aware from chatting with him that Milburn's appointment was not a popular one.'

'Why?'

Warlow sent her a why-do-you-think look.

'Because of who he was?' she asked.

'Because of *what* he was. The NHS, and all who sail in her, is a contentious sacred cow. Milburn got appointed from an English Hospital Trust. The circulating rumour is that he was brought in to wield a hatchet.'

Jess looked intrigued. 'Did you get that from Tom?'

'Yep. And he got it from his mates in the local hospitals.'

'So, how do you go about using a hatchet in a creaky old vessel that is the biggest employee in the area?'

Good question. A sixty-four-billion-dollar question. And

one that could not be answered without addressing an entire herd of elephants in the room.

Whenever he'd discussed this kind of thing with Gil, or even Jess, it always seemed such a mountain of a problem that clutching at soundbites were as worthy as they were ineffectual.

'No idea.' Warlow's answer grated in his own ears because, like most people, he would have dearly liked to know.

He abhorred the shouted rhetoric from across the political divide. Equally, tales of fifteen hours in A and E, or sitting on a concrete patio under a makeshift tent with a fractured hip, waiting for an ambulance to arrive, sounded so third world as to be hardly credible in the UK in 2025. But the nameless and persistent anxiety of having a safety net of a free service —albeit the social contract meant that you paid for it if you worked through a national insurance contribution—slowly disintegrating before your eyes, buzzed like a persistent wasp. In no small part, thanks to the media headlines and horror stories of a failing service.

'All I know is that his appointment had not been met with open arms. The Health Board is not in special measures, but it had come close.'

'Special measures?'

'A plan to fix problems in a hospital service. Specific steps to make things better for patients. The goal is to improve the quality of care quickly. So, Milburn was an instrument of change. Efficiencies needed to be made, and what better way than bringing in a fresh suit with no true skin in the game.'

'That's lead balloon territory right there.'

'Exactly.'

They fell into a lengthy silence as they processed all of this. Finally, Warlow broke it. 'Looks like we won't be calling in on Rosebush today, though.'

Jess shrugged. 'I trust them to get on with it.'

'Totally, Alwyn and Bryn are great. Salt of the earth guys.'

'You trust them. So, I do too. But I hear so many horror stories about building projects spiralling out of control.'

'Alwyn's a good project manager. They've factored in a percentage margin. Are you worried about the money?'

She didn't need to be. For one, there was enough in the pot. For another, Warlow could, and would without having to be asked, help.

Jess sighed. 'I'm not, really. But I got a text from Ricky this morning while I was shopping. He's asked to borrow some.'

'Oh?' Warlow's brow furrowed. 'Hang on a minute, what about the money he got from the sale of your house?'

A derisive snort followed. 'That is a very good question.'

'So, what has he done with it?'

'God knows. I mean, we had to pay off the mortgage, but it still left a tidy sum. Maybe he's used it on a new place.'

'How much are we talking about?'

Jess hesitated.

She'd fished out a hand wipe from a sealed package in the door bin and was over-zealously cleaning away the last remnants of ice cream from her hands. She didn't look at him when she said, 'Six grand.'

'*Sapristi*,' Warlow muttered. 'That's not exactly pocket change. Did he say what for?'

Jess let out a bitter laugh. 'Oh, he spun some story about needing it for a "business opportunity." Said he's got a mate who's starting up a security consultancy firm, and they need investors.'

'Do you believe that?'

Jess's scathing look answered that question.

'And he thinks you're his personal ATM?'

'Apparently.' Jess squeezed the wipe into a tiny ball. 'It's bullshit. I can smell it a mile off.'

'What makes you so sure?'

Jess's eyes narrowed. 'Because it's Ricky. Ever since… well, you know… the crap with going undercover. The mess he got himself into. It's like he's given up on being responsible. Drinking more, gambling. I've heard rumours he's had formal warnings, though of course, he'd never admit that to me.'

Warlow nodded slowly. 'You think the money's for something else?'

'Almost certainly. Probably to cover some debt he's racked up.' Jess sighed heavily. 'The thing is, part of me wants to help. For old times' sake. But I can't keep bailing him out.'

'It's not the first time?'

Jess exhaled and shook her head. 'I don't trust him with that kind of money.'

'Six grand.' Warlow sucked in some air.

Jess's face morphed into a mix of frustration and lingering hurt. 'I just… I hate that I still care enough to even consider it. After everything.'

Warlow shrugged. 'He sounds desperate. Has he paid back other loans?'

'Some. Others he's conveniently forgotten.'

Classic.

Warlow's mother had run the family finances. She'd never owned a credit card. Though she'd used a credit facility from some of the bigger stores in Swansea when he'd been a child. Mostly, she only ever spent what she'd saved. It sounded light years away from today's modern maxed-out credit card lifestyles.

'Can you ask him for more detail why he wants the money?'

'I could, but he'd only come back with more BS.'

They lapsed into a leaden silence again.

Though it was none of his business, Warlow sensed her anxiety. With exes and money, things had a way of getting messy. He knew that only too well. Denise, his ex, had taken her pound of flesh when they split—she'd made damn sure of that—but in the end, she'd done the right thing. Not that it made the ending any less bitter.

———

'Gᴏᴛ ᴏɴᴇ.' Rhys pushed the Audi up to the speed limit on the A48, which they'd accessed from HQ with no need to go back through Carmarthen town itself.

'Really? Well, you have my sympathies. Haemorrhoids can be a bugger. Like jack-in-the-box zombies. As soon as you push one back down into its hole, another one pops out.'

Rhys's face distorted. 'Who said anything about haem-orrhoids—'

'I can recommend a good proctologist. One not with fingers like bollards, which seems to be part of the bloody job description—'

'I mean a song title,' Rhys insisted.

'For a proctologist? Okay. *Lipstick on your colon*—'

'You said a Welsh karaoke songbook,' Rhys snapped, though he did so through a throaty giggle as Gil's pun hit home.

'I did, indeed. Right, let's have it. I'm sure it'll be worth hearing, judging from the way you've been chewing your lip since we started off from HQ. You've had enough time to come up with a belter.'

'The Whitney Houston classic. *I will always love Ewe…* ewe, as in female sheep?'

'Yes, no need to jokesplain. And not an awful effort, though the sheep reference is a bit stereotypically naff. Not a patch on lipstick and colon, though. And frankly, going the smut route is beneath a man of your talent. That's low-hanging fruit. All been done before.'

'Has it?'

'Oh, come on. Surely you've heard tha classic, *Don't let the nun go down on me?* '

The car lurched as Rhys spluttered with laughter.

'See what I mean?' Gil's face was as straight as a Roman road. 'I'm talking about subtlety. Something like… *I left my Harp in San Francisco.*'

'That's stretching it for Welsh,' Rhys objected.

'Artistic licence. And lipstick/colon is a bloody good title for a smutty song if you could ever write lyrics for it.' Gil shifted in his seat and found something to listen to on the radio.

'Do we need the satnav?' Rhys asked.

'No. I know the way,' Gil said. 'There is only one road up to where they found the body. That reminds me, *Is this the way to Llandisilio*? There's another one for you.'

Rhys refused to grace the joke with the noises of a laugh. But his shoulders shook silently in recollection more than once as they settled into the journey. 'How's the shoulder, sarge?'

Gil rolled his left arm in demonstration. 'Remarkably good, considering the skewering it got. Physio is pleased with it, though.' He did not mention the Bowman, the psychotic killer who had used him as target practice. There seemed no need. 'Only so much time you can spend stuck in the office. *Mam fach*, I've been ensconced with our brothers in financial crimes as it is.'

'Ah, yes, the Napier case. How is that going?'

'Like a snail on diazepam. There is a great deal of stuff to wade through and more arriving each week. Ninety-nine point nine percent of it is irrelevant to me. And guess what? Napier had links to some high-ranking officers who are jittery about giving us access. No one has said anything to me, but there is scrutiny.'

The recent case involving solicitor John Napier's murder by Roger Hunt continued to reverberate. However, posthumous allegations of fraud against Napier opened new avenues of investigation, and Gil, at the behest of higher-ups, had been tasked with delving into the illegal online activities that had initially motivated Hunt.

Gil's motivation remained the faint possibility of uncovering any potential connection to the disappearance of a young boy, Freddie Sillitoe. While the link seemed tenuous, with his extensive experience with Operation Alice, Gil was uniquely qualified to pursue this lead. With Financial Crimes disrupting the Napier estate's delaying tactics, Gil had been eager to seize the opportunity and investigate thoroughly.

'Have you made any progress?'

'A little. But this will be a distraction, no doubt. And talking about distractions, how's Gina's brother... uh, Dan, wasn't it?'

Rhys coughed. As if he was expelling an unwanted crumb. 'DD as we, okay I, like to call him. Desperate Dan. He's back in Cambodia. Apparently, he's done the right thing and moved in with his pregnant girlfriend. In fact, the baby is due any day-ish.'

'He's seen the light, then,' Gil said.

The grin Rhys sent him was impish. 'I never asked you what you actually said to him?'

Not too many months ago, while Dan played cuckoo in Gina and Rhys's terraced rental property and felt entitled enough to smoke pot with his "friends" and fall asleep with earphones on while the TV blared, much to the annoyance of their neighbours, Rhys had asked for Catrin's help in getting Dan to smell the coffee. She had reached out to Gil.

'I said not much at all. Only that we were likely to be keeping a weather eye on comings and goings. Anyone with a firing neurone would interpret that as stop and search. The way his backpack took on a life of its own on his jittery shoulders, I suspect that was something he preferred to avoid.'

'It worked,' Rhys said in a low and appreciative whisper.

'Either that or he caught sight of Catrin knocking on your next-door neighbour's door. That would put the fear of God into anyone.'

They were approaching the Cross Hands roundabout.

'Pull off into the Home Bargains car park. It just so happens that the Lady Anwen was on her way to Aldi, and she has kindly agreed to meet us with a flask of tea and some refreshments for the quest.'

Rhys's eyes lit up. 'I've missed these trips with you, sarge.'

'I think you've earned the right to call me Gil out of the office, Rhys. Once a sergeant, always a sergeant, even if you were acting up.'

'My mother says I've always acted up.' Rhys indicated left and headed up the hill to the car park.

Gil's turn to smile. 'A woman with my sense of humour, if ever there was one.'

CHAPTER FOUR

GINA AND CATRIN sat in front of Catrin's computer screen.

'Righty-ho,' Catrin said, twirling a dry-erase marker between her fingers. 'Welcome to my kingdom of chaos.'

Behind them, the boards that Catrin had placed into position, the Gallery, and the Job Centre, in beige material, stood empty. But on Catrin's screen, photos of the boards from previous cases were kept in a file.

'I photograph them every night in case a cleaner or someone rubs something off. And yes, it's anal, but it has saved my bacon more than once.' Catrin blew up one image.

Gina's eyes widened as she took in the explosion of photos, notes, and scribbles covering the boards. 'Wow, I've sat and looked at these during briefings but seeing this now… it's like arts and crafts for CSI.'

Catrin laughed. 'Trust me, there's a method to the madness. I like to think of the Job Centre as our time machine.' She gestured to a neatly organised timeline at the top. 'I prefer Post-it notes, but I also pin them up in case they decide to un-stick themselves. Past, present, future—all laid out like a demented family tree.'

'And the Whiteboard?' Gina asked, eyeing the photos.

'That's where the magic happens.' Catrin winked. 'The "what if" wonderland. Photos, crazy linking arrows, and basically, it's detective Pictionary until something clicks.' She pushed away from her desk and turned to the actual boards. 'Right, grab a marker. Let's see if you can keep up with my colour-coding system.'

'Bring it on,' Gina said.

Catrin picked up a red marker. 'I use red for active persons of interest.' She wrote POI on the board. 'Green for victim-related things. Blue for us.'

'Seems simple enough,' Gina agreed.

'Questions?'

'Yes, how's it going?' Gina asked, leaning against the desk. 'Three days a week back in the madhouse—are you holding up okay?'

Catrin sighed, placing the marker in a holder attached to the Gallery.

'It's… a change, that's for sure. Some days I feel like I'm winning at life. Other days…' she trailed off, shaking her head.

'That bad?' Gina's voice softened with concern.

'No, not bad, exactly… more challenging.' Catrin's eyes flickered to the framed photo of eleven-month-old Betsi on her desk. 'Especially when she's not feeling well. Last week, she had this really nasty cold and a rash, and I swear, I nearly called in sick myself to be with her.'

'The Wolf would not have minded,' Gina said. 'Still, it must be hard, leaving her when she's poorly.'

'It is. But I remind myself how lucky we are.' Catrin's lips curved into a small smile. 'Mum and Craig's parents have been absolute lifesavers. We've got a shared-care system, and honestly, I don't know what we'd do without them.'

'That's brilliant,' Gina said, a wistful note creeping into her voice. 'Must be nice, having that kind of support network.'

Catrin caught the change in the younger woman's tone.

'We're so fortunate. The cost of childcare these days is astronomical. It's at least £250 a week for someone Betsi's age —how people manage without family nearby.' She shook her head.

Gina nodded, her gaze drifting to the window. 'Yeah, I've heard. It's pretty scary, actually.'

'Gina? Everything okay?'

Gina shrugged, trying for a nonchalant smile that didn't quite reach her eyes. 'Yeah, course. Thinking about the future, that's all.'

'Ah,' Catrin said softly. 'You and Rhys talked about it?'

'A bit,' Gina admitted. 'My parents aren't the hands-on type. My mum said as much. Don't blame her because I'm one of five. Rhys's mum would be all in, but his dad's been ill. So, I don't know how much help we'd get.'

Catrin reached out, squeezing Gina's arm. 'That must be daunting to think about.'

'It is. I mean, I want kids. I think. But I look at you, juggling everything, and even with all the support you have, it's still tough. How would we manage?'

'Hey,' Catrin said firmly. 'People manage. And you're one of the most organised people I know—I remember the invites you did for Jenna's hen do.'

Gina laughed, some of the tension easing from her shoulders. 'God, yeah. Now that I think about it, my colour-coding system was way better than yours.'

'In your dreams, Mellings,' Catrin teased. 'I don't think Mr Warlow would appreciate bubble-gum pink and banana yellow.'

Then, more seriously, she said, 'But when the time comes —if that's what you want—you'll figure it out. And you've got friends here who'll help, right? I have a list of emergency babysitters and wine nights when it all gets too much.'

'Wine nights sound good.' Gina grinned. 'I should practise with a few of those before any hypothetical babies come along.'

'Now that,' Catrin declared, 'is an excellent idea. How about Friday night? I'll get Mum to watch Betsi, and we can have a proper catch-up.'

'You're on,' Gina agreed. 'Thanks, sarge. For listening, and… stuff.'

'Anytime.' Catrin smiled. 'Now, speaking of organising,

why don't you start with the Gallery? Get a photo of Milburn up, and I'll get the tea on.'

As they bent over the desk, the earlier heaviness dissipated. They chatted and laughed, slipping easily between work talk and personal stories. And if Gina occasionally glanced at Betsi's photo with a mix of longing and apprehension, Catrin pretended not to notice. For now, they had work to do, and a Friday night wine session to look forward to. The rest would sort itself out in time.

———

THERE WAS a bit of catching up to do regarding Milburn. His partner had rung the police to register his failure to return home the previous evening. That he had not contacted her since 5:05pm that afternoon had her very worried.

'She rang it in, and the call is logged.' Jess read the messages that Catrin was sending her.

What had also been recorded was the fact that Milburn was a fit, experienced cyclist who had told his partner that he was off on a ride after work. He fancied a spin and intended to go "over the mountains". Perhaps as far as Swansea, up the Valley, and back around to where he'd parked his car in the community hospital where he'd been for his meeting. Not a long trip by cycling standards. Not for a man with his experience, given that he regularly did a couple of hundred miles on a weekend.

'How far is that?' Jess asked Warlow as she related what little knowledge they had of the situation in the car as they headed west.

'If he set off around five, which would give him a couple of hours of daylight, he'd be coming back on A roads. Only thirty miles all told. But with the terrain and hill climbs, etc, it's not a straight run.'

'Returning in darkness?'

'Definitely.'

They both were aware of the standard procedure in cases like this. Initially, a local duty officer would take the report and assess the risk. They'd gather information on the person of concern, their habits, and planned route.

'I doubt they considered him vulnerable because of his age and fitness level.'

'No,' Jess agreed. 'But the fact of him being a cyclist and the planned route raised concerns. By now they'd have begun initial searches along his expected routes.'

Warlow glanced over. 'Had the partner contacted hospitals?'

Jess nodded.

'And the kid finds him with her drone,' Warlow said.

'She does.'

Jess's phone chimed with a message.

'Gil and Rhys are there now,' she said.

'Okay. Tell them we'll be with them in half an hour.'

Warlow chose the quickest route, though not the most scenic. He stayed on the A48, branching east at Cwmgwili. He'd made the run dozens of times. This same route took them to Ammanford town and the police station custody suite that, before the opening of the custody Hub in Llanelli, served as a place to hold suspects, which HQ sadly lacked.

The change from rural to post-industrial always struck him as soon as they reached Cross Hands. Cwmgwili itself once had a colliery, as did most of the villages they now passed through. Tycroes (tee-croees), Pantyffynon, (Pant-uh-fun-on), Warlow kept up a bit of a running commentary and a lesson on pronunciation for Jess as they approached Ammanford, a literal translation of its Welsh name, Rhydaman.

'So, where did it end, the coal?' Jess asked.

'The anthracite field spread west towards Llanelli from here and a long way east, of course. But if you think of a line about halfway between here and where Gil now lives—'

'Llandeilo?'

'That's it. The last coal was mined in and around here in the early 2000s. They say there's more coal there still than was ever taken out.'

'So, why shut it all down?'

'Economics. Cheaper to import it.'

'I bet the communities loved that explanation,' Jess said.

They crossed the River Amman, and Warlow turned south, passing remnants of old pit baths finally being repurposed as the road began to ascend and open out into farmland once more.

'We're at the eastern edge of the patch here,' Warlow explained.

They climbed steadily, the land gradually opening out on either side, passing the Scotch Pine Inn, just a mile and a half from the town, but looking like almost the last property on earth with sheep and open high moorland only as neighbours.

'Wow,' Jess exclaimed, looking around. 'Where the hell did everything go?'

'Welcome to Betws Mountain.'

They climbed past the pylons and turbines marching like a spindly mechanical army across the open, wild wilderness.

Response vehicles had parked in the viewpoint parking area where, earlier, Megan Llewellyn sat while her father rang the police.

Warlow didn't stop at the viewpoint but drove on to the Y-shaped junction that had become the staging post for the crime scene itself. He pulled the Jeep onto the rough grass, leaving two tyres on the tarmac.

There had been rain, and the ground remained soft. Ahead, cars lined the roadway and beyond them stood the unimpressive mound of the highest point in this vast expanse. Where once a Norman stronghold stood against the indigenous marauding Welsh princes to the north and west.

'Gil's up there,' Jess said, reading another text as they unbuckled. 'With Tannard.'

'No Povey?' Warlow was surprised that the chief scientific officer was not around.

'She's caught up with that drowning case in Aberystwyth.'

'Okay. Well, Tannard is no slouch as we all know. Who's the HOP?'

'Sengupta. She's already been. They're waiting to move the body.'

'Okay, let's not hold up the train any longer.'

They got out of the Jeep.

Immediately, the wind began tugging at their clothes, and Warlow reached for a waxed jacket from the back seat. He tasted the promise of rain and a tang of salt in the breeze. From the summit, they would have a view of Swansea Bay, but the weather was reminding them already that here the hills and the ocean were aeons old bedfellows.

CHAPTER FIVE

PENLLE'R CASTLE. Another one of those places with the dreaded double 'l' that had non-Welsh speakers flummoxed in a tautological mouthful. Literally, the summit of the place of the castle. Now there was no castle as such. Not that there ever had been much of one. At least nothing like the imposing structures dotted all over this land.

While Warlow and Jess trudged up the hill, the wind whipped around them. Under what had become a dull white sky, the mountain grass rippled and swayed like waves about them.

Historians had this isolated spot as a blockhouse to house border troops. What stones had been laid were long since taken or fallen back into the earth. All that remained were earthworks with surrounding ditches that might have been water-filled at one time but now were only V-shaped gouges in the ground. Still there as reminders of the "Strive" lands this place sat in.

The words "motte and bailey" rumbled in the back of Warlow's head somewhere, like distant thunder, and equally intangible.

Where was Rhys when you needed a medieval explanation?

On the south side, a Tyvek tent set up precariously over

the ditch provided a focal point, its white surface stark against the muted greens and browns of the landscape. Another had been set up not far away, flapping noisily in the gusty breeze.

All of this only became visible as Warlow and Jess crested the rise along a marked-off path to stand and consider the view, their eyes squinting against the wind.

To the north, the misty silhouettes of the Black Mountains brooded. Southwards, the lowlands of the Gower Peninsula stretched out, the sea beyond it a steely grey line merging with the horizon.

'I was about to say that this is hardly the place to hide a body, but most of this is invisible from the road.' The wind blew strands of dark hair over Jess's face, and she wiped them away with a finger, her cheeks pink from the climb.

Tannard appeared from behind a tent. She was hardly recognisable in her white and blue Tyvek suit, but the detectives recognised her posture and stance before she spoke. Her voice carried on the wind, tinged with a hint of wry amusement.

'I recognise that voice,' she said, her words almost lost in a sudden gust that brought with it the faintest trace of decay, a grim reminder of why they were all gathered on this desolate hilltop.

She was younger than Povey but possessed a sharp mind and her boss's attention to detail. A trait that spilled over into her appearance.

The Tyvek hood was down now, and she had her hair in a ponytail, her gaze intense beneath striking brows that arched with precision. So flawless that Warlow often wondered if they'd been artfully inked, though he freely admitted to not understanding what micro-blading was. But he had lived in a house with a teenage girl for many months, and so the term had entered his lexicon.

'Sengupta say much?' Jess asked.

'Not much. She'll do the PM tomorrow.' With the hood down, Tannard's features were striking, with those perfectly sculpted eyebrows framing sharp eyes. High cheekbones gave her an air of authority, and her lips, set in a determined line, suggested a methodical approach.

She led the way and lifted the tent flap, revealing the grim scene within.

Although both Jess and Warlow were old hands, seeing a body that had been vital and active a day before, now reduced to a lifeless shell, still sent a chill through their veins.

Jess inhaled sharply, her jaw clenching as she fought to maintain her composure. Warlow's eyes softened for a moment, a flicker of sorrow crossing his weathered face before he steeled himself for the task ahead.

Russell Milburn's body lay sprawled in the ditch, his Lycra-clad form a jarring sight against the dun backdrop. Death had drained the colour from his skin, leaving it ashen and waxy under the harsh lights set up by the forensic team.

His face wore a grimace, hinting at his last moments being filled with pain or fear. His right arm was twisted at an unnatural angle, confirming the broken shoulder the pathologist had noted and the fracture the drone had picked up. Scrapes and bruises mottled his exposed skin, telling the tale of his fall.

'He's positioned oddly,' Jess observed, her eyes tracking the awkward twist of Milburn's torso. 'It's as if he tried to turn over but couldn't manage it.'

Warlow nodded, crouching for a closer look.

'His fingers are caked with mud. He must have been conscious for at least a short while after he ended up here. Sengupta couldn't determine the cause of death?' Warlow asked, standing up with a grunt.

Tannard shook her head. 'No. The obvious injuries aren't severe enough. We'll need the postmortem for more answers.'

The damaged bicycle lay a few feet away, its front wheel bent and spokes broken. It seemed to underscore the violence of Milburn's fall. Yet, as Tannard had said, these circumstances alone didn't explain his death.

As the wind whistled around the tent the detectives exchanged troubled looks.

When they got back outside, Gil and Rhys were waving to them from below, but Tannard hadn't finished.

'We've identified some skid marks from the cycle on the road below and some drag marks suggest the cycle was pulled up here. No useful footprints, as the grass masks all of that. I'll post what we found on the roadside later.'

They thanked her and walked back down to join the others.

Gil and Rhys took the two senior officers to another cordoned-off area where the crime scene techs had identified markings which might be consistent with Milburn's bicycle crash. Warlow and Jess had driven past it some fifty yards from the Y junction in the road.

'Not much to see. But the techs spotted some blood a little further on from the tyre markings.'

'So, he came off his bike, fell into the road and… what?' Warlow asked.

'Either dragged himself and his bike up the mound to the remains of the castle…' Rhys suggested.

'Or someone else dragged him up there,' Jess said.

Of the two scenarios, Warlow suspected one as being far more likely.

'Therefore, are we thinking hit and run? Panicked driver kills cyclist and tries to hide the body?' Warlow's theory had lots of holes but, for the moment, was probably the most plausible.

'It's bloody Silverstone up here after five, or can be,' Gil said. 'Boy racers who all think they're Michael Schumacher. Not beyond reason to believe one of them might've knocked Milburn off his bike.'

'Or possibly the driver was drunk,' Jess suggested, 'and wanted to hide things.'

If anyone considered it unlikely that a half-decent person might act in that way, no one said it. They'd all been on the job long enough not to be surprised by anything one human being could do to another.

'We have the drone footage.' Rhys waved a tablet.

He'd become something of a drone footage expert, having

recruited a friend with an interest on more than one occasion to help with cases. Though in this instance, they had only the Llewellyns' images to work with.

'I sent Megan and her dad home,' Gil explained. 'They'd hung around long enough. The poor kid was terrified.'

'They local?' Warlow asked.

'Cwmgors address. I said we'd pop over and take a statement later.' Gil looked around at the scene. There was little more to do here.

'Where's Milburn's car?' Warlow asked.

'Black Mountain Hospital,' Gil explained. 'You know it?'

Warlow nodded. 'Know of it. It's a community hospital and where they do all the eye stuff, the macular degeneration clinic, isn't it?'

'Yes, we have a neighbour that pops over once every six weeks to have that done,' Gil said.

'Is there anyone we can speak to over there?' Jess asked.

'A ward manager.'

'Okay,' Warlow confirmed. 'We'll do that if you speak to the Llewellyns.'

————

WARLOW TOOK the mountain road back to the town. And though he'd heard of the hospital, it took a bit of finding with the help of the satnav, which took them up the valley and over the river to an easy to miss sharp right.

'Bit out of the way, isn't it?' Jess said as they climbed the steep accessway off Folland Road.

'If I'm right, this was once a private house, donated to the community before the NHS ever existed.'

Jess nodded. 'Looks like an old house from here.'

'No surprises there, then. Look it up.'

Jess did and read out the background she found.

"Like so many community hospitals functioning or moth-balled, The Black Mountain Hospital had its roots in the industrial heart of Wales. Originally a private home for a family involved in the tinplate industry, it was indeed donated to the community in the 1920s to serve as a much-needed medical facility well before the NHS came into existence. After years of debate and fundraising efforts, the hospital officially opened its doors on June 3, 1936, when the local economy was struggling, making the hospital's establishment a remarkable achievement for the community.

"Over decades, the hospital evolved to meet changing needs, with the addition of a maternity wing in 1950, which operated until the mid-1980s when it was closed due to changing demographics and financial constraints. The main hospital block has one ward of twenty-eight beds offering recuperation, palliative care and treatment, as well as a day hospital for the elderly, offering services such as physiotherapy and occupational therapy. Some out-patient clinics still run, with the added idiosyncratic ophthalmology services that had been shoehorned in thanks to the developments of treatment for the commonest blinding condition in the United Kingdom, age-related macular degeneration."

Warlow grunted. 'Amazing to think it's still here and adapting to change. A mix of the old and new. A symbol of industrial philanthropy and community perseverance. And, as such, I expect despised by the men in suits who consider these things as expensive white elephants.'

'Really?' Jess asked.

'Pick up any local paper, or rather, find one online, and you'll see some community or other trying to fight closure. It's the way of things. Aren't we always being told there's only so much money to go around?'

Jess's lips compressed in a half-smile. 'I'm guessing you and Tom have chewed the fat on this one more than once.'

The road looped to the side of the main "house", passing an ugly hotchpotch of utility buildings and the block of the ward unit, doing its bit for the environment with a roof full of solar panels.

Warlow kept on driving until the road curved into an elevated parking area.

Police tape had been wrapped around some bollards in a square around a Black BMW to the right of the steps that led down to a lower single-storey building that housed an eye operating theatre, designed with steel-framed windows and rendered walls that screamed hospital construction.

Jess got out and stood stock still, staring at the building behind where they'd parked, further up the hilly terrain.

'What is that?' She pointed at the long, low building on an elevated area a few yards away with boarded-up windows, grey walls, and a red-tiled roof.

A corridor ran off to one side to a separate building, this one with corrugated steel wall and roller shutters on the windows. Temporary, anti-climb steel fencing had been erected around this second, two-storey section, though it projected an unloved appearance.

'The old maternity hospital. Shut for years.'

'Spooky,' Jess commented.

'Spooky death trap, I suspect,' Warlow commented.

'It looks like it should be demolished.'

'I think they've tried. I remember reading about plans, and not so long ago. But we're on a mountainside here, and voices were raised in objection.'

'Why?' Jess looked aghast.

'Why don't we ask someone who'd know?'

CHAPTER SIX

THEY WALKED through some doors into a reception area and, after some introductions and explanations, met with the ward manager in a cramped office in the main hospital block. The small room was dominated by a large desk, with filing cabinets along one wall. A well-used wall planner hung above these, covered in colourful notes.

Deena Barton greeted them with a tired smile. She was a short, compact, middle-aged woman with a pleasant smile and dark hair that fell to her shoulders. As she sat behind her cluttered desk, her chair creaked softly.

The office smelled of coffee and antiseptic. The manager brushed back a strand of hair and focused on Warlow, ready to cooperate.

'I won't keep you long,' he explained. 'We're here about Russell Milburn.'

Deena nodded. 'Have you found him?'

She had an accent that took Warlow a while to figure out. In the end, he settled for somewhere east of Ipswich.

'We are looking into his disappearance,' Jess said with deliberate vagueness. Relatives needed informing and the body formally identified. 'Can you tell us why he was here yesterday?'

'A fact-finding mission, he called it. I'd never met him

until yesterday, even though he's the Health Board's Chief Exec.' She compressed her lips. 'We are off the radar up here.'

'So, that was it, just a tour?'

Deena shook her head. 'Afterwards, he'd arranged a meeting with the local head of the Hospital's action group and community fundraisers, a GP, and me. Six people, including Milburn and his PA.'

'Was there a reason for the meeting?'

Deena nodded, her nostrils tightening a little. 'The same reason that every Chief Exec comes here for. He'll be the fourth in fifteen years. To tell us what a great job we're doing and then to tell us that there would be a rapid series of consultations regarding a restructuring, and he wanted everyone's opinion.'

Warlow shifted his weight. 'What opinions were there?'

'Too many to mention.'

'Did he have an opinion?'

'Oh, yes. He didn't say as much, but he'd like to shut us down. There's no doubt about that.'

'Why?'

'To re-utilise resources. Move the nurses across to Llanelli. Use a mobile unit for the eye treatments. Encourage more care at home, like virtual wards. He had all kinds of ideas.'

'What was the reaction?'

'Did you not hear the gnashing of teeth?' Deena's response made Warlow smile.

'What was your impression?'

'That he'd done all this before. Soft soap before the guillotine comes down. It's a bitter pill.'

'The hospital looks busy, though,' Jess observed.

'It always is. Twenty-eight beds. Two rooms for palliative care.'

'What kind of care do you offer here?'

'People recovering from surgery, respite care, some chronic gerontology. It's a mix. But we also run Outpatients, and the eye unit is manic.'

Someone knocked on the door, and a head appeared

around the frame. It belonged to a man in his mid-thirties, with a face as plain as unbuttered toast, a mop of unruly ginger hair, and a small crescent scar below his left eye.

'Alright for the off, Deena?' he asked, barely glancing at the two strangers in the room.

Deena looked up from her desk. 'Yes, Gary. I think so.'

'Nothing extra needed?'

Deena flicked her eyes to the screen in front of her, jiggling a mouse to bring up a spreadsheet. She skimmed through it and shrugged. 'We're good. Off you go.'

Gary nodded, his eyes turning with the briefest of apologies for the intrusion to Warlow and Jess before he retreated, closing the door with a soft click.

Deena turned to the detectives. 'Sorry about that. Gary's one of our drivers. They're the lifeblood of this place, you know. Three runs a day between here and the General in Llanelli—laundry, sterilised equipment for theatres, drugs, you name it. Keeps us ticking over.'

'Seems efficient,' Jess commented.

'Has to be,' Deena replied. 'Gary's as reliable as they come. Good as gold, that one.'

Warlow glanced at his watch.

'Is this when Gary normally does his run?'

'One of them,' Deena said.

Warlow got up and called to Gary as he headed for the door. 'Mind hanging on for five minutes?'

Gary shrugged, and Warlow hurried back into the office.

'You're not local, Deena?'

She smiled at his observation. 'Worked my way west from far-flung Suffolk. I went where the jobs took me.'

'Can I ask you about the other building?' Jess asked.

Deena appeared nonplussed.

'She means Arkham Asylum at the back.' Warlow immediately regretted his Batman reference but was relieved to see that Deena had DC comic awareness, judging by her smile.

'Tragic. You know its history, I guess? The first maternity unit in the country?'

'I did not,' Warlow admitted.

'Built for that purpose in 1948. Closed in the '80s. A reorganisation and cutbacks.'

Warlow's ears perked up at the mention of cutbacks. He reined in a snort at how ironic it was to hear governments promising a bigger spend but that the realpolitik was so often very different. And, as Deena explained it, this sounded like a complete casserole of a set up regarding the old hospital's complex ownership structure—the main building sold off to developers, while the NHS clung to the annexe.

'So, the NHS still owns that end bit?' he confirmed.

'Yes, we used it for storage until recently. The vandalism in the old building forced us to close it off. The old place has become an internet-fed destination for urban explorers, complete with ghost stories.' Deena said all this with resigned disgust. 'You can find amateur trespasser videos online showing the inside.'

Jess, intrigued, inquired about plans for the site.

Deena outlined the unsuccessful planning applications, citing various reasons for rejection. However, she hinted at potential changes under the new government's housing commitments.

'How do you feel about it?' Jess probed.

The manager's response remained measured. 'Renovation would be wonderful, but that's... unlikely. It's old, poorly located, and expensive to update. Even though it holds a special place in people's hearts, what's the point of a moth-balled building?'

The conversation shifted to Milburn's interest in the annexe. Deena revealed his plans to assess its potential use or demolition, much to Warlow's concern. 'He wanted a tour. But we'd need to clear out the storage spaces. We keep gas cylinders in there. Away from the vandals.'

'Not exactly encouraging, then,' he remarked.

'I know that if we spend money tarting-up the annexe, we could use it for something, I'm sure. We never have enough room. But I was told it would need a business plan for it to be considered… it might mean severing the corridor linking it to the original maternity unit, some landscaping and better access, and as you can see, the road up is degrading, too.'

Warlow remembered the grass growing in the parking area between the two buildings.

'But why expend all that energy on a business plan when there is to be a bigger reconfiguration?' Deena said.

'Are those Milburn's words, too?' Jess asked.

Deena wasn't giving much away, yet Warlow sensed her professionalism fought against some unreadable emotion.

'That's why they bring the Milburns of this world in from outside. They have no local connections. They can look at it all coldly. Treat it like a business, that's what I keep hearing. But it isn't a business, is it? It's people and raw emotion.'

Warlow and Jess grimaced. Raw emotion, in their book, never aided clarity and could complicate any murder inquiry.

The DCI steered the conversation back to their case in point. 'Sorry about nabbing space in the car park, too. We'll be moving Milburn's car, but only once our forensic people have finished with it.'

Deena shrugged. 'We'll manage. We always do.' She let out a thin laugh. 'It's odd seeing all this activity up here. We're normally very much Cinderella to the big ugly sisters of the two main county hospitals. Hardly anyone comes near.'

'And we'll get out of your hair as soon as we can.' Warlow announced. Once the press were informed, things would escalate quickly. 'I can't tell you any details, but I think it's only fair to warn you to expect some press activity. Chat with the people who deal with them on the mother ship. That would be my advice. And I'd chat with your staff, too. The hyenas will latch on to anything for a headline.'

'Oh, dear.'

'Not the word we normally use,' Jess said, 'but wise to be aware. The good news is that they're not allowed on the property without your permission and usually only take shots from outside the main entrance. And for this hospital, that means the bottom of the hill, which will not give them much of a shot, will it?'

Deena grinned, finding a sliver of silver lining in their isolated location. 'That it will not.'

'Excuse me for a moment while I talk to the driver,' Warlow said.

Gary was outside, sitting on a low wall of covered walkway, looking at his phone.

'Thanks for waiting.'

The hospital-supplies driver, bearded, late thirties, wearing a Health Board polo shirt and black cargo pants, shrugged.

'Were you in the car park when Milburn left?' Warlow asked quietly.

Gary nodded. 'Yeah, I was loading up. Didn't pay much attention, except for the shouting.'

'Tell me what you saw.'

'They all came out of the meeting. The suit went to the BMW and grabbed a kit bag.'

Warlow struggled to place Gary's accent, but it was not local. At least it had not been local, though it seemed to struggle now against the vernacular. Accents, like old habits, faded but never fully vanished, their edges softened by time and place, yet still with roots tied to places left behind.

'There were some verbals between him and some others. I didn't take that much notice. They weren't kids. Some of those sods can be feral these days.'

Warlow probed. 'And then?'

'Nothing. This Milburn guy, he just ignored them. Went back into the hospital. To a changing room or the toilet, maybe.'

'Why do you say that?'

'Because ten minutes later, he comes back out in Lycra.' Gary snorted. 'Prancing about like he's in the Tour de France. Gets on his bike and off he goes.'

'Remember anything they said in the argument?'

Gary shook his head. 'Nah, not really. Except Milburn saying something like, "Face the facts." That's all I caught.'

Warlow nodded, his mind racing. 'Thanks, Gary. That's useful. Somebody will be in touch for a formal statement.'

Gary pocketed his phone and moved off as Warlow re-entered the hospital block to thank Deena Barton.

Back outside, Warlow did not stop at where the Jeep was parked. Instead, he trudged up the overgrown path.

Jess followed, taking in the moody sight of the derelict maternity hospital.

'Doesn't look like much, does it?' Jess muttered, eyeing the squat, red-brick building.

Warlow grunted.

The single-storey structure crouched against the autumnal landscape, its boarded-up windows like sightless eyes staring blankly at the world it once served.

They rounded the corner, and the true state of decay revealed itself. Here, away from prying eyes, the building's wounds were laid bare. Several windows had their coverings torn away, leaving jagged edges of splintered wood and rusty nails. Shards of glass glittered ominously in the fading light.

'Ugh.' Warlow stepped carefully over a scatter of broken tiles and crumbled mortar. 'It really is a bloody death trap.'

Jess peered through one of the exposed windows, her torch beam cutting through the gloom inside. 'Looks like the local kids have been having themselves a time in there.'

The beam illuminated graffiti-covered walls and piles of debris—broken furniture, overturned metal trolleys, soggy cardboard, and unidentifiable detritus. A musty, damp odour wafted out, tinged with something sharper. Urine? Or worse.

'She wasn't kidding about those urban explorers,' Warlow said, his voice tight. 'One wrong step in there and you'd be in a world of trouble.'

A sudden gust of wind whispered through the building, moaning through gaps to remind the listener of its history. Birth, death, joy, and sorrow. Nothing but memories now, yet still haunting these crumbling halls.

'Come on,' Jess said, suppressing a shiver that had nothing to do with the chill in the air. 'We've seen enough. Let's head back before we lose the light completely. This is interesting but not relevant.'

She was right. But as they turned to leave, Warlow cast one last glance at the building.

Empty windows watched them leave. If the building could talk, it might have told them something worth hearing. From its perch above the main hospital car park, it had been the last to see Russell Milburn alive.

CHAPTER SEVEN

GIL TOLD Rhys where to go as they headed east, out of the town of Ammanford.

'You familiar with this road, Rhys?'

'Only for passing through. We used to come this way when we had that case where Mr Warlow grew up. Down in the Swansea Valley.'

'Ah, yes, the Geoghans' murders. Tiger country,' Gil observed.

'But these houses, they were all built when there were collieries, right?' Rhys looked out at the rows of terraced housing along roads made narrower by the parked cars.

None of these properties had garage facilities.

'Mining and tinplate. This is the western edge of the anthracite field. Black gold in its time. All these houses were built at the beginning of the last century during the mining boom. And almost every village had, still has, a rugby club.'

'So, coal and rugby. Bit of a cliché,' Rhys said.

'Cliché? Yes, well, there isn't all that new under the sun, is there? Best not to throw the baby out with the bathwater, and the tried and tested generally win the day.'

Rhys shook his head.

'The men and boys who worked underground, believe it or not, had some energy to expend when they came up into the fresh air. Why not do that by belting seven bells out of each other on the rugby pitch in all weathers? And out of that fire has been forged some of the greats. Shane Williams and Gareth Edwards are both from this tiny patch.'

'Something in the water, Gil?'

Gil stared out at the small houses as they drove past.

'It certainly isn't money,' he muttered.

'What really happened to the mines, though?'

Gil seemed to struggle to respond. 'Time has a funny way of diluting things. Evan knows more than me, but the economists will say that the mines were inefficient. Nothing but nationalised money pits, excuse the pun. The people in the thick of it call it a class war, pure and simple. Unions versus a political sledgehammer. Scargill versus Thatcher.' Gil sighed. 'It's forty years since the miner's strike, but when they shut the collieries, it ripped the heart out of these valleys.'

Rhys nodded solemnly. 'I've heard stories. Must have been rough.'

Gil's expression remained unusually sombre. 'Generations of miners suddenly found themselves unemployed and no prospect of work for their kids. Mining is a hard, dirty job, but it was the lifeblood of these communities.'

'Surely, there were other opportunities?'

Gil let out a bitter laugh. 'Where? The closest city's an hour away, and not everyone can afford to move. Once the pits shut, the shops, pubs, and clubs that depended on miners' wages started closing, too. Like dominoes falling.'

They passed a boarded-up Workmen's Hall. A magnificent, three-storey, red-brick building built by a committee of workers and owners in the 1920s.

'See that?' Gil pointed. 'That's the entire story in one building. Used to be buzzing with life, staging operas, and showing films. And yes, times changed. But guess what happened in the naughties?'

'Strip club?'

'In Glanamman? No. Someone started using it as a cannabis farm.'

Rhys frowned. 'But the mines, I mean, that was decades ago. Surely, things have improved?'

'Improve is an odd word. Scars run deep in this part of the world. The valleys have one of the highest unemployment rates in the UK. Youngsters leave as soon as they can, looking for work elsewhere. Those who stay… well, let's just say food banks aren't exactly going out of business.'

'I know it's bad in some places.'

Gil's eyes softened. 'It's not all doom and gloom, mind. There's still a fierce pride here. People look out for each other. And rugby… rugby's still the body and soul of these villages.'

Rhys nodded. As a rugby player himself, he worshipped at the same altar.

They were on the border of the Black Mountains here at their most northerly point. The road led them through Gwaun Cae Gurwen, swinging south again along the A474 linking the Amman and Swansea valleys.

The Llewellyns lived on this road. A three-bedroomed semi-detached with a white door and just enough room for a car to sit at a clumsy angle between the bay window at the front and the pavement.

Gareth Llewellyn opened the door himself to Rhys's knock. Introductions weren't necessary since they'd all met earlier.

The house was compact, the kitchen opening into a cosy dining area linked to a light-filled extension at the rear.

Llewellyn took them through to sit looking out onto a long garden with views of the hills and the inevitable wind turbines behind.

'It is just me, or do you want to speak to Megan, too?' Llewellyn asked.

'Both of you, if possible,' Gil said.

'She's badly shaken up by it,' Llewellyn said. Not objecting to the inclusion of his daughter as such but laying the ground.

'That's partly why we're here, Mr Llewellyn,' Rhys said. 'And for our records, you have no connection with anyone in the NHS?'

'Me? No, why?'

'Does your wife work?'

'She does. She's a teaching assistant in the comp.'

'And the plumbing business? It's yours?'

'Llewellyn and Walters. It's a partnership.'

Gil grinned. 'You'll never be out of work, then.'

Llewellyn responded with a half-smile. If he still wondered about the NHS connection, Gil's quip about plumbing sidetracked him.

Llewellyn left them to fetch his daughter. She shyly sat next to her father on the sofa. The purple drone that had been Megan's birthday present sat on the coffee table.

'Now, Megan, your dad has told us all about what happened, but I want to hear what else you saw when the drone was flying.'

Megan's lower lip trembled, her eyes darting to Gareth's face for approval before she whispered, 'There was a man lying down in the field. He wasn't moving.'

'I know, but what else did you see?'

Megan wiped moist eyes with her sleeve. 'I saw some rocks and the Turbines and some big birds.'

'Red kites,' her father explained.

'Dad said the rocks might have been put there by really old people. Iron Age, he said.' She hesitated, her eyes wide. 'Was… was the man dead?' she asked, her voice barely audible.

Gil exchanged a look with Rhys before nodding solemnly. 'Yes. I'm afraid he was.'

The admission sparked a silent cascade of tears from Megan, her slight frame shaking with quiet sobs.

Gareth wrapped an arm around her, murmuring soft words of comfort.

Gil felt a familiar ache in his chest. Memories of tough conversations with his own daughters and granddaughters reverberated ion his mind. The need to make it all okay. He leaned forward.

'Listen to me, Megan,' he said, his voice low and kind. 'What you and your dad did today was a very good thing.'

Megan looked up, her tear-stained face a mixture of confusion and distress.

Gil continued, 'That poor man might not have been found for a very long time if it wasn't for you and your drone. You've helped us and his family.'

Megan sniffled, considering his words as her gaze drifted to the peaceful vista outside. 'But I don't want to find any more dead people,' she said. 'I don't want to fly the drone anymore.'

Rhys spoke up. 'You know, Megan, your drone won't just find sad things. It can do a lot of good.'

Gil nodded, building on his colleague's words. 'That's right. Search and rescue teams use drones to find lost hikers in the mountains. Scientists use them to study wildlife without disturbing animals. And in some countries, they use them to fly medicine to difficult to reach places. And think of all the amazing photos you could take.'

A glimmer of interest animated Megan's expression, but uncertainty still lingered.

Rhys took up the baton. 'What happened today was unusual. Most of the time, your drone will show you amazing sights no one else can see. It's like standing on top of one of those wind turbines and looking down.'

Gareth squeezed his daughter's shoulder. 'He's right, *cariad*. Remember how excited you were to see our house from high up?'

A ghost of a smile touched Megan's lips as she nodded.

Gil smiled. 'Tell you what,' he said, reaching for a notepad. 'Rhys will send you some websites where you can learn about all the amazing things people do with drones. He's a bit of an expert. Perhaps your dad will look them up for you and then you can both go on some better adventures.'

Megan's tears had subsided, replaced by a thoughtful expression. She reached out, tentatively pulling the drone back towards her.

'Maybe I could help find Mrs William's cat?' she suggested quietly.

Gil beamed at her. 'Syniad da.' He complimented her on

it being a great idea in welsh. 'You know where she might have gone, and the drone can go there while you watch from your garden. Use the drone for detective work. Like us.'

The interview wound down, but a spark of resilience shone in Megan's eyes.

Gil felt confident they'd get through this.

Five minutes later, Rhys eased the Audi onto the road and away from the Llewellyns' house, fiddling with the radio, searching for the traffic report.

'Motorway or mountain, sarge? For the return journey, I mean?'

'Motorway. I've seen enough of mountains for one day.'

After half a mile of silence, Gil cleared his throat. 'Perhaps, in a couple of weeks, check in on Megan and Gareth. Just a phone call, or if we're up here, call in. Make sure this ordeal hasn't cast too long a shadow. In case I forget.'

Rhys nodded. 'You're worried about the girl?'

'In my book, it's equally important. We can't have a bright young thing like that losing her spark because of one grim day.' He paused, then added softly, 'I've seen it happen before. Best to nip it in the bud. Shall I text you a reminder?'

'No need, sarge. It's locked away.' Rhys tapped his head. 'The websites and YouTube stuff is a good idea. Could be a good ice breaker.'

Gil's lips curved into a small smile. In this line of work, it was easy to forget the living in pursuit of justice for the dead.

But not today. Not on his watch.

'*I'm a Barry Girl,*' said Rhys.

Gil sent him a side-eyed glance. 'Is this pronouns related?'

'No, the song.'

Some might have found Rhys's non sequitur style a tad confusing, but Gil had worked with him long enough to tune in on how the DC's mind worked. And this little gem meant only that Rhys's mind had slipped effortlessly back into the challenge of earlier in the day.

'I'm a Barry girl, to the tune of *I'm a Barbie girl*, I presume?' Gil asked.

Rhys grinned.

'Nice,' Gil replied.

'Gina texted me one earlier on.'

'Go on, then.'

'*Help me, Rhondda.* It's an oldie, sarge. I had to Spotify it.'

That earned him a scathing glance from the sergeant. 'That is a Beach Boys classic. Not just an oldie. Are you telling me you do not know the words to *California Girls*?'

Rhys threw Gil a wary, negative glance.

'Right, enough of this.' Gil took out his phone and found the track on his music app, spent ten minutes trying to link to the sound system while Rhys watched, not saying anything.

Eventually, Gil set the system up. As they bypassed Pontardawe on the way to the M4, Gil began telling Rhys, in song, how hip East Coast girls were regarding the styles they wore.

By the time he got to wishing the female population could all live in California, Rhys was tapping his hand on the steering wheel in time to a sixties' classic about surfing on the West Coast of America. About as far from the remains of the mining culture in West Wales as it was possible to get.

CHAPTER EIGHT

RUSSELL MILBURN and his partner rented a large, modern, grey stone house in Llanedi, a hamlet on the South Eastern fringe of Carmarthenshire with a functioning pub. Some people's idea of heaven.

By the time Warlow and Jess arrived, Russell's partner had already been visited by uniformed officers and the news broken. She'd had time to process some of her grief. Enough to agree to answer Warlow's questions when he politely asked if she could.

Maeve O'Connor's angular frame made her look taut with unspoken anguish. Warlow put her at around forty. Styled hair, attractive features, even makeup free, or perhaps because of it. She wore jeans and a baggy sweater. If there had been tears, there were none now in the fragile composure she'd cobbled together for their visit.

There were no children, and Milburn's job as a kind of managerial troubleshooter had taken them from Sussex to Liverpool and now to West Wales.

O'Connor worked as a freelance web designer, creating and maintaining websites for small businesses. The kind of thing you could do from anywhere as long as you had a reasonable internet connection. The house had come fully furnished and had an echoing new feel to it when the detectives followed the woman in.

On the surface, she looked to be holding it together, but the jittery movements of her hands and an inability to sit still spoke of a turmoil under the surface.

Warlow and Jess accepted the offer of tea, and they sat in a room with laminate wood flooring and glass-fronted seascape photographs on the wall. The kind with no frames.

'You should know that we are treating Mr Milburn's death as suspicious,' Warlow said gently.

'Some bastard knocked him off his bike. Of course it's suspicious.' Maeve threw back the response. But something in the detectives' expressions fanned the flames of suspicion. 'That's not what you mean, is it?'

'No, we think there was some kind of collision,' Jess said carefully. 'But given the circumstances of how his body was found—'

Maeve stood up stiffly.

'What circumstances?' she demanded, her voice rising.

Warlow explained, 'We know he was not where he came off his bike. He was moved somewhere out of view.'

'Moved? Why?' Maeve's voice cracked.

'That's what we're here to find out,' Warlow said.

'I don't understand. What aren't you telling me?'

Warlow kept his gaze on her when he spoke. 'Mr Milburn was found away from the road. We do not think he arrived at that point on his own.'

'You're not making any sense.'

Jess leaned forward, her voice gentle. 'Someone put him where he was found, and it was in a place we would not have expected to find him. In fact, had it not been for a piece of luck as a father and daughter flying a drone, he might still be missing.'

'But—' Maeve's words caught in her throat, a horrified expulsion of denial mixed with disbelief. 'Why would anyone do that?'

'We're going to find out, Maeve,' Jess said. 'That's why we need to ask you these questions. If you're up to it.'

The woman sat down again, visibly struggling to process the information.

But Warlow pressed on. 'Was there anything out of the ordinary yesterday? Or in the days leading up to yesterday? Was he stressed?'

Maeve's shoulders slumped. Part misery, part disdain. 'He was the Health Board's Chief Exec. Of course he was bloody stressed. Have you any idea what he did?'

'Manage the local health service,' Jess said, deliberately vague in her response.

'Yes. Well, he's known as a turnaround CEO. The most unpopular kind. This Health Board is in enhanced monitoring for planning and finance status. In bad trouble. Bottom line, he was brought in to shake things up. It's one up from being in special measures. We've been here fifteen months, and the environment he worked in has become none the less hostile.'

'Hostile?' Warlow asked.

'Patients hate change, doctors hate change. Even when change is the only answer. And Russ was an agent of change. But just mention the word closure and you have to call the bloody fire brigade in this part of the world. In any part of the UK, I'd say. So, he was in a fight, and he knew it. And that is stressful. But had someone posted dog shit through the letterbox? No. Russ was very private.' She hesitated, reassessing her answer, assimilating the genuine horror of Warlow's question again. 'You don't think he's dead because of that, do you?'

'We must consider all angles. We'll probably know more after the postmortem.' Jess's phone buzzed with a message. She read it and looked up. 'A liaison officer is on the way. They've explained that we'd like you to confirm the identification. They've taken the body to the hospital at Llanelli. She'll accompany you there.'

'Is there anyone we can call, Maeve?' Warlow asked.

She clasped her arms over her chest as if caught in a sudden chill. 'I've already rung my sister. She's in Ireland. She'll come over tomorrow.'

The FLO arrived ten minutes later, and Warlow and Jess left with the promise that they would be in touch once they knew more.

'Not a job I fancy,' Jess said as they drove away, heading back to Pembrokeshire and Ffau'r Blaidd, the cottage they shared in Nevern.

'A turnaround CEO. No,' Warlow agreed.

'What could possibly motivate someone to do that? Is it the money?'

'There is that. But you're putting yourself in the firing line. Some of them are doctors, some not. Either way, for some, it's a calling. If I was generous, I might say it gives you the chance to improve the lives of thousands of people.'

'Or make it worse,' Jess observed.

'I suppose,' Warlow agreed. 'I'll do some reading about Health Service CEOs tonight and give Tom a ring for his input.'

'Fancy a fish supper, then?'

Warlow turned to her and grinned. 'Ready-made and throw the plates in the bin. Thought you'd never ask.'

———

CATRIN PETERS EASED her car into the driveway of her parents' house. The porch light flicked on as she approached and the front door opened the minute she pulled up. A warm aroma of shepherd's pie wafted out into the cool evening air as Catrin crossed the threshold.

'Sorry I'm late. Got caught up with some paperwork.'

Eunice Richards waved away the apology. 'Don't you worry. Betsi's splashing in the bath with her *Tadcu*. He'll be as wet as her, you watch. We thought we'd save you a job.'

Catrin followed her mother into the kitchen, where a pot of tea sat steeping on the counter. The familiar layout and smells of a house she'd spent twenty-one years living in comforted her, as did the mug of hot, brown liquid that magically appeared at her elbow.

'How's she been?' Catrin asked.

'Fine. Up and down, but then she's had that cold. She was grizzly this morning but perked up after her lunch. That new teething gel seems to help.'

Catrin nodded, a mix of relief and guilt washing over her. 'The rash?'

'Much better. That cream is working wonders. How about you? You're looking a bit peaky.'

Catrin ran a hand through her hair, aware of the dark circles under her eyes. 'I'm fine, Mam. It's been a busy week, what with Betsi's cold waking her, and us, up. And it looks like we have a nasty case brewing at work. I am going to be busy.'

'Hmm,' Mrs Richards murmured, unconvinced. 'And Craig? Working late again, is he?'

'He's on nights this week. We're like ships in the night at the moment.'

Eunice reached across the table to pat her daughter's hand. 'It'll get easier. These first few months back are always the hardest, they say.'

As if on cue, a raucous laugh drifted down from upstairs.

Catrin made to stand, but her mother waved her back down. 'You finish your tea. I'll go. You father will be there for ever.'

Catrin listened to her mother's footsteps on the stairs, the soft murmur of her voice. The giggles were replaced by happy gurgles.

A few minutes later, Eunice reappeared with Betsi in her arms, her husband, Lou following. The baby's cheeks were red from the bath and her eyes bright.

Catrin felt the stresses of the day melting away.

'There's my girl,' she cooed, reaching out to take the baby, who immediately nestled into her chest, small fingers curling into Catrin's blouse.

Eunice busied herself at the counter, warming a bottle. 'I've got some of that pie in the fridge for you and Craig. There's plenty for tomorrow too if you need it.'

Catrin breathing in the sweet scent of her daughter's hair. 'Thanks, Mam. You're a lifesaver.'

As she gathered the baby's things and prepared to leave,

she felt the familiar tug of guilt and gratitude. But for now, with her daughter in her arms and the promise of home ahead, everything else, including Russell Milburn, could wait.

———

GINA STOOD at the kitchen counter of the maisonette flat she and Rhys shared on Tabernacle Terrace in Carmarthen, spooning leftover lasagne onto two mismatched plates. The tiny kitchen in their rented terrace on Tabernacle Street barely had room for one person, let alone two, but they'd made it work for the past year.

'Smells good,' Rhys said, appearing in the doorway. He planted a quick kiss on her cheek before grabbing cutlery from the drawer.

They settled at the small table in the living room, knees bumping underneath. Rhys dug in immediately, while Gina picked at her food.

'Hungry, were you?' she asked, amused.

Rhys nodded, mouth full. 'Didn't get much of a lunch break. Gil made me drive.'

'You love it,' she said. 'Starsky and Hitch.'

'Hutch,' Rhys corrected her.

'Sounds exciting,' Gina said, trying to keep the envy out of her voice.

Rhys paused, fork halfway to his mouth. 'It wasn't, but probably more dynamic than being bored stiff, stuck in the office all day.'

Gina shook her head. 'Actually, it was really interesting. Catrin's brilliant at running the boards. I learned loads.'

'Yeah?' Rhys looked surprised. 'Gil and I were chasing our tails most of the day. Dead ends everywhere.'

They ate in companionable silence for a moment before Gina spoke again. 'Rhys… do you think I'm cut out for this?'

'For what?'

'Running the office. When Catrin's away, I mean.'

Rhys put down his fork, reaching across to take her hand. 'Of course, you are. Why even ask?'

Gina shrugged. 'It's just… Catrin makes it look so easy. And she's only part-time. What if I can't keep up?'

'Geen, you're mega organised. You'll be great. I'm telling you, the Wolf doesn't do dead wood. If he didn't think you could hack it, you wouldn't be there.'

'You have to say that,' Gina said, but she was smiling.

'True.' Rhys grinned. 'But it doesn't make it any less true. Besides, Catrin wouldn't have relied on you if she didn't have confidence in your ability to handle it, either.'

Gina nodded and smiled. 'Thank you.'

'Anytime,' Rhys said, squeezing her hand before returning to his food, but unable to resist looking at Gina's plate. 'You aren't going to leave that, are you?'

'I'm full. You finish it.'

'Sure?' Rhys asked.

Gina swapped plates with him. It was like having a dog around to clear away the leftovers. And Rhys was just as easily pleased, even if he didn't quite sit up and beg, though he did like his back rubbed, come to think of it.

'Why are you smiling?' Rhys asked, narrowing his eyes.

'Just thinking what sort of dog you'd be if you were one.'

'Pirra neon mountain dog, I reckon,' Rhys said.

'Don't let Gil hear you say that. It's Pyrenean. And I'm thinking more Golden Retriever.'

'Loyal and lovable, right?' Rhys agreed. 'What about you?'

'I don't know. You guess.'

'Afghan Hound?'

'Aren't they meant to be the least obedient?'

'Exactly that. Plus, cool-looking and aloof, stubborn and great hair.'

'Wow, obviously you've thought about this.' Gina half-laughed.

'You asked,' Rhys replied.

'I did.' Gina got up and took Rhys's plate to the sink, her expression fixed in an over-bright smile. 'Now you finish all that up like a good boy while I stubbornly and aloofly put fresh water in your bowl.'

Rhys paused in his eating to look over at her. 'Am I in the doghouse now?'

'Woof,' came the reply from Gina.

CHAPTER NINE

Eight am. An early start. Sengupta had pushed the postmortem because of another drowning. This time of a thirteen-year-old. Another moronic internet challenge gone awry. There'd been a spate of them of late across the country, but it meant the team could meet and kick off early. A miserable fact that made none of them feel good about it.

Warlow let Catrin open things up.

'Russell Milburn, forty-four years old. Chief Executive Officer Dyfed University Health Board. We've confirmed he spent an afternoon at Black Mountain Hospital in meetings. A keen cyclist, he'd brought his bike with him since he was "heading for the mountains", which is how he'd explained his late afternoon bike ride. His last known contact was at 5:05pm, a text to his partner, Maeve O'Connor.' She pointed to some of the scene of crime photographs. 'Found in Penlle'r Castle at 10:15am the following morning by the Llewellyns flying a drone. A birthday present for their daughter, Megan, who had the day off because the school she attends had an In-Service day. The HOP's report from the scene shows bruising that matches a fall from the cycle.'

'Thrown from his bicycle,' Jess said for confirmation.

'It seems the most likely explanation,' Catrin said.

'Is there any trace of his phone?' Gina asked.

'There's a possibility that it's lying somewhere on the mountainside, but I doubt it,' Gil said.

'My bet is that whoever knocked him over took his phone and disabled it.' Warlow was half-seated on the desk. He got up and moved to the Gallery. 'It's a desolate stretch of road that leads eventually to the Swansea Valley and then to Swansea itself. So, options…' Warlow picked up a whiteboard marker and wrote on the board, speaking as the letters and numbers appeared.

'One. Knocked off his bike accidentally. He was simply in the wrong place at the wrong time. But that doesn't explain the reason for him being where we found him. So…'

He wrote 1A underneath. 'The driver panics and hides victim.' He wrote 1B under that. 'Hit by accident and somehow drags himself and bike to a high point, then collapses.'

He looked around and registered the team's scepticism. 'Unlikely, I realise, but he might have been disoriented by a bang on the head. For now, though, it remains possible.'

Warlow wrote the number 2 on the board. 'Deliberate hit and run, and the driver chooses that point closest to the ditches at Penlle'r Castle so that he could hide the body.'

He turned again and saw a couple of people wincing at the idea. 'Jess and I interviewed the partner last night. She says he'd been in post for about fifteen months. They don't know many people in the area. But of course, his job is high profile.'

'What is a CEO, sir?' Gina asked. 'I mean, I know what the CEO is in a business, but in a Health Board?'

Warlow still had the marker in his hand. He replaced the top but did not put it down, preferring to use it to tap against his palm as he recalled his research and answered Gina's questions.

'Basically, he's the top dog in charge of running all local health services. Think of him as the captain of a massive ship —responsible for steering the entire operation. His job is to make sure hospitals and other health services in the area are working properly and efficiently. They deal with everything from managing budgets and staff to improving patient care. It's a high-pressure gig—they're constantly juggling demands from the government, local communities, and their own staff. They have to make tough decisions about where to spend money and how to improve services.'

'He was the top of the pile?' Rhys asked.

'Indeed. CEOs spend a lot of time dealing with regulations and inspections. They're always under scrutiny from various watchdog organisations. When things go wrong—like long waiting times or safety issues—they're the ones in the hot seat. It's a bit like being a football manager; when the team's doing well, you're a hero, but when things go south, you're the first one they look to blame. The job's got its perks, like good pay and the chance to make a real difference, but it's also incredibly stressful and can be somewhat of a political minefield.'

'They're not political appointments, though, right?' Gil asked before adding in a low rumble, 'I've had enough of politicians after the last case.'

No one could argue with that. The murder of a disgraced politician in the sleepy Pembrokeshire seaside village of Solva remained fresh in everyone's minds.

'Apolitical,' Warlow replied. 'But in Milburn's case, things were even more complicated. He'd been brought into a Health Board that was already under what they call "enhanced monitoring" by the authorities in Wales. That's basically a polite way of saying the Board was in deep doo-doo, particularly with finances and planning. Milburn's job was to turn things around, which is never easy. In NHS speak, he was probably tasked with "service reconfiguration" and "efficiency improvements".'

Rhys was frowning.

'In plain English,' Warlow explained, 'that meant he was looking at closing some hospital beds and possibly merging or centralising certain services. They call it "optimising resource allocation" and "streamlining service delivery". At least, that's what Tom said.'

'How is Tom?' Gil asked.

'He's fine. He's had his run-ins with hospital managers over the years, so he has a bit of insight. But CEOs often make tough, unpopular decisions. Milburn would have been under pressure to implement a "financial recovery plan" and improve "performance metrics" while also maintaining quality of care. It's a balancing act that puts them in the crosshairs of both the public and their political masters in Cardiff since Health provision has been devolved to the Welsh government.'

'Are we thinking disgruntled employee as a person of interest?' Catrin asked.

'It's a thought.'

'There won't be a press announcement until after the PM, so we can still get ahead of this,' Jess said.

'We've already spoken to the ward manager at the community hospital. I'm taking Gina to the postmortem at two. But, on the way to Cardiff, we'll call in on the GP who was at the meeting with Milburn if we can.' Warlow nodded to her.

'That leaves Milburn's PA and the local councillor,' Gil said.

'Who is he?'

'Huw Leyshon,' Gil replied. 'Ex miner. Sings in a local choir. Rugby fan.'

Warlow nodded. 'Catrin can chase up phone records and do some background on Milburn while we wait for the post-mortem. Meanwhile, let's get as much information as we can on the scene. Is there any work going on up there? Maintenance for the turbines. Anyone we might contact as witnesses?'

A fishing expedition. But if you didn't cast far enough into the water, you'd never catch anything.

Tea got made. But despite the lubrication, progress remained slow.

At ten thirty, Tannard strode into the Incident Room, her face a mask of concentration. The team looked up expectantly as she nodded at Warlow. She waved some papers and strode to the Whiteboard.

'I've got some information on the bike,' she began, reading from the written report. 'The damage to the rear wheel is consistent with a side-impact collision. There is significant deformation of the rim, with multiple spokes broken or bent at the point of contact.'

She paused, gauging the room's interest before delving into the technical details. 'As yet, no evidence of obvious paint transfer in the distorted areas of the frame and wheel.'

'From the impact vehicle?'

Tannard nodded. 'It might be microscopic.'

Unlike Povey, she liked to present her findings personally. She was a team player. So was her boss, but usually Povey was being pulled in a dozen directions at once and delegated.

'Good work,' Warlow said.

'No evidence of a phone at the scene. But I thought you'd want to know this about the bike.'

'We did,' Warlow said. 'It's confirmation.'

Tannard gave him a perfunctory smile and left.

Gil cleared his throat, a mischievous glint in his eye. The team braced themselves, recognising the telltale signs of an impending Gil monologue.

'Imagine if you had to explain the concept of the NHS to an alien,' Gil began, earning a collective groan from his colleagues. 'Everyone knows it isn't fit for purpose, and yet…'

Warlow pinched the bridge of his nose but motioned for Gil to continue. 'You've obviously thought about it. Go ahead.'

'Picture this,' Gil said. 'You're trying to explain to some green blob with antennae—'

'Where from?' Rhys asked.

'I see your ruse, DC Harries. Tricking me into saying something puerile like Uranus, but I refuse.'

Rhys shook his head.

'So, explain to some green blob with antennae,' Gil continued, 'that we have this massive, lumbering beast of an organisation that's supposed to keep us all healthy. It's free at the point of use, which sounds great until you realise that "free" means "paid for by eye-watering taxes" and "point of use" means "after waiting in a queue longer than the Great Wall of China".'

Rhys and Gina exchanged amused glances.

Gil pressed on. 'So, you tell this alien that we've got hospitals bursting at the seams, GPs who are harder to get an appointment with than the Pope, and waiting lists so long they've got their own postcodes. But here's the twist—we're all so bloody proud of it, we pillory anyone who dares suggest we change it.'

Catrin rolled her eyes, but there was a hint of a smile on her face.

'We're all in an abusive relationship with a giant bureaucratic octopus,' Gil continued, gesticulating wildly. 'It keeps letting us down, but we keep defending it to outsiders. "Oh, but it's lovely when it works properly." It's like someone trying to set up their friend with a notoriously dodgy date.'

Warlow narrowed his eyes. 'We get the gist, but is this going anywhere?'

'It is. Now imagine explaining to this alien that we put people in charge of this institutional behemoth who've never so much as put a plaster on someone. It's like asking a fish to manage a wedding cake shop.'

'And Milburn had never baked a wedding cake,' Rhys pointed out.

'Exactly.' Gil pointed a finger at Rhys in agreement.

'Luckily, we aren't aliens,' Jess said.

Gil, finger still pointing, cocked an eyebrow. 'I wouldn't be so sure of that.'

'What did I do?' the DC objected.

'I saw you trying to dance at Catrin's wedding. It could have been that the booze counteracted your human disguise because it looked very much like an extraterrestrial's first attempt at locomotion to me.'

'That was Beyoncé. *Texas Hold-em.*'

'Someone needed to hold 'em because they looked like they might fall off.'

Gina nodded exaggeratedly.

'Not fair,' Rhys said.

'No, it isn't,' Warlow said. 'But I remember seeing that, and I'm with Gil on the dancing. I'd like you to have a DNA test just to be sure.'

Laughter skittered over the room. But it faded quickly. There was too much work to be done.

CHAPTER TEN

THE HEALTH BOARD's Corporate Offices stood on a site next to the old mental hospital at the north-western edge of Carmarthen town. A repurposed red-brick facility that had once been a giant psychiatric unit. You could throw a stone, and it would hit the University of Wales Trinity Saint David campus. Someone, given the unit's history, probably had.

Jess and Rhys parked up on a damp, grey morning and walked to a nondescript entrance with doors opening into a vestibule that required intercom access. Shades, no doubt, of the previous security arrangements. They were buzzed through to another area where a security man behind a plexi-glass-protected desk gave them visitor badges. It all seemed a tad overzealous, as they were both wearing their ID lanyards. He also made them sign the visitors' book.

Jess didn't object. Though, her compliance was made in complete silence and a tight mouth. Through glass panels in doors that were also security locked, they could see carpeted, silent corridors. An attempt, no doubt, to lessen the slightly eerie "Shining" feel of the place.

While the security man rang the PA's number, Rhys studied the big poster on the wall containing the Board's mission statements while Jess looked at her phone.

Another missed call from Rick. Well, a call she'd have refused to answer, anyway.

She'd told him she'd think about the loan but hadn't given him a timescale for her decision because he had not responded to her text about the £6000 she'd already lent him the year before. Instead, she'd received a:

Can we talk about this, please?

To which she had not replied either.

With no hint of cynicism in his voice, Rhys read the mission statements. Or muttered them loud enough for Jess to hear.

'"Prioritising humanity in our operations. Relentless pursuit of service excellence."'

Rhys paused before continuing. '"Collaborative efforts towards peak performance" And get this: "Embracing accountability at all levels".'

He turned to Jess, a wry smile on his face. 'Why do they have to write this stuff down?'

The DI pressed her lips together. Thinking about her ex had made her less than receptive to blandishments. She gestured at the framed words with a dismissive wave.

'"Prioritising humanity"—as if every other Health Board is running a butcher shop instead of a hospital. "Teamwork and excellence"? Right. Because otherwise, we aim for mediocrity and infighting. It's all to make it sound special. Just like every other bureaucratic nightmare in the country.'

Rhys's mouth had dropped open.

She turned to him, rolling her eyes. 'I don't blame them. I bet if we walked into any corporate building in the UK, we'd find the same load of tosh plastered on their walls. It's as if they're all following the same plan, believing they're inventing something groundbreaking.'

'Everything alright, ma'am?'

She tilted her head and reset. 'Yes. And thank you for finding me something to vent on.'

She turned back to the security man at the desk, who had also been listening.

'She's on her way,' he said hastily.

'Good,' Jess replied and though she smiled, it stopped long before it ever reached the top half of her face, where her eyes remained steely.

"She" turned out to be a young PA called Sharon Higgs. Dressed in a white blouse, navy straight-legged trousers, and sling-back kitten heels. Her smile twitched with anxiety. Jess put her somewhere in her late twenties, pale colouring, blonde hair. They followed her along the corridor.

'Tim said I should let him know as soon as you arrived.' Sharon spoke as she walked.

'Okay,' Jess agreed.

They stopped outside a door. The nameplate read: Tim Riggon, Assistant Chief Executive.

Sharon knocked and pushed open the door gently, revealing a man in his mid-fifties with salt-and-pepper hair and a pinched expression.

Jess and Rhys stepped inside, followed by a wan-looking Sharon Higgs.

'Mr Riggon,' Jess said, extending her hand. 'I'm Detective Inspector Allanby, and this is Detective Constable Harries.'

Riggon's handshake was firm, his eyes shrewd. 'Tim Riggon. I understand you're here about Russell.'

Rhys cleared his throat. 'Yes. Obviously, you've been made aware. I did phone Ms Higgs before we came.'

'I got a call last night from Maeve, too. Russell's partner. It's difficult to believe. Shocking business,' Riggon muttered. 'We're all in a state here, as you can imagine. How can I help?'

Jess's gaze flicked to Sharon, who stood quietly by the door. 'Actually, Mr Riggon, we need to speak with Ms Higgs. And we'll need to see Mr Milburn's office.'

Riggon's brow furrowed. 'I'm not sure that's wise. There's sensitive information—'

'Mr Riggon,' Jess cut in, her tone brooking no argument, 'there's an easy way and a hard way. It is likely we will need to remove some personal and some Health Board items. There will definitely be a warrant for that. But at this stage in the investigation, time is a priority and letting me look now would be of significant advantage.'

Riggon's mouth tightened, but after a moment, he nodded. 'Of course. Full cooperation, that's what I meant to say. Sharon can show you to Russell's office. But I must insist—'

'Thank you, Mr Riggon,' Jess said, already turning away. 'We'll be in touch if we need anything further.'

As they left the room, Rhys muttered, 'Well, that went smoothly.'

Jess's lids became slits. 'As sandpaper, you mean? Come on.'

They waited for an unhappy Sharon to emerge.

Jess followed her a dozen yards up the corridor but stopped before they entered Milburn's office and addressed the young woman. 'Sharon, whatever you've been told to do, just forget it. We are not here to interfere, but nothing is off the table. I want you to be honest with me because we need to find out everything we can about Mr Milburn and quickly.'

Sharon frowned and then nodded. 'It's so unfair, though. Accidents happen, I realise that—'

'I'm going to stop you there,' Jess said. 'One of the reasons we're here is that, as yet, we are uncertain this was an accident.'

Sharon's pale face became rigid with horror. It took her a moment to close her open mouth. 'But—'

'Let's talk in the office, shall we?'

———

Dr Anjali Joshi's manicured nails clacked against her keyboard as Warlow and Gina settled into the cramped confines of her office. The faint murmur of phone consultations drifted through the thin walls.

'Right,' Warlow grunted, eyeing the clock. 'We won't keep

you long, doctor. Just a few questions about your meeting with Russell Milburn.'

Dr Joshi's eyes flicked to her computer screen. 'I have patients waiting.'

'Ah, the wonders of modern medicine,' Warlow drawled. 'Time was, you'd sit in a waiting room, thumbing through ancient copies of Country Life until your name was called. A time suck, admittedly, but at least you got to see a real person, not chat to someone faceless on a phone.'

'We're more efficient now,' Dr Joshi replied tersely.

Not the first time the current tele-medical approach to practice had been in the line of fire, by the looks on her face.

Gina got down to business. 'You meeting with Milburn. How did it go?'

Dr Joshi's lips thinned. 'It was… one-sided. He set it up as a forum, but he wasn't interested in anyone's opinion. Already made his mind up, hadn't he?'

'About what, exactly?' Warlow prodded.

'Local services. Cuts. Centralisation.' Dr Joshi's voice dripped with disdain. 'Progress, he called it.'

'Did things get heated?' Gina asked.

Dr Joshi hesitated. 'The Friends of the Hospital… they weren't pleased. Or rather, he wasn't pleased. Raised voices. Promises had been made by the old Chief Exec. Not worth the paper they were written on, obviously. Because they had been written down.'

'And Milburn's response?' Warlow asked.

'Times are changing,' Dr Joshi mimicked, her accent sharpening. 'That's all he'd say.'

She paused, frustration etching lines around her eyes. 'He doesn't understand the challenges we face here, but he should, because that is his job. We're chronically short-staffed, scraping by on outdated equipment. Finding doctors willing to work in an area like this is like pulling teeth.'

The GP's carefully maintained composure cracked.

'We're running on fumes. No slack in the system whatso-ever. And yet, Milburn waltzes in, ready to cut and run with what little we have left. It's...' she trailed off, shaking her head.

'Maddening?' Gina offered.

'Bloody criminal,' Dr Joshi muttered, then seemed to remember herself. She stopped glancing at her screen and turned a full-on glare towards Warlow. 'This job... it isn't...' Suddenly, she looked on the verge of tears. 'It's like climbing Snowden in flip-flops.'

'That bad, eh?'

'Worse.' She sighed, rubbing her temples. 'We're under constant pressure. Time's always against us.'

'My son's a surgeon. Almost finished his training,' Warlow said. 'I know a bit about what's going on.'

'It's the disconnect. We're losing the ability to truly interact with our patients. Their stories, their lives... it's all getting lost in the rush.'

'Ah.' Warlow nodded, a hint of nostalgia creeping into his voice. 'I recall a time when my GP knew my entire family history.'

'Exactly,' Dr Joshi agreed, warming to the subject. 'Now, we're expected to be hi-tech wizards, specialists in everything. Yet, we're sacrificing the heart of what distinguishes general practice.'

'Which is?'

'Connectedness. Continuity of care. Building relation-ships.' She shook her head. 'With all this fragmentation, those values are being eroded. Milburn's changes will only make it worse.'

Warlow frowned. 'How so?'

'We're already fighting to balance care with the numbers. His so-called "efficiency measures"', she practically spat the phrase out, 'will tip us straight into chaos. This isn't the job I signed up for."

Warlow noticed the tension in her shoulders.

There was more here than just professional frustration. He made a mental note to dig deeper into Milburn's proposed changes. Something told him that in the gap between efficiency and care, he might find some of the answers he was looking for.

'My apologies,' Joshi said, sitting back. 'I shouldn't speak ill of the dead. Even if they are managers.'

'But no threats were made at the meeting?' Gina asked.

'Threats?' Joshi looked mildly alarmed. 'No. No threats. Everyone in that room was a grownup.'

Warlow and Gina exchanged glances.

After extracting a few more reluctant details, they found themselves back in the surgery carpark, squinting in the daylight. Clouds still blanketed the sky, but it had brightened.

'Would you call that enlightening?' Warlow grumbled, not expecting an answer as he dug keys out of his pocket. 'I remember when doctors actually saw their patients. Sat down, had a proper chat, maybe even offered a cuppa.'

Gina raised an eyebrow. 'Sounds like ancient history.'

'Funny old word, "efficiency",' Warlow said. 'They fling it around like holy water, hoping it'll fix everything. But we both know better. You can't run a service built on human beings like a business chasing neat little outcomes.'

Gina's expression shifted into a smirk. She caught Warlow's quizzical glance and apologised. 'Not a laughing matter, sir, I realise, but I've remembered something Sergeant Jones said to Rhys the other day.'

Warlow hesitated at the Jeep's door. 'I might regret this, but go on.'

'He told Rhys he tried to get his boil treated over the phone. And it didn't work out too well.'

Warlow snorted. 'And?''

'He said it made him wish he was in Camelot,' Gina added, her eyes twinkling. 'No boils there, he said. Thanks to Lancelot.'

Warlow groaned. 'That's bad, even for him. But I am delighted to see you are embracing the team ethos, Gina. When in doubt, crack a joke.'

They got in the Jeep, and Warlow took the route Gil and Rhys had taken, looping east and south along the valley towards the M4 and all points east.

After a few moments, Warlow voiced his ruminations. 'What do you make of our miffed Dr Joshi and the meeting with Milburn, Gina?'

Her face became serious. 'I think it was less than joyful, and we need to have a word with this Friends of the Hospital chap.'

'Agreed. But that ball is in Gil's court. We, the lucky pair that we are, are heading for the big city and its deluxe pathology suite. Bring the Polo mints?'

'Yes, sir.'

'Good. Now, let's have a chat about strategies for the morgue.'

'Oh, Rhys has already told me what to do, sir. Have a paper bag handy in case I throw up and never inhale when you're leaning in.'

Warlow couldn't help but laugh a little. 'Did I ever tell you he was a keeper?'

CHAPTER ELEVEN

DETECTIVE SERGEANT CATRIN PETERS negotiated the drizzle outside HQ, her mobile pressed to her ear while her other hand juggled an umbrella and a shopping bag.

The call came through as she'd slammed her car door shut after a quick trip to Tesco to replenish a very depleted Human Tissue for Transplant box and, more importantly, the team's tea supply. She made it to shelter in the main entrance and accepted the call.

'Dr Forrester speaking,' came the crisp voice at the receiving end.

She knew who Forrester was; clinical director of the Northeast University Health Board.

'Good morning. This is Detective Sergeant Catrin Peters, Dyfed Powys police. Thanks for returning my call. It's in relation to Russell Milburn, your ex-CEO.'

After a short, but in Catrin's mind, meaningful pause, Forrester replied, 'I see. How may I assist you, Sergeant?'

She picked up the wariness in his tone.

Nothing strange in that. Calls from the police made a lot of people nervous.

'I appreciate you taking the time to speak with me. Have you been informed—'

'We got the news this morning. That's… it's a shock.'

'This is never easy, but I'm afraid Mr Milburn's death is being treated as suspicious. I'm gathering background information about his professional life.' Catrin pushed through the front door, walked inside out of the rain, flicked water off her umbrella and continued her call in a quiet corner of the reception area.

'Suspicious?' Forrester's voice sharpened. 'That's concerning.'

'Indeed,' Catrin agreed. 'I'm particularly interested in Mr Milburn's time with you. I gather you and he worked together. So, anything you can tell me about his working methods, his reputation would be useful. I understand he was an agent of change there?'

The line went silent briefly, and Catrin could practically visualise Forrester weighing his words. 'Russ Milburn was a... mover and a shaker. An efficient mover and shaker,' he finally said. 'He came in and agitated things here, no doubt about that. Made changes that were long overdue if I'm being honest.'

'But not popular, I take it?' Catrin pressed.

A dry chuckle crackled over the line. 'Popular? No, I wouldn't say that. But Russ wasn't the sort to lose sleep over congeniality contests. He was here to do a job, and he did it.'

Catrin nodded to herself, sensing an opening. 'Were there any particularly contentious issues during his time there, Dr Forrester? Anything that might have made him enemies?'

The silence stretched longer this time.

When Forrester resumed speaking, his voice had lowered. 'One notable incident springs to mind. A consultant who... let's just put it this way, whose colleagues had concerns, serious ones. It got ugly, as these things so often do.'

'And how did Mr Milburn handle that?'

'Not well, I'm afraid.' Forrester sighed. 'The consultant in question is currently on gardening leave, but the whole affair spiralled into a mess from start to finish.'

'Can you elaborate?' Catrin asked.

'There are underlying psychological issues at play. Though the party in question disputes that. However, we pursue that line. It might be as simple as stress management problems; it might be something else. These things are seldom clean cut. It raised questions about how the doctor in question had been vetted for the position in the first place. But that didn't change the fact that he simply couldn't cope with the demands of the job.'

'And Milburn's approach?'

'Russ wasn't one for kid gloves,' Forrester said, a note of disapproval creeping into his voice. 'He went in hard, all business. There were subsequently accusations of bullying, counteraccusations of incompetence. As I say, it got very ugly, very quickly.'

'Two sides to every story,' Catrin murmured.

'Precisely,' Forrester agreed. 'The consultant clearly needed support, perhaps a gentler touch. But Milburn... well, let's just say "gentle" wasn't in his vocabulary.'

'Can I ask about the outcome?'

'A tribunal is scheduled. These things do not move at Mach speed. But Russ left before it took place. It's likely he would have been called back as it involved the Royal College. The whole thing was hanging over him when he departed.'

'I see,' Catrin said. 'I'll need the name of the consultant involved.'

The line went silent again, and Catrin could almost hear Forrester's internal debate.

'I'm hesitant to—'

Catrin interrupted, her voice firm but not unkind, 'I understand your reservations. But as mentioned, we're dealing with a possible unlawful death here. Any information could be vital. You have already told me this dispute had been escalated, and a tribunal scheduled. It would not take much for me to find out that information. By not telling me, all you're doing is delaying the inevitable.'

She heard Forrester exhale heavily. 'The consultant's name is Jeremy Latimer. He's a Urologist.'

Catrin put down her shopping and took out her notebook to jot down the name. A small thrill of satisfaction ran through her as she did. Some calls were more fruitful than others. 'Thank you, Dr Forrester. You've been very helpful. One last question, if I may. In your professional opinion, was Russ Milburn good at his job?'

'He was. Very competent, if not exactly empathetic. I'm not sure that answers your question, but it's the best I can come up with,' Forrester said. 'He got results. Made unpopular but necessary changes. As for his methods...' He fell silent for a moment. 'Let's just say he left behind plenty of bruised egos and ruffled feathers. Effective, sure. But not always in a way that served the greater good of the institution.'

Catrin ended the call, retrieved her shopping, and stood, mulling over Forrester's words.

Russ Milburn, it seemed, had been a man who got things done, regardless of the collateral damage. The kind of man who made enemies easily and friends rarely. The kind of man, perhaps, who might push someone too far.

She hurried back to the Incident Room, her coat shedding droplets across the corridor floor.

This lead needed following up and, as per her way with all things, no time like the present.

She fired up her computer, fingers flying across the keyboard as she accessed the police database.

'Jeremy Latimer,' she muttered, entering the name.

While the system churned, she stared at the goodies she'd gone out to get. Essential supplies for the smooth running of the operation. A box of biscuit-flavoured tea poked out of the open bag. Risky choice that one. She wondered what the aficionados on the team would make of it.

Then her computer came back with the response to her enquiry. She speed-read the results and settled into her work.

———

GIL TOOK two calls on his way up to meet with the chair of the Friends of the Hospital. The first, from a detective inspector in Financial Crimes, told him that at last they'd had a van full of material from a storage facility that John Napier's firm had used and which had not come to light until fairly recently, thanks to all the obfuscation from Napier's legal team.

Gil thanked the detective inspector and said he'd be more than happy to look, but that the Milburn case would take up much of his time for the foreseeable. The DI had reassured him that the files were not going anywhere soon.

Five minutes later, he took a second call. He knew who it was even before he picked up his mobile. All confirmed when his screen flashed "Superintendent Drinkwater". He took a deep breath, steeling himself for what was sure to be a less than pleasant conversation.

'Jones.'

'Sergeant. I trust I'm not interrupting anything vital?'

Gil opted for the lie. 'Not at all, sir. How can I help?'

'I've been hearing strange stories, which are my least favourite kind, as it were, concerning your investigation into the Moyles and Napier case.'

'Sir?'

'You're aware, I'm sure, that this is a sensitive matter. High-profile victim, not the best optics…'

Gil felt his jaw tighten.

Bloody optics.

'Of course, sir. We're proceeding with all due caution.'

'Caution. Yes. That's precisely what I wanted to discuss.' Drinkwater's voice took on a patronising tone that set Gil's teeth on edge. 'I understand you've been making some… intriguing connections, interesting connections. Between the Napier bombing case and potential missing persons?'

'We're exploring all avenues, sir. Standard procedure.'

'Standard procedure, indeed. And I'm sure you're aware of the parameters of your investigation?'

Gil's free hand clenched into a fist. 'To assess any potential links between missing persons from the illicit filming of visitors related to the Moyles murder, sir.'

'Precisely. And yet, I understand you are going to have unprecedented access.'

'With respect, sir, we can't ignore potential motives just because they might be inconvenient.'

There was a long pause on the other end of the line. When Drinkwater finally resumed his voice had a dangerous edge to it. 'Inconvenient, Sergeant? I'm not certain I appreciate your implication.'

'No implication intended, sir. Just stating the facts as we see them.'

'Facts can be tricky things, Jones. Especially when viewed through the wrong lens.'

Gil bit back a retort. Lens, optics, it was worse than being at the bloody opticians. 'We're simply following the evidence, sir. Wherever it may lead.'

'And where exactly do you think it's leading?'

'It's too early to say, sir. But there are certainly some interesting connections emerging.'

'Connections.' Drinkwater practically spat out the word. 'Let me be clear, Sergeant. Your task is not to uncover "connections". Your job is to eliminate any link to a specific missing person.'

'With respect, sir, if those connections lead us down different avenues—'

'Then you bring those avenues to the attention of a senior officer. Superintendent Buchannan, I'm sure, will be on hand. And my door is always open. But tread carefully. Carefully. There are people watching this case who won't take kindly to any… unnecessary distractions, as it were.'

As it sodding were.

Despite the irritation at Drinkwater's verbal tick, Gil felt a chill run down his spine.

'Stick to your brief, Sergeant. Focus on what's relevant. Nothing more, nothing less.'

The threat hung in the air, unspoken but unmistakable.

'Was there anything else, sir?' Gil asked because he felt he needed to say something.

'No, that will be all. Keep me updated on your progress. The actual progress, mind you.'

'Of course, sir.'

Gil ended the call, his hand shaking slightly as he grasped the steering wheel.

Drinkwater had the reputation of someone who'd always had his foot on a slippery rung of the promotional ladder. Added to that simmered a puritanical streak such that Drinkwater liked to think of himself as a guardian of order, a bulwark against chaos.

To some, that made him the enemy. Protecting the system, they'd say, with a sneer in their voice. And maybe there was some truth to it, but it wasn't as simple as all that. The system didn't need protecting. It adapted, developed, always staying one step ahead. What needed protecting, in Gil's mind, was the application of fairness. The idea that justice was blind, that the law applied equally to all. It was a noble lie, perhaps, but one he believed necessary.

And Gil wasn't naïve.

The Police Service was caught in the middle of it all. Budget cuts, political pressure, the constant scrutiny of social media—it was enough to make a man long for simpler times. But there was no going back. The best anyone could do was navigate these treacherous waters, try to keep focused on the job at hand.

That was what Warlow did. What he expected of his team. Gil could live with that.

CHAPTER TWELVE

TWENTY MINUTES LATER, Gil pulled up to Huw Leyshon's house near Garnant. A former colliery manager's residence, it stood as a solid stone bastion against the backdrop of the hills, a testament to a bygone era when the valley bustled with industry. But two hundred years was a very long time.

Although some coal was still extracted through open cast mining until the 1990s, even that site had been reclaimed and turned into a golf club. You needed a bag of extra balls there as the rough was brutal. One day, when someone finally invented a mechanical mole that could slice through brambles as thick as your arm to retrieve lost balls, they'd make a fortune

Gil stepped out of the car, his shoes crunching on a stoned drive. Cool air carried the sharp scent of engine oil and diesel. From the far end of the yard came the distant clang of metal, drifting from the workshop where Leyshon's son, Ian, was at work.

The senior Leyshon appeared at the door before Gil could knock, a wry smile on his weathered face. '*Bachgen*,' he said, the greeting naturally in Welsh. 'I was expecting some nice, young woman in a uniform and instead, I get MI5.'

'I gave up kissograms a while ago,' Gil replied. 'Besides, your angina would never stand it.'

The two men shared a laugh, the insults a comfortable dance between acquaintances. They made their way into Huw's living room, where family photos adorned the walls, telling the story of a life well-lived and love lost too soon.

'How are Anwen and the girls, Gil?' Huw asked, settling into his armchair.

'Can't complain. The grandchildren are growing like weeds. Yours?'

Huw's eyes flicked to a photo of his late wife and back again. 'Ian's keeping busy. The trailer business is doing well, all things considered.'

Gil nodded, sensing the undercurrent of grief that still ran through the Leyshon household. He moved the conversation on to safer waters, swapping choir gossip and rugby predictions before broaching the real reason for his visit.

'So,' Gil began, leaning forward. 'Russell Milburn. Tell me about the meeting at the hospital.'

Huw's face darkened, the jovial mood evaporating like so much morning mist. '*Na beth oedd pwrs,*' he spat, the insult instantly regretted. 'Sorry. But he came in like he owned the place, all slick suit and PowerPoint bloody presentations.'

Gil watched as Huw's hands clenched and unclenched, knuckles white against his weathered skin.

'He used all those words, the ones that are supposed to excuse the execution, "centralisation" and "rationalisation",' Huw continued, his voice dripping with disdain. 'Like the hospital was just a line item on his bloody spreadsheet.'

'Were there any concrete plans?' Gil asked.

Huw stood, pacing the room like a caged animal. 'Closure, plain and simple. Oh, he dressed it up in fancy words—"service consolidation" and "efficiency improvements". Thanks to a brand new all-singing, all-dancing hospital west of Carmarthen.'

He came to a halt. 'But we all knew what he really meant. Why he'd called the meeting.'

Gil could feel the anger radiating off the man in waves. A man whose life had been embroiled in the place he grew up in. A place that most of the world had never heard of, unless you were into the Velvet Underground, and everything they spawned, in which case you obviously knew where John Cale was born.

Gil's shoulder twinged as he shuffled in his seat. A reminder of recent adventures with a crossbow-wielding killer he could have well done without. He'd taken much longer to recover than he would have done had he been younger. Getting older was a right sod. He hadn't quite got to the stage where he was saying this out loud, but that day was fast approaching. 'And the promises they made before? About bringing surgical services back?'

Huw let out a bitter laugh. 'Promises? To people like Milburn, they're someone else's smoke. He had the gall to tell us we needed to separate "practicalities from emotion". To him the hospital was an anachronism. A waste of time and resource.'

The man's eyes grew moist, his gaze fixed on a point somewhere beyond the room. 'If they'd expanded Outpatients like they've said they were going to for a decade or more, if we'd had some of those services here, who knows whether Val...'

The unfinished sentence hung in the air, heavy with unspoken what-ifs.

Gil's gut churned as he remembered the vibrant woman who had once cheered her husband on at local *eisteddfodau*. An old school advocate of the language and culture.

'I'm sorry,' Gil said, and meaning it. 'This... it must be difficult for you. Hearing that after all you've done.'

Leyshon wagged his head, as if trying to clear away the memories. 'It's not just about Val, though God knows that's part of it. It's about all of us. We've already lost so much—the pits, the shops, the young people moving away. That hospital... it's more than just a building. It's a beacon, Gil. Hope. That we haven't been forgotten.'

Gil nodded, fully comprehending the fear of being left behind that haunted these once-thriving communities.

'And Milburn?' Gil pressed. 'How did he react to the pushback?'

'Like water off a shiny duck's back. A stuck record, he said. Told us we were being unrealistic, that times have changed. As if we don't know that better than anyone. The meeting broke up at four, though I hung around talking to the GP and Deena. But I left then. I was on grandchild-care duty while Trudy was at work and Ian was out on a job.'

'You last saw him in that meeting room?'

'No, in the car park. Our "discussions" continued outside.' He paused, his eyes meeting Gil's. 'I could happily have strangled him; I will admit that. I was angry, but mostly I was disappointed. You know, we're here for the long haul and these… these people come and stay for a few years and then they're off with no thought of what they've left behind. I saw Milburn as a climber. And I suspect his ambition made him cold. Perhaps it's a requirement, who knows. I mean, what was Milburn's stake in all this apart from a bonus if he delivered?' It isn't fair and sometimes, I despair. I know the NHS isn't perfect and needs something doing to it, but people like Milburn do not help.'

They talked for a while longer, but the heat had gone out of Leyshon's anger. Neither man mentioned it, but Milburn's loss would no doubt put any changes on hold for a while. If this thought occurred to Leyshon, he wisely kept it to himself, though it had not escaped Gil's thinking.

As he prepared to leave, Gil sensed the toll the meeting had taken on Leyshon. The older man seemed diminished somehow, the weight of his community's future pressing down on his shoulders.

Outside, a breeze orchestrated the gorse bushes on the hills into a shimmy. Huw stood in the doorway.

As Gil was about to get into his car, he heard footsteps behind him. He swivelled and caught sight of Ian walking up from the yard, coveralls stained with grease and a determined set to his jaw. The younger Leyshon was heading in for a late break with his father, no doubt.

'Afternoon, Ian,' Gil called out. 'How's the family?'

Ian's face softened slightly. 'Can't complain.'

Gil nodded, thinking how Ian was one of the lucky ones.

With Huw's support, he'd carved out a niche for himself, applying his formidable work ethic to the trailer and plant repair business. It wasn't glamorous, but it was an honest job that kept food on the table.

'I was just catching up with your dad,' Gil volunteered, instantly regretting his words as he saw the man's expression harden.

'You mean that farce at the hospital?' Ian's voice took on a sharp edge. 'You here about that CEO bloke?'

Gil nodded cautiously. 'Yes, Russell Milburn.'

Ian's lip curled in a sneer. 'Accidents do happen. That one couldn't have happened to a nicer bloke.'

'Ian,' Huw chided his son.

'*Na.* Be honest, dad. He was a waste of bloody space. Maybe now they'll send someone who actually gives a damn.'

The vehemence in Ian's tone caught Gil off guard.

As he drove off, the detective couldn't shake the sense that here, in the shadow of the Black Mountains, anger and resentment ran as deep as the old mine shafts beneath their feet.

———

Sixty miles away in Cardiff, the autumn chill nipped at Warlow's ears as he and DC Gina Mellings trudged along the leaf-strewn pavement. They'd left the Jeep several streets away from the University of Wales Hospital. A crafty move Warlow had perfected over the years.

'Believe me, it's a lot quicker,' he'd assured Gina as they'd set off on foot. 'Beats circling the carpark like vultures for half an hour.'

As they rounded a corner, a gust of October wind whipped up a small cyclone of crisp leaves. Gina tugged her coat tighter and glanced sidelong at her superior.

'We can't be that far from John Lewis, can we?' She floated the question in a suspiciously innocent tone. 'If I needed to pop in, I mean?'

Warlow's brow furrowed, his mouth opening to bleat out a

retort. Something along the lines of needing to keep one's mind on the job, when he caught the mischievous glint in her eye. He shook his head. 'Alright, which one of them put you up to that?'

'DI Allanby suggested I mention it,' Gina admitted with a grin. 'Said it was a rite of passage.'

'Cheeky sod,' Warlow muttered, but there was no malice in it.

They lapsed into preoccupied silence, broken only by the need to pay attention to traffic as they crossed roads to enter a park gate, the noise of cars mingling with the wail of an ambulance.

As the hospital loomed ahead, Gina's stride faltered slightly.

'Bit nervous about the postmortem, sir.'

Warlow raised an eyebrow. 'You don't strike me as the squeamish type, Gina.'

'First time for everything,' Gina muttered. 'Plus, I'm not Rhys.'

She was stating the obvious, there. By this stage of their visit to the morgue, Rhys would be like a kid at Christmas.

'Ah, yes, DC Harries. Never far from our minds when we near the house of the dead.' A smile tugged at his lips. 'He's a one-off.'

'Sergeant Jones says he's not sure where he came from, but there's probably an alien spaceship somewhere missing a passenger.'

Warlow's smile blossomed into a grin. 'But we wouldn't swap him, would we?'

'No, sir.' After a few more silent yards, Gina added, 'Do you think he'll make sergeant?'

'Absolutely. He's already proven himself in the field,' Warlow said, and couldn't resist adding, 'and in a hayloft, a few rough pubs, and a snake-infested airfield.'

Gina's turn to nod with a half-smile, remembering the cases and scrapes Rhys and Warlow had been involved in of late.

'We need to keep him close, mind. Can't have him shipped off to darkest Powys, chasing sheep rustlers.'

Gina exhaled through her nose. 'I'll tell him you said that, sir. He'll be chuffed. It might cheer him up. He's miffed at missing this one.'

As they approached the hospital's Pathology suite entrance, the levity in their conversation ebbed away. Warlow's expression grew serious, his eyes taking on a steely glint that Gina recognised all too well.

'Right, then, DC Mellings,' he said, his voice low. 'Let's see what Milburn's body has to share with us. Polos at the ready?'

With a shared nod of determination, they stepped into the sterile confines of the morgue, leaving the autumn day behind and entering a world where death held all the answers.

CHAPTER THIRTEEN

THE DOUBLE DOORS of the morgue swung open with a soft hiss, releasing a gust of cold, antiseptic-laden air.

Warlow strode in, his plastic overshoes shuffling against the polished floor.

Gina followed, her steps more hesitant, one hand tucked in the one pocket of her coveralls, fingers wrapped around her roll of Polo mints. She'd already put one in her mouth, and it rested against her palate, clearing her sinuses at the same time. She slid up a surgical mask and tucked a strand of hair under her hat. Doing it sent an odd ripple of recollections through her.

She and Warlow were in full PPE and with it came memories of lockdown. Long days trapped and bored in her mother's house. She and Rhys had not hooked up at that point. Lockdown with him in Tabernacle Terrace might have been a lot more fun.

But then, no one should have had fun during lockdown. She gave herself a mental kick.

Come on, Gina. Get it together.

Dr Sengupta glanced up from the body on the stainless-steel table, her gloved hands pausing mid-gesture. 'Ah, DCI Warlow. Good timing. I was just about to begin the cranial examination.'

Warlow nodded, his eyes already fixed on the pale form of Russell Milburn. The Y-incision on the chest had been neatly sutured. 'Dr Sengupta. Good to have you back. How's the little one?'

'A beautiful handful,' Sengupta replied, her eyes softening above her mask before her professional persona reasserted itself. 'Shall we begin?'

Gina dragged her eyes away from the white tiles on the wall towards the reason they were all there.

The HOP. The assistants. The police officers. The corpse.

Sengupta's voice took on a clinical tone. 'Subject is Russell Milburn, male, forty-four years old.' She worked efficiently, pointing out salient features. 'We have bruising and contusions on the left side of the face and a fractured ulna on the left as well. It's displaced. It would have rendered that arm painful and unusable. External examination has also revealed petechial haemorrhages on the conjunctivae and facial skin. These were separate and not related to the fall.'

Warlow leaned in, his brow furrowed. 'Asphyxiation?'

'Consistent with that, yes.' Sengupta nodded. 'We also observed facial congestion and cyanosis. But there's more. Fundoscopy showed dilation of the retinal blood vessels.'

Gina found her voice. But only after clearing her throat because it had become thick with minted saliva. She moved the sweet away with her tongue and asked the question. 'Is that inside the eye?'

'Yes.' Sengupta looked up. 'It's DC Mellings, right?'

Gina nodded.

'That's one side of the exam that doesn't involve cutting things open,' the pathologist explained. 'Looking into the eye. And the findings tally with the conjunctival changes. But neither are marked. In fact, I had to look hard to be convinced.'

Sengupta moved to the head of the table, carefully manipulating Milburn's skull. 'I'm about to open the cranium to assess the extent of the injury.'

The high-pitched whine of the bone saw filled the room.

Gina ground her back teeth, her hand instinctively

moving to her mouth, forgetting the intervening mask briefly. But, to her own surprise, curiosity won out over queasiness. She stepped closer, watching intently as Sengupta worked.

The metallic scent of blood mingled with the sharper smell of cerebrospinal fluid as Sengupta removed the skullcap.

'There's a small subdural hematoma consistent with the external bruising,' she reported. 'But note the petechial haemorrhages in the brain tissue as well.'

Gina leaned forward to look more closely at the pinpoint-sized red and purple spots scattered across the surface and within the tissue of the brain.

Warlow spoke. 'So, head injury first, then asphyxiation?'

'That would be my initial evaluation, yes,' Sengupta agreed. 'The head injury likely incapacitated him, as did the arm fracture, but wasn't the direct cause of death.'

Gina cleared her throat, her voice slightly muffled by the mask. 'What caused the asphyxiation? Did he end up face down?'

Warlow shot her an approving glance as Sengupta nodded.

'Good question, DC Mellings. And the answer is no. There'd be evidence of flora or fauna in his mouth. But it's all clean. There are some marks on the neck. At the moment, it's difficult to separate those out. The chin strap from the helmet caused some bruising. But, if I was asked to hazard a guess, I'd say perhaps a plastic bag. Sometimes with bags, there are nil signs unless there is constriction around the neck, as in a ligature. And these are subtle signs, but they are there. We'll need to run some tests on trace evidence around the mouth and nose. That may confirm, it may not.'

The pathologist moved back to the chest cavity. 'I've already examined the thoracic and abdominal organs. The lungs showed significant congestion, and there were petechial haemorrhages in the kidneys as well.'

The mint clicked against Gina's teeth as she asked, 'Is that also consistent with asphyxiation?'

'Indeed,' Sengupta replied. 'It's one of the less obvious signs, but important in building the overall picture.'

Warlow straightened up, his eyes still on the body. 'Anything else of note, Doctor?'

Sengupta nodded, moving to a nearby table where several vials were arranged. 'Negatives, mainly. Preliminary toxicology came back with nothing, but we'll run a more comprehensive panel.'

She picked up a clipboard, flipping through the pages. 'Based on stomach contents, his last meal was approximately four to six hours before death. Salads, chicken. No alcohol in the stomach, though we're still waiting on blood alcohol levels.'

'Given the head injury and the asphyxiation, could you estimate how long it was between the two events?' Gina asked.

Sengupta's eyebrows rose slightly. 'Another excellent question, DC Mellings. It's difficult to be precise but based on the degree of swelling around the head trauma, I'd estimate not much separation between the two.'

Warlow's jaw tightened. 'Incapacitated by coming off his bike and then killed shortly afterwards.'

'That would be my assessment, yes,' Sengupta confirmed.

The DCI's phone buzzed, breaking the tense silence that had fallen. He glanced at the screen, then back at Sengupta. 'Anything else we should know?'

'It'll all be in my preliminary report. And you'll get that as soon as possible, of course.'

Warlow nodded. 'Thank you.' He turned to Gina. 'Anything else you want to ask?'

Gina shook her head. Asphyxiation seemed enough to be getting on with.

As they changed in the small area outside the morgue doors, Warlow discarded his mask and considered Gina. 'You survived.'

'Thanks to the Polos,' she said.

'Not just the Polos. Some people are too overwhelmed to think. Those were spot-on questions.'

Gina smiled, the last of her mint dissolving. 'Thanks, sir. It's fascinating, really, once you get past the… well, you know.'

Warlow's lips twisted in a half-smile. 'Indeed I do.'

That the inanimate corpse on the trolley was walking around a few days ago and did not deserve what was done to him. They'd peel away layers of the Milburn onion and no doubt find some bruised, even rotten spots. But rotten enough to condemn him to an untimely death? Warlow thought it unlikely.

There'd be a reason this had happened. Their job now was to dig through the mire to find the motive.

'Just imagine the stories you'll be able to swap with Rhys now that you're a veteran,' Warlow added.

'But a plastic bag? What does that all mean?' Gina matched Warlow's stride as they reached fresh air.

'It means we can put all thoughts of this being an accident to bed.'

Gina shuddered. 'It all happened in broad daylight, though.'

'But somewhere very remote. Let's consider that for a moment. Let's think about the motive. You suggest some and then tell me why they don't apply.'

They walked on a few strides in silence before Gina said, 'Road rage? Someone fed up with him not letting them pass. The road is pretty narrow.'

'Good. And why is that unlikely?'

'The plastic bag.'

'Exactly. Now run with that and remember your five Ps as motivation.'

Gina thought before answering. 'Panic. We can eliminate panic. The unplanned moment.'

'Exactly. Rage incidents don't end up in asphyxiation. Go on.'

'The same probably could apply to passion as a motivator. Only in that it's usually unplanned, too.'

'I agree. This has all the makings of Milburn being a target.'

'So, that brings us to psychosis. Someone who hated him so much—'

'They could follow him in a vehicle and run him off the road. And instead of helping him after he'd fallen, they held a garbage bag over his head.'

'Oh, God. Now I do feel sick,' Gina said.

'Keep going. You're doing well. Psychosis can't be eliminated. Someone he's wronged. But it might be low on the list.'

'That leaves us with protection. Someone saw him as a threat to themselves or… the community?' Gina suggested.

'Correct. And one more.'

'Profit, sir. Someone would gain from not having him around.'

Warlow grinned. 'Deductive reasoning, detective constable.'

Gina didn't smile. 'It doesn't help us all that much, does it?'

'It all helps. Taking a piece off the chessboard helps. We suspected this was no accident by him ending up where he was found. Now we can be certain it was not. How are you in typing up notes as we drive?'

'That's Sergeant Peters's speciality, sir, isn't it?'

'It is. I don't know how she does it. I get car sick reading the paper if I'm not driving.'

'Oh, that doesn't bother me at all.'

'Good.' Warlow headed across the hospital grounds. 'We need to get this information to the others, and we'll stop for a cuppa in McArthur Glen. It'll make a change for the staff in Costa to see me with you. They think Rhys and I are joined at the hip. Or at least my hip and his mid-thigh.'

This time, Gina did laugh and out loud.

CHAPTER FOURTEEN

JESS COULDN'T REMEMBER BEING in any ward manager's office where there were table lamps. There were in Milburn's office. This was a side of the NHS not many people saw.

Foxtrot, foxtrot, sierra.

Jess's eyes swept the room, taking in the ergonomic chair, the state-of-the-art computer setup, and the minimalist artwork adorning the walls. Such a far cry from Deena Barton's cramped room at the Black Mountain Community Hospital. The difference spoke volumes about the priorities of the Health Board's upper echelons.

Because we're worth it?

Right.

Besides the desk chair hunkered a couple of upholstered seats for visitors, and a few more plastic stackers for when the room got busy. Rhys had taken one of those out to sit on, his long legs making the seat look like it belonged in a kid's nursery. Jess took the comfy chair at right angles to Sharon, who sat, unsmiling, hands in her lap.

Jess kept her tone hushed and measured. 'You didn't travel to the hospital with Mr Milburn, Sharon?'

'No, I went on my own. Earlier. There were some papers I needed to sort out. For the meeting with Mrs Barton before we met with the others.' Her fingers fidgeted with the crease of her trousers.

'And you left before he did?' Jess probed, her eyes never leaving Sharon's face.

Sharon swallowed. It made a hard noise. 'He was going to ride his bike, he said.'

'Did he do that often?' Rhys asked.

'More sometimes than often. Occasionally, he'd go out at lunchtimes. If the weather allowed.'

'You didn't think it strange when he told you he'd be doing that?'

'No.' Sharon's response came over as clipped, her jaw tightening as she struggled to maintain composure.

Jess sensed the woman's reluctance, recognising the internal tug-of-war between loyalty to her deceased boss and the need for honesty. 'How long have you worked together?'

'Since he was appointed. Fifteen months ago.'

'Easy to work with?' Jess asked, her tone gentler now.

The young woman's brow furrowed, conflict etched across her features. 'I wouldn't say easy. The job he did wasn't easy. He could be blunt with people. But he was… clever. He could read something and understand it in ten minutes.'

'But some people didn't like what he was doing, did they? People at the Black Mountain Hospital, for example.'

'No, they didn't. He had ideas for them, to help them. But they only heard the word "reorganisation" and they flipped.'

'Would you say you knew him better than anyone else here?' Rhys asked.

Sharon flinched, her eyes widening. 'I suppose. I worked with him the most. I organised his diary and set up his meetings.'

Jess leaned in. 'So, you'd be aware of anyone with ill intentions towards him?'

A strange tinkling laugh escaped Sharon's lips before she realised Jess wasn't joking. Her face paled. 'No, I mean, yes… I mean, there was no one.'

'But some changes he proposed made big waves, right?'

'Yes.' Sharon's voice trembled. 'But no threats.'

Rhys went for the jugular. 'No direct threats?'

'No,' Sharon insisted, her knuckles white as she gripped the thumb of one hand in the palm of the other. 'I mean, if you're foolish enough to look at social media, then all kinds of strange people are out there. But no direct threats.'

'Why is Riggon worried about us going through his papers?' Rhys asked.

Sharon's lips quivered. 'Mr Milburn's plans. They're not actual blueprints, but proposals. For discussion first with the Health Board and then perhaps in the communities. But none have been released yet. He was meeting with the Welsh government next week. They have to sanction them.'

'Big changes?' Jess prodded.

Sharon nodded, her expression growing more miserable. 'Not everyone liked Russ, I admit that. And he used to tell me the changes would put some noses out of joint.'

Jess's tone softened again. 'On a personal level, no suggestion of him being involved with anyone other than his partner at work?'

Sharon shook her head vehemently. 'When he came back from his visits to the hospitals and wards, he used to say that it was good to see that the obesity gene was alive and kicking in the nursing community.'

Jess raised an eyebrow. 'Hmm, a nice bit of casual fat shaming then.'

'He could be sharp sometimes, like I said,' Sharon muttered, her cheeks flushing. 'He concentrated on the preventative side. Not just for us here, but in the country. He was part of a think-tank for a while. He had a bit of a bee in his bonnet about it. Wanted to guide the GPs towards obesity treatments.'

'Do, can you think of anyone who might want to do him harm?' Jess asked one last time.

Sharon's composure finally cracked. 'Look, Russ could be sarcastic, I admit, but he was kind to me. And he didn't care what people thought of him.'

She hesitated, and Jess urged her on. 'It's okay to be open,

Sharon. We'll take a formal statement later, but you can say whatever you want here.'

Sharon's gaze flitted between Jess and Rhys, her internal struggle evident.

'I've been here five years, and at least with Mr Milburn… Russ… you felt things would get done. So many people here are content to settle for their salaries and wait for pension day, but not Russ.' Her voice broke on his name, and she looked away, blinking back tears.

————

THE KITCHEN DOOR SLAMMED SHUT, and Huw Leyshon winced at the sound. His son Ian stormed in, face flushed with anger. They spoke entirely in Welsh.

'*Beth odd y mochyn moen?*' Ian demanded, which translated into 'What did the pig want?'

Huw sighed, running a hand through his thinning grey hair. 'You know what. He was asking about the meeting at the hospital. About Milburn.'

Ian's eyes narrowed. 'And?'

'And nothing. I told him what happened. How Milburn didn't want to listen, how he—'

'How he killed Mam, you mean,' Ian interrupted, his voice sharp as flint.

Huw's shoulders sagged. 'Ian, *er mwyn yr arglwydd*, we've been over this. Milburn wasn't even here then—'

Ian snapped. 'He's like all the other bastards, Dad. If they'd have kept their promises, Mam might still be here.'

Huw turned away without answering, preferring to fuss with the kettle.

'I won't be two-faced. I won't say I'm sorry he's gone,' Ian said, his voice low and dangerous.

Huw turned, kettle in hand. 'Don't say things like that. Whatever Milburn did, he didn't deserve—'

'Didn't he? How many lives will his precious "efficiency" ruin? How many families will suffer because of his decisions?'

Huw set the mugs down with a clatter. 'That's as may be, but we can't go wishing death on people. It's not right.'

'Always the voice of reason, eh, Dad? Even after everything that's happened?'

Huw's eyes darted to his son's face. Searching, willing himself to ask the question that had been preying on his mind. 'Where were you that afternoon? When you called me to pick up Celyn?'

Ian's face hardened. 'What are you asking me, Dad?'

'I'm not… I'm just…' Huw fumbled for words. 'If the police come asking, it might be good to have an alibi, that's all.'

Ian exploded from his chair, sending it clattering to the floor. 'An alibi? You think I had something to do with this?'

'No, of course not!' Huw protested. 'But we know how the police think.'

Ian's laugh was bitter. 'Don't protect these buggers, Dad. Where were they when we were begging for help? When they cancelled three bloody appointments for Mam.'

Huw reached out, but Ian recoiled.

'I was on a job, alright? Fixing Lewis Bryn Du's trailer over in Trap if you have to know. You can call him yourself if you don't believe me.'

Huw knew the farmer and Bryn Du, the farm. But he wouldn't call. Instead, the words hung in the air, sharp and accusing.

Huw nodded slowly, but something in his son's eyes—a flicker of… what? Fear? Guilt?—left him unsettled.

'Sorry,' he said softly. 'I just… I worry, that's all.'

Ian's shoulders slumped, the fight draining out of him. 'Yeah, well. You don't need to worry about me, Dad. I didn't do anything.'

As his son trudged out of the kitchen, Huw stared after him and then into his cooling tea.

He wanted to trust Ian, desperately wanted to. But as the silence settled over the house once more, Huw couldn't shake his disquiet.

Ian's mother's death festered like a blackthorn in his son's heart. He'd not had a good word to say about hospitals or doctors since it all happened. Since they'd seen her suffer so much when the syringe driver stopped giving her any relief.

He hated himself for having these thoughts, but Ian's bitterness simmered under the surface as a constant reminder of the horror they'd endured. He'd changed since they'd lost Val, they both had. He'd controlled his own anger, channelling it into work on improving the lot of others. But Ian was a long way from that. All Huw wanted now was to make sure Ian's temper didn't get him into trouble.

He picked up his mug. On the wall hung some of Val's wisdom. Old sayings she had loved, framed with the words arcing over a print of the mountains.

Gwyn y gwêl y frân ei chyw

A crow sees its chick as white.

Even Gil had laughed on seeing that writ large. A truism about how a parent never saw its own child's faults. Especially apposite now that both men were grandparents, though Gil had remarked acerbically that these days, someone would undoubtedly twist this innocent saying into a battleground.

'They'd claim it's a micro-aggression, perpetuating systemic oppression through linguistic colonialism,' he'd remarked gruffly.

'Do those words actually mean anything?' Huw had asked.

'Buggered if I know,' had been Gil's pithy answer, and they'd shared a rueful laugh.

Men from a generation that understood where they'd come from and the history it contained and refused to have it rewritten.

And perhaps what Huw was doing was the exact opposite to a crow seeing its chick as white. He might be seeing fault in Ian where there was none.

He sincerely hoped so.

CHAPTER FIFTEEN

WARLOW TREATED Gina to a flat white with oat milk. DCI and DC retreated to the Jeep to drink the coffee.

Warlow wanted a little peace and quiet, which, given the hoard of shoppers at the outlet mall where Costa was situated, half of whom had opted to queue for a sticky bun and a beverage, was about as likely as a bank holiday heat wave.

He parked in a quiet corner. Coffee'd up, he set up the work phone on a holder on the dashboard, adjusting it with decreasing patience.

'One day, so Rhys says, we'll have sim cards implanted in our heads and all that would happen now is that a holo-screen would drop down from the rearview mirror.'

Warlow gritted his teeth and tightened a knob on the holder for the third time. 'Don't get me wrong. It is still bloody incredible to think that I could talk to someone on top of Everest at this very minute.'

'Do you know someone up there, sir?'

'I have a list of people I wish were up there, but no, sadly I do not.'

The phone, stubbornly, refused to sit and dropped forward again at a drunken angle.

'An implanted sim and images in our brain would be a lot quicker than this sodding thing.'

Gina glanced at him over the rim of her cup, before saying, warily, 'You've had the lecture too, then? From Rhys? About the "future"?'

'Rhys would've made a great Tomorrow's World presenter,' Warlow said, the phone finally deciding to play ball as he took his hands away and held them up either side of it, waiting for it to slip again.

'Tomorrow's World? Is that on Amazon Prime?'

Warlow threw her one of his best sideways glances. 'No. Very BBC. I think it started off in black-and-white and, according to them, by 2025, we should all be in flying cars.'

Gina drew air in through her teeth. 'I wouldn't mention flying cars to Rhys, sir. That's at least forty minutes of regurgitated TV documentary stuff right there.'

'Noted.' The phone burped a warning, and DS Catrin Peters's face appeared. Followed by four other faces arranged in slightly different-sized rectangles.

'Always nice to have these family catch-ups,' Gil said.

'I'm hoping we all have something useful to say. Catrin, you are first. '

'How did the postmortem go, Gina?' Catrin asked.

'The Polos worked a treat, thanks, sarge. But I won't steal Mr Warlow's thunder on that.'

'Ooh, sounds intriguing,' Gil said.

'Right.' Catrin was suddenly all business. 'I had an interesting call with a clinical director from the Health Board where Milburn worked previously. One that threw up the odd skeleton.' She explained what Forester had told her about the disgruntled suspended consultant, plus the grumbling and still-to-be-resolved inquiry into both the consultant and Milburn's handling of it.

'Sounds as if we'll need to visit,' Warlow said.

'In the meantime, I'll do some background on the skeleton, a Dr Latimer,' Catrin added.

'Jess?' Warlow prompted.

'I'll let Rhys fill you all in on our visit to the Health Board.'

Rhys waved from his phone. 'It's a bit like lockdown, this,' he said. 'But without the fear and paranoia.'

'Oh, that's all still there,' Gil said. 'Just wears a different set of clothes.'

Just as Rhys recounted their visit, Warlow's personal phone pinged a notification. Another text message. He glanced at the phone on his lap and frowned.

From Jodie, his soon-to-be daughter-in-law:

Can you ring? Urgent.

Jodie, a nurse, was not a woman given to exaggeration. Warlow felt something unpleasant ripple inside him. He looked up at the assembled team.

'Carry on. I need to take this.'

He stepped out of the car and walked a few yards between the parked vehicles, his fingers pressing on the little icon that would return the call.

Jodie picked up after two rings. 'Evan, thanks for calling back.'

Something in her voice made the ripple double down into a full-blown wave of anxiety.

'Jodie, what's wrong?'

Jodie exhaled. A quick, tremulous sound. 'It's Tom. He was on a late shift. Starting at one. He's been thrown from his bike. They've taken him to A and E. I'm on the way there now.'

'What?… How?' There were words in his mind, but he couldn't articulate them.

'He's conscious but confused. Done something to his shoulder. That's all I know. They rang me at work.'

'How long does it take him on a bike from Walthamstow?' Warlow asked. It sounded like a whine of protest in his own ears.

'He catches the Tube to Hampstead and bikes it from there. Takes him about fifty minutes. He insists on it for the exercise. You know Tom.'

Warlow did. His clever, funny, stubborn son.

'Okay, I'm on my way.'

'I'll be there in under an hour. Why don't you wait until—'

'I can be halfway there in an hour.'

The line went quiet.

'Are you okay, Jodie?'

'Yes. I'm a nurse, remember? I'm supposed to be able to handle this kind of thing.'

'Crap. It's never the same when it's someone close.'

'No,' she said, quietly. 'Thanks.'

'Keep me informed.'

'I will.'

Warlow ended the call and stood, for a moment, with his back to the Jeep and his face pointing towards the grey sky.

Complications were never welcome. And he was heading up another murder investigation.

He rang Buchannan and explained.

'Go,' said the Buccaneer. 'Jess can run this until you get back.'

'I could wait and let Jodie go alone. She's—'

Buchannan cut him off. 'Do you want me to send a car for Gina?'

'No. I'll drop her at the railway station at Bridgend. Rhys can come and pick her up from Neath or Swansea.'

'Keep me informed, Evan,' Buchannan said, with an unusual degree of earnestness.

Warlow rushed to the car. The group call was in full swing. Gina was talking.

'I was just telling everyone about the GP at the meeting with Milburn, Dr Joshi—'

Warlow cut her off. 'Apologies. Something has come up and I'm going to have to end this call. Tom's had an accident. He's in hospital. I'm going to London.'

After a moment of stunned silence, everyone started speaking at once.

Warlow held up his hand. 'I'm going to drop Gina off at the train station. Rhys, can you get to Neath to pick her up? Jess, you run the show.'

'What happened?' Jess spoke for everyone.

'Knocked off his bike. And yes, I know, bloody ironic doesn't come near.'

No one spoke. They'd moments earlier been talking about someone who'd died from that same trauma. Almost.

'I have no details, but, is there anything anyone needs to know?'

'Why are you still here?' Gil said.

Warlow's smile was fleeting but grateful. He picked out the phone from the cradle and pressed the end call button. Next to him, Gina looked anxious.

'Sorry—'

'There is no need to apologise, sir,' Gina said. 'Let's get going.'

———

GINA GOT BACK to HQ well before Warlow reached North London. They were all waiting, but her first action was to ask Jess about the DCI.

'No news, I'm afraid. I spoke to him briefly half an hour ago. He told us you'll fill us in on Sengupta's findings.'

Gina barely had time to shrug off her coat before Jess called an impromptu briefing with the young DC at the centre of attention.

'Asphyxiation,' she said. 'Sengupta was certain it was the cause of death. He might have had some concussion from falling off the bike, but she felt that had not killed him.'

Everyone stared at her. A kind of what-is-this-alien-species stare.

'How?' Gil demanded. 'Did his helmet chin strap get twisted or something?'

'It's a "something", I'm afraid, sarge.' Gina suspected Warlow would have made her deliver the autopsy findings, but it felt much more nerve-racking with him not there.

'Did Sengupta have any suggestions as to what?' Jess asked.

Gina nodded. 'The findings...' She quickly consulted her

notebook as an aide-memoir. 'Haemorrhages and petechiae in the conjunctiva and kidneys and retinal vessel dilation.'

She looked up and saw several raised eyebrows. 'I saw some of them. She admitted they were subtle. She also suggested that this kind of subtle change could have been from a plastic bag.'

'What?' Rhys expressed his surprise, which echoed the look on everyone else's face.

'Mr Warlow suspects he was followed to the mountain, driven off the road by another vehicle, and then attacked while he was incapacitated. Possibly by someone holding a plastic bag over his head. He'd broken his arm, by the way. Which meant he'd not be in much of a position to resist.'

'That sounds ugly,' Rhys said.

'Malice aforethought,' Gil muttered.

Jess spoke up. 'I'll speak with Evan later. We need to press on. There isn't much left of the day, but enough time to set some things up. Tomorrow, we need to take a deep dive into Milburn's recent activity.' She turned to Gina. 'Catrin is off tomorrow, so you'll be running the Incident Room. Okay?'

Gina nodded.

'I could come in, ma'am,' Catrin volunteered. 'My mother would have Betsi in a heartbeat.'

Jess smiled. 'At this stage, it's all discovery. We'll manage. But I might hold you to that offer in a day or two.'

'I hope Mr Warlow's son is okay,' Catrin said by way of an answer.

'Amen to that,' Jess replied.

CHAPTER SIXTEEN

NORTHWICK PARK HOSPITAL sat under the umbrella of the London Northwest University Health Trust. They were all bloody University Health Trusts these days, even though Warlow struggled to find out which university they were alluding to more often than not.

Once, he dared not think how long ago, the place may have been considered of modern construction. Nothing like the brick or stone buildings in Central London, like the old Middlesex Hospital, once on his Metropolitan beat, built in the eighteenth century and now sadly gone.

Northwick Park had been someone's idea of modernity. But it had not aged well. Grey concrete and dirty glass windows looked out over London. Wembley's arches were visible from here, too, and behind was the famous hill on which sat Harrow School.

Warlow didn't give a monkey's for any of that.

He found the assessment unit after asking for directions. Found Tom sitting up with a vomit bowl at his side. And, once his heart had finished clenching, he sputtered, 'Christ, Tom, you've looked better.'

Tom attempted a smile, wincing as it pulled at the sutures above his left eye. His right eye was nearly swollen shut, his face a canvas of cuts and bruises. 'Cheers, Dad.

And please don't make me laugh. I've got stitches inside my mouth, too.'

Warlow pulled up a chair, eyeing the sick bowl in Tom's hand and the strapping on his shoulder. 'How bad is it, then?'

'Possible concussion, sprained ACJ. They're going to do an MRI.'

Warlow tilted his head.

'Acromio-clavicular joint. Point of the shoulder. Nothing broken, thankfully.' Tom's words slurred slightly. 'Feeling a bit queasy, though. Shock or maybe the drugs.'

'What happened?' Warlow asked.

It was impossible to read his son's features, inscrutably swollen as they were.

Tom sighed, closing his good eye briefly. 'A van turned right at some lights. No indicator. I swerved, came off. Nearly ended up under a bus.'

Warlow felt a chill run through him. 'Bloody hell, Tom.'

'Or words to that effect. Police are interviewing the van driver and there were a load of witnesses. They'll keep me in overnight, just to be safe. I honestly do not know if I passed out or not. It's all a blur, and my head feels like someone has an anvil in there and they're shoeing a horse.'

'I'll stay with Jodie tonight,' Warlow said immediately.

Tom shook his head slightly. 'Dad, there's no need—'

Warlow cut him off. 'No, but I'm still staying. I'm sure she'll be glad of the company. My decision. Anything I can get you?'

'No, I just want to sleep, but probably not a good idea at the moment.'

A nurse appeared, clipboard in hand. 'Sorry, I need to do some observations.'

'Okay. I can come back.' Warlow nodded, standing. 'Right. See you later.'

He wandered the corridors, not sure why his pulse refused to slow down. To his surprise, he sensed a lump forming in his throat, and his eyes stinging.

This wasn't in the script.

He kept walking, got to the exit, turned around and

walked back again. Several times until eventually he found a quiet corner to settle into.

This was not like him. And he struggled to assimilate it. Gil would have a field day. The tough-as-old-boots detective overwhelmed by… what? Emotion? He wasn't big on that as core curriculum subjects went. But the reality of how close he'd come to losing Tom now hit him like a physical blow.

This man in the hospital bed, a skilled surgeon in his own right, was still his boy.

The realisation jarred Warlow. He wasn't accustomed to this… vulnerability. Where the hell was the hard-nosed cop? He pondered, tried to resolve it. Something to do with the current case, perhaps?

Milburn, the cyclist, knocked off his bike and killed. But deep down, he accepted it was more than that. The image of Tom almost under that bus kept flashing through his mind, irrational as it was.

He'd seen people who'd been struck and gone under buses. Seen the way those enormous wheels stripped the flesh like flaying a bloody rabbit—

'Evan?'

Hearing his own name startled him. He looked up to Jodie, see Tom's partner, concern etched on her face. Before he could stop himself, words tumbled out. 'If anything happens to Tom… Denise will never have forgiven me.'

His chest tightened, and a sudden and overwhelming sense of loss overtook him.

He caught himself. These were words that should have stayed locked in his head, but they'd escaped, irrational and gut-wrenching and shocking, even to his own ears.

What the hell did his dead ex-wife have to do with any of this?

But Jodie's eyes softened with understanding.

'Oh, Evan,' she breathed. She sat next to him and took his hand.

Warlow stared at it, befuddled.

Jodie, the nurse half his age, should have been the one he

was comforting. But someone had turned the table when he wasn't looking.

'Is that what this is about?' she asked.

Was it?

Warlow blinked, unable to speak.

Jodie pulled him into an embrace, and he let her, his usual stoic façade crumbling.

'You never really grieved for her, did you?' Jodie murmured. 'None of you did.'

Warlow shook his head, surprised to find tears threatening. This wasn't like him at all, but the fear of losing Tom had cracked something open inside him, releasing emotions he'd long suppressed.

'It's okay to feel like this,' Jodie said softly. 'But Tom's okay. And it's okay to miss Denise, too. To remember her. Even after all this time.'

In that quiet hospital corridor, Warlow allowed himself a moment of rare openness. Held by a young woman as he confronted the complex tangle of fear, relief, and long-suppressed grief for a woman he had truly lost many years ago, but who he had helped bury only a year or so ago.

'Funny how you can love someone, but sometimes not like them very much.'

Jodi's smile dripped sympathy. 'I think most couples can say that if their honest.'

Seeing Tom hurt, and knowing how close it had come, had cracked something in him. Underneath the hard edges he showed the world, there was still a father there, raw and unguarded, whether he liked it or not.

————

Afternoon became evening. Much of it spent doing little but waiting for more assessments and the MRI. Northwick Park wasn't where Jodie worked, but the ward staff knew what she was—one of theirs—and with that came respect and an effort to make sure she was kept well informed. When a tired-looking ward manager explained the MRI would probably not be until 8pm, they both said their goodbyes to Tom, whose nausea had eased but whose headache remained.

'What are you going to eat?' Tom asked as they left.

'Don't worry about us,' Warlow replied.

'There's a great Himalayan place around the corner from ours.'

Jodie smiled and leaned in to kiss her partner. 'You're obviously feeling better if you're talking about food. Has your boss been to see you?'

'She has. She was nice about it, but she thought I was a total prat for letting it happen.'

'The accident has nothing to do with that. She thinks you're a total prat, anyway.' Jodie beamed.

'Kick a man when he's down, why don't you?' Tom winced as he moved his strapped arm in order that Jodie could give him a peck on the cheek.

Warlow observed these bluff insults with amusement and fondness. They were good for each other, these two. Tom was a lucky boy.

Warlow put the Jeep in a long-term parking spot at Northwick Park station at Jodie's suggestion. She sorted it all out on his phone at £4 a day. She'd argued that ULEZ and congestion charges made driving across North London a non-starter.

It took them a long hour on the Tube to get back to the flat. By the time they arrived, Jodie had ordered pizza at Warlow's insistence. Tom considered it an evil form of carbohydrate overdose, but Jodie loved it.

'While the cat's away,' Warlow had muttered. It also meant getting away with just eating a slice since he had never been less hungry.

Jodie, over the food and an Italian beer from their fridge —strangely enough not considered in any way a waste of carbs by Tom—told him everything that the ward manager and the medics had told her. They stated Tom had been concussed, but that the MRI was only a belt and braces check.

'Thanks for coming up. And thanks for staying with me. I'm glad I'm not alone here tonight,' Jodie said. She hugged him once more. When she pulled back, her eyes were smiling. 'You Warlow boys. You all think you're as tough as nails, but not one of you is bulletproof.'

In the tiny spare room, Warlow sat on the bed, whilst Jodie showered in the one bathroom. He rang Jess. He'd kept her informed by text, but now he needed to hear her voice.

'How is he?' were her first words.

'Banged up. Had an MRI this evening, and they're keeping him in for observation. He won't be operating for a few weeks, that's for sure.'

'But he's okay?'

'Yep. They say he'll be fine.'

'Thank God. How are you holding up?'

Great question. 'Realising that I'm getting far too old for this.'

Jess rolled out a breathy laugh. 'My mother used to say, whenever I got in too late, "When you stop worrying about your kids-ah, you'll be hearing the last nail in the coffin lid."'

'She got that right. And I like the Italian accent.'

'Makes it more dramatic. I sometimes use that same accent and the same phrase when I want to wind Molly up.'

'And how is she?'

'Fine. I still can't believe she's already in her second year at uni. Working hard and there might even be some romance on the horizon, though she's keeping those cards very close to her chest. No name yet, just a "someone" she is going to a party with.'

Warlow sensed Jess was secretly pleased by that.

'How did vespers go?'

'Gina's asphyxiation bomb came as a bolt from the blue.'

'I bet it did.'

'Catrin's off tomorrow, so I'm going to leave Gil to support Gina. But we'll have the catch-up meeting tomorrow morning and decide actions from there. I'll take Rhys up to visit the suspended doctor from Milburn's last place of work.'

'I'll leave that up to you, but it sounds like a good idea. I could try to sit in via video link, but I don't know quite what my movements will be. Jodie's been amazing. But she feels she ought to go to work because they'll be assessing Tom anew at dawn and there's nothing she can do. So, I want to be free to make myself useful if I can.'

'Absolutely. We'll crack on down here.'

'How's Cadi?'

'I've got the phone on speaker so she can hear your voice. Her head is tilting at all angles.'

Sitting on the bed, Warlow smiled. 'Thanks, Jess.'

'For what? Sitting in a nice warm cottage in Pembrokeshire with a fierce guard dog to look after me?'

'There's another dog there then, is there?'

Jess's laugh was soft. 'Take no notice, girl.'

'I meant thanks for being there.'

The line went quiet. 'Tom's going to be fine, you know that, right?'

'I do… It's just that there was a sodding bus that only just managed to stop in time, and it could have been a lot worse.'

Jess sighed. 'I wish I was there.'

'Yeah. I wish you were too.'

'Get some sleep, Evan. I bloody hate clichés, but things are always that much better in the morning.'

CHAPTER SEVENTEEN

As WARLOW FINISHED the call with Jess, back at police HQ in Carmarthen, a different call began. The phone trilled, and Maggie Pearce suppressed a sigh as she saw the familiar number. She took a deep breath, put on a warm smile that translated into her voice, and answered.

'Dyfed Powys Police. How can I help?'

'Maggie? It's Ivy. Ivy Pugh. You remember me, don't you, love?'

'Of course, Mrs Pugh. How are you this evening?'

'Oh, it's terrible, Maggie. They're at it again. In the old hospital. I can hear them clear as day from my house.'

Maggie's hands stayed poised over her keyboard, ready to log the call. 'What can you hear, Mrs Pugh?'

'Chanting, love. And singing in tongues. It's not right, I tell you. And the kids! They're always up there, spray painting and whatnot. It's not safe, is it?'

Maggie nodded, though Ivy couldn't see her. 'I understand, Mrs Pugh. Can you tell me exactly where you are?'

'You know where I am, love. The little place off Folland Road. About two hundred yards up the lane. The council can't be bothered to put a name to it, but everyone knows it as Ffordd y Berach. Berach way. You'll have it written somewhere, won't you, Maggie?'

'Yes, of course. I need to confirm for our records. And you say you can hear sounds coming from the abandoned hospital?'

'Clear as a bell, Maggie. It's not right. Someone needs to do something.'

Maggie typed quickly, logging the details. 'I hear you, Mrs Pugh. I'll pass this information along to our officers. We'll get someone to check things out, but it might not be right away. Is that alright?'

'Well, I suppose it'll have to be, won't it? But you promise they'll come?'

'I promise, Mrs Pugh. We always look into these reports.'

After a few more reassurances, Maggie ended the call. She turned to her colleague, Dave, who'd been half-listening with a smirk.

'Ivy again?' he asked.

Maggie nodded. 'Yeah. Same story. Noises from the old hospital.'

Dave rolled his eyes. 'Christ, how many times is that now? You're too soft on her, Mags.'

'She's lonely, Dave. And scared. Costs us nothing to be kind.'

'Costs us time,' Dave muttered.

Maggie shrugged, turning back to her screen. 'I'd rather be the one who listened than the one who didn't.'

Dave shook his head, but there was a grudging respect in his voice. 'You've got more patience than I have, Mags. I'll give you that.'

Maggie, a good fifteen years younger than Dave, sent him a look. 'That's a low bar.'

Dave grinned. 'None taken.'

As she finished logging the call, Maggie couldn't help but wonder what it might be like being alone, worrying about noises in the distance. But then the next call came in, and thoughts of Ivy and her fears were pushed aside by the never-ending stream of emergencies, real and imagined, that made up a night shift in the control room.

———

DETECTIVE CONSTABLE CRAIG PETERS stood in the kitchen, his police uniform pristine, save for a small coffee stain he was furiously dabbing at with a damp cloth.

In the living room, Catrin moved about with their ten-month-old, Betsi, perched comfortably on her hip, the baby's bright eyes darting from object to object with insatiable morning curiosity.

Catrin spoke entirely in Welsh. Craig's family were not natural Welsh speakers, but he was trying since Catrin made no concession with the baby.

'*Pwy 'di hwna? Pwy yw'r blodyn bach pert na?*' Catrin pointed to the large mirror on the wall, asking the child to recognise her own reflection and comparing it to a pretty flower.

Betsi gurgled, reaching out to pat her reflection.

Catrin moved on, scooping up a threadbare stuffed lion from the sofa.

'*A dyma Llew.* Rawr!' She made a gentle growling noise, eliciting a peal of laughter from her daughter.

Craig's phone buzzed, and he chuckled, shaking his head as he read the message.

'What's got you grinning this early in the morning?' Catrin called out.

Craig wandered into the living room, coffee mug in hand. 'Text from Sammy. Sixth sense Ivy's been at it again. Phoned the station last night about "strange goings-on" at the hospital.'

Catrin's brow furrowed. 'The hospital? Glangwili?'

Craig shook his head, still grinning. 'That's the point. Not Glangwili. She's up in the Amman Valley. The hospital on your watch. Where your dead cyclist was visiting before his untimely end.'

'Sh… ugar,' Catrin muttered, but quickly added, 'Sorry,' to Betsi, who was contentedly gumming on the lion's ear. 'He's not my dead cyclist, thanks. But that's a coincidence, right?'

'Don't worry yourself.' Craig dismissed Catrin's curiosity

with a wave of his hand. 'Ivy phones in at least once a fort-night. Hearing noises, seeing lights. Lives alone in a cottage that overlooks the hospital site.'

Catrin nodded, but she'd worked with DCI Warlow for too long to accept coincidences without stopping to think. 'You reckon she's a bit fixated, then?'

Craig shrugged, downing the last of his coffee. 'Ask the call handlers. They're thinking of inviting her to their Christmas party. I'll keep an ear out, just in case.' He kissed Catrin on the cheek, kissed the baby next, and ruffled Betsi's wispy hair. 'Right, I'm off. Looks like a nice day. You two off to the park?'

'On the list,' Catrin said.

But as the door clicked shut behind him, she found herself pondering. Something DCI Warlow encouraged. A very underestimated skill was pondering, according to him.

The hospital, Ivy's calls, the dead cyclist—all swirled in her mind as she carried Betsi through to her room to sort out some clothing for the day. By the time she'd picked out trousers, top, and jumper for the baby, she'd filed Craig's information away, knowing full well she'd revisit all when she got back to work.

Or, better still, she'd maybe drop Gina a text when Betsi was having her first nap. The child's insistent babbling brought her back to the present.

'Alright, alright.' Catrin laughed, bouncing the baby gently. 'Let's get you dressed, *cariad*.'

As she passed through the kitchen to fetch some more disposable nappies, she stopped at the whiteboard hanging on the fridge and wrote the word 'IVY' in red. Since having the baby, she'd found the whiteboard invaluable as a list maker.

Catrin turned back to see the sunlight starkly illuminating the morning's breakfast adventures, with a teaspoon spilling the remains of a hard-boiled egg onto the surface of the table next to a sipping cup. Adjacent to that stood her own half-drunk morning tea, made for her by Craig in the mug he always used these days. One with the words: Sergeant Recharging. Please wait. I said…WAIT.

She liked the mug, but not as much as she liked the one she'd bought for him with an image of a blue-and-yellow-chequered pursuit vehicle and the words: It's Not Road Rage if you have a Siren.

Betsi had begun pointing at things when she wanted something, and now she was pointing at the bowl.

'More breakfast, madam?' Catrin asked.

She reached for a safety chair that sat on the table and put the baby in it, wiped her hands clean and spread some bits of egg on the slotted-in tray.

Betsi, using all her concentration, did her best to pick up some egg white and mash the lot into her mouth.

Catrin threw her tea into the sink and started a coffee pod percolating, all the while encouraging Betsi with descriptive words. Five minutes later, most of the egg had gone from the bowl, though a significant proportion remained randomly distributed around Betsi's mouth rather than in it.

'Ooh, you've inherited Dad's eating style.' Catrin grinned. She made her eyes wide with excitement. 'Blueberry yoghurt? Let's see how much you can get into your hair, shall we?'

———

THE AIR SMELLED stale as Rhys entered the Incident Room, redolent with yesterday's theories and frustrations. They were the first in, at Gina's insistence, and she hurried straight to the Job Centre, Post-it notes in hand.

'Fancy a brew?' she called over her shoulder.

'Go on, then,' Rhys replied, booting up his computer. and scrolling through his inbox, pausing at an email from Tannard, the CSI manager.

His fingers hovered over the phone for a moment before he dialled.

'Morning, Rhys,' Tannard's voice crackled through the speaker. 'Bit early for you, isn't it?'

'Oi, watch it.' Rhys feigned offence. 'What's this about Milburn's helmet?'

Tannard's voice came back all business. 'It's an expensive

model, the kind with a ratcheted wheel at the back that tensions a cradle around the back two-thirds of the helmet to keep it snug. We found a tiny fragment of plastic lodged in the ratchet wheel. No more than about three by two millimetres and with ragged edges. We've checked with the manufacturer and there is no plastic wrapping involved in packaging. Plus, it's white.'

'How did it get there, you reckon?'

'Based on the photos and tear vectors, it was noticeable that a certain level of tearing occurred, implying the action of someone putting on, or pulling off a plastic bag over said helmet and, by implication, the head.'

Rhys leaned back in his chair, the implications sinking in. 'Sengupta was spot on, then.'

'Appears so,' Tannard agreed. 'We'll run DNA, but it's possible someone might have slipped the bag over the head while the helmet was on and cinched it shut. Could be a fold of the top of the bag got caught.'

'Cheers. Keep us posted.'

He hung up just as the rest of the team trickled in, bleary-eyed and chatting. Rhys waited until they'd settled, the scraping of chairs and murmured greetings fading into expectant silence as they noticed the way he stood, like a kid at a Sunday school concert bursting to do his party piece.

'Right. I've just got off the phone with Tannard. Her team found plastic fragments in Milburn's helmet. All fits with the pathologist's theory of suffocation.'

The room fell quiet as the news sank in.

DI Allanby, who'd slipped in unnoticed, spoke from the doorway. 'It's all adding up, isn't it?'

It wasn't a question. Rhys swivelled to nod, meeting his boss's grim gaze. 'Yes, ma'am. It looks that way.'

Jess shrugged off her coat. 'Okay, then let's get cracking.'

CHAPTER EIGHTEEN

WARLOW GOT UP EARLY.

The noise of the city, the sirens, refuse trucks, a drunk shouting for 'Maria' at three in the morning delivered with more angst than an audition for West Side Story, had given him a restless night.

Yet these were sounds that had once been familiar, part of a rhythm he barely noticed. Now they felt distant, the hubbub of a metropolis growing more diverse in every imaginable way, and drifting further from the rest of the country as a result. Warlow held no strong brief either way, seeing the arguments on both sides, but it struck him that those in charge, of all political stripes, often missed the point. They had no language to explain what kind of society they were building, no plan they could share honestly with people outside these urban mixing bowls. Instead, everything seemed as if it were a runaway train with no brakes and the conversation turned into labels—progressive, reactionary, nostalgic, right and left—leaving most people feeling unheard in the places they still called home. Not for the first time, he relished the fact that he'd done his time in the Smoke and those that chose to be here now were welcome to it.

Once morning light crept through the curtains, he got up in time to see Jodie off for her early shift and played the waiting game with only the radio and his phone to keep him company in their flat.

The call came from the hospital at around 10:15. Tom had a reasonable night, his vitals were stable, and the consultant had seen the MRI and found nothing to be concerned about. Once they got his pain meds sorted out from the pharmacy, he'd be free to go.

Warlow showered, put on yesterday's clothes, and headed back out to travel across London by Tube. When he got to Northwick Park, Tom was waiting, sitting up in a very fetching and unflattering tied-at-the-back robe, eager to go home.

The ward manager read Warlow the riot act in Tom's presence. 'He's to take it easy for at least a week. Any odd symptoms, worsening headaches, vomiting, double vision, ring this number.'

He handed Warlow a printed sheet of A4 with a high-lighted number.

'I'll pass the message on to his nurse,' Warlow replied.

'There is that,' the ward manager conceded in a way that suggested such warnings were all too often ignored.

Warlow had brought a backpack with some fresh clothes for Tom, and forty minutes after arriving, they were returning to the flat on the Tube.

'What about your bike?' Warlow asked as they boarded the Metropolitan Line at platform two of the Tube station.

'Your lot have it,' Tom said. 'I spoke to someone yesterday. Front wheel is crushed, and the handlebars are knackered, but the frame is okay, so they said I can pick it up next week. Fixing it will give me something to do while I'm in the flat, waiting for my shoulder to get better.'

Some of the swelling had receded from Tom's right eye, but he still looked like a loser in a vicious street fight.

'You'll be lucky if Jodie agrees to you biking during the winter.'

'Fair point,' Tom said. 'Maybe I should shelve the idea until next spring. By then, I'll only have three months of the Northwick Park rotation left.'

'Then what?'

'I'm waiting to hear about a research job. Get my Master's done.'

They were getting odd looks on the train, but eyes slid away as soon as Warlow engaged with them. It was a look he'd perfected over the years, guaranteed to make people feel uncomfortable. Designed specifically for perpetrators. Or rubberneckers on a Tube train.

'Is that something you want to do?' Warlow continued.

'Not want but probably need. As I say, WLGOCV. Will look good on CV,' Tom said, as well as he could from a mouth still not opening properly.

It made him look and sound like a terrible ventriloquist.

At home, Warlow made some tea and tomato soup at Tom's request. As long as he could remember, it had been both his sons' go-to recovery food for all kinds of illnesses, including severe hangovers.

'How is your case?' Tom asked, gingerly sipping a spoonful.

'I've deliberately stayed off radar. Jess is in charge. That means, it'll probably be sorted by the time I get back.'

'I can't imagine her as fierce,' Tom muttered.

'Yes, well, Belgian Malinois can look friendly, but I've seen one fly through a car window and disarm a man with a knife.'

Tom paused in his soup ingestion to stare at Warlow with his good eye. 'As references go, that one might be best kept between you and me, Dad.'

'You know what I'm saying. Jess is a tough cookie at work.'

'What does it feel like to be back up in the big smoke?' Tom's mood seemed surprisingly light, all things considered.

Warlow suspected it was related to the painkillers. Then again, Tom had dodged a very nasty bullet. That sort of thing did wonders for self-appraisal and gratitude for being able, once again, to sit in your own home and slurp tomato soup.

'I'd forgotten how bloody noisy it is at night.'

Tom chuckled. At least that's how Warlow interpreted the sound emerging through his half-paralysed mouth. 'Compared to Nevern, everything is noisy.'

'And Walthamstow wasn't my patch.' Warlow went back to the original question.

'No, but you were in North London, weren't you?'

'North of the river, yes.'

'Was it Special Branch?'

Warlow let out a laugh. 'Good God, no. I was based out of Holborn.'

'Funny, I thought Mum mentioned you had an involvement with Special Branch.'

Was that after the first or the third bottle of vodka? Those were the words that Warlow wanted to say, but he didn't. No need to gild the prickly lily with that. Besides, he'd become momentarily lost for words because a very distant and vague bell rang somewhere in the back of Warlow's mind.

Special Branch hadn't existed as a unit in the Met since 2006.

But the link didn't register. Not then. And seconds later, they were chatting about Tom's brother, Alun, and the very uncomplimentary message he'd sent Tom from Perth in Australia, having seen the startling image of Tom's cut and swollen face in the hospital bed that Jodie had forwarded.

But then, that's what brothers did.

———

THE INTERVIEW ROOM in York Police Station was sterile and functional, its beige walls a sharp contrast to the vibrant "personality" of the man seated at the table.

Jeremy Latimer, or Mr Jeremy Latimer, as befitted his position as a consultant urologist, sat with perfect posture, his crisp white shirt and silk tie a statement of professionalism despite his current circumstances. He sported dark, wavy hair streaked with grey and full lips set in a perpetual, almost-smirk, exuding an air of intellectual superiority that barely masked his deep-seated insecurities and inflated sense of self-importance.

Jess's face filled the screen of the laptop positioned on the table. Her colleague, DS Martin Graves of North Yorkshire police, sat opposite Latimer out of shot, his presence a physical anchor in the room.

'Mr Latimer, thank you for agreeing to speak with us,' Jess began. 'DS Graves has given you the background, and I apologise if some of this sounds repetitive, but could you tell us how you knew Russell Milburn?'

Latimer's smile was practised, charming. 'Of course. Though I must say, I'm curious why you're asking me about Milburn.'

Jess paused, considering her response. 'DS Graves has explained that Mr Milburn died under suspicious circumstances. We're building a picture of him as part of our investigation. In doing so, we are interviewing a range of people who knew him.'

A flicker of surprise crossed Latimer's face, quickly replaced by concern. 'Fair enough. Russell Milburn and I had our differences, but suspicious circumstances, you say? How did it happen?'

'We're still investigating those circumstances,' Jess replied. 'What about your professional relationship with Mr Milburn?'

Latimer smiled. 'Professional relationship? That's a generous term for our run-ins. Russell Milburn was a bureaucrat who failed to understand the complexities of modern urology.'

'Could you elaborate on that?' Jess prompted.

'Certainly.' Latimer leaned forward, his voice taking on a lecturing tone. 'I was bringing innovation to a stagnant department. My methods may have been unconventional, but they were necessary. Milburn, in his short-sightedness, saw only inefficiency where I saw potential for excellence.'

DS Graves interjected, 'Your colleagues reported concerns about your ability to manage your caseload. Can you expand on that?'

Latimer's eyes flashed away from Jess to a point to the left of the laptop camera. 'My colleagues? You mean those so-called professionals content with mediocrity and milking the system to enhance their private practices? Look, everyone knows there has been a plot to oust me from the post. Jealousy, bullying—I've documented everything. Your reference to caseload mix is interesting. If I refuse to rush through consultations like a production line, that is because I have always put patient safety and diligence before being slipshod. Each of my patients deserves, and receives, thorough attention.'

Back in the interview room at Carmarthen, Jess waited.

Latimer's preoccupation had been a bone of contention. She'd read reports from patients. They described him as very attentive. Obsessively so. Hardly surprising since he spent almost an hour with each of them, resulting in clinics that overran by hours. But as a patient receiving that attention, who wouldn't think the consult top-notch?

'Even if that means other patients wait months to be seen?' Jess asked.

'Quality over quantity, Detective Inspector,' Latimer replied, his tone condescending. 'Something Milburn never grasped. I'm happy to explain my rationale since you've asked.'

Jess hadn't. But for a while, she was prepared to let the man have his head.

As the interview progressed, the surgeon's responses became increasingly erratic. He talked about his innovative research on chronic bladder inflammation and the use of cannabis oil. He dismissed patient concerns about his occasionally strange recommendations as misunderstandings and criticised the narrow-mindedness of the medical establishment.

The cannabis oil research, she'd read, was genuine. But suggesting to patients that they might consider using krill and ashwagandha oil as alternatives had marked him out as... eccentric.

'Look, the urology department's shared-care model was a mess. Patients didn't have a specific consultant, which meant communication had to be top-notch. But it wasn't. You'd have one consultant seeing a patient and another doing the surgery, often without proper handover. This led to many problems—patients not knowing who was in charge of their care, surgeons showing up to operate on patients they'd never met before. There were incident reports and investigations showing this was an ongoing issue and a recipe for poor patient experiences and confusion all round. I put myself forward as the clinical lead to overhaul all of this, many times.'

'Even though you were the most junior consultant?'

'Junior, but most skilful.' Latimer said this with no hint of deprecation.

'Mr Latimer,' Jess said, her patience wearing thin, 'is it true that you were heard threatening to kill Russell Milburn?'

Latimer's charm vanished entirely. 'Nothing but a turn of phrase. No one who knew me would take that seriously.'

Jess shifted some papers on her desk and read out. 'I hope you and your wife get cancer, so that if I don't fucking murder you, the big C will.' Jess looked up. 'Did you say that?'

'That's… it's completely out of context. Some things Milburn accused me of made me furious. He said I was not fit to be a surgeon. That I needed help. From a bloody manager, I ask you. And the world will soon understand the true scope of my work, despite Milburn's attempts to silence me.'

'I understand you're on semi-permanent leave while the Royal College conducts its investigation into the department.'

'They're swimming in shark-infested waters there. I have warned them. And I have given them a dossier on every other consultant in the department. In fact, I suspect some of them of criminal behaviour. Claiming additional activity sessions while they're swanning off—'

By now, forty minutes had gone by, and Jess had had enough. 'DS Graves will need details from you of your movements.'

'Hang on, I haven't fully explained myself here.'

'Sorry, Mr Latimer. This case is complex, and we have other interviews to conduct. But please make sure your contact details are left with DS Graves.'

A few minutes later, the link was up again, this time with no Latimer. 'Well, that was… illuminating,' Graves commented, his face appearing in a separate window on the screen. A seasoned detective with weary eyes hinting at a long career of seeing both the best and the worst of humanity.

'What he didn't tell you about was the time he locked himself and a nurse in a room to discuss his preference of having the catheter laid on the left side of the trolley instead of the right. She was in there for an hour and a half with him while he vented on how important it was to be able to reach the instruments without having to think too hard and used a measuring tape to show her exactly how he wanted things.'

'Did she report that?'

'She and a dozen others. He'd become… in their words… a bit odd.'

Jess rubbed her temples. 'How does someone with those… challenges make it through medical school, let alone become a consultant?'

Gil, who had been observing silently, spoke up. 'Mental illness doesn't discriminate based on intelligence or achievement. Sometimes, it's those same qualities that mask the underlying issues.'

'True,' Jess conceded. 'But surely, there were signs along the way?'

'Narcissism can be bloody insidious,' DS Graves added. 'In small doses, I suspect it might even help in certain high-pressure fields. It's when it tips over into disorder that problems arise. And here…' He shook his head. 'He doesn't have much of an alibi for the day in question. Rides a motorbike in leathers, so he has transport. But from us to you is, what, a good five or six hours?'

Jess nodded, her mind already moving forward. 'Right. Well, as unpleasant as that was, I don't think we can eliminate him until we establish where he was the afternoon Milburn went missing.'

'I'll get on to it, ma'am,' Graves said.

Jess thanked him and shut the laptop. Another loose end yet to be tied off.

CHAPTER NINETEEN

DC RHYS HARRIES stood in the doorway of Russell Milburn's office, overseeing the warranted search. It was a modest space, barely large enough for the four of them to move around comfortably. Apart from the artwork, the tastefully painted walls were adorned with a couple of framed certificates, but none of the bland motivational posters he'd seen downstairs.

'Right, let's get cracking,' Rhys said, gesturing to the three uniformed officers. 'Bag and tag everything. Pay special attention to any documents or electronic devices.'

The team set to work methodically. One officer carefully unplugged and bagged Milburn's computer, while another began sifting through a filing cabinet. The third started on the desk drawers. Sharon Higgs, the PA, stood outside in the corridor, ready to answer Rhys's questions if he had any. She had her arms crossed over her body, no less anxious about it all than she had been before.

Rhys watched the Uniforms work, the monotonous routine of an office search unfolding before him.

Staplers, paperclips, and half-used notepads were catalogued with the same care as financial reports and meeting minutes. The room smelled of plastic and laundry air freshener.

One of the officers called out, holding up a mobile phone charger. 'Should I bag this?'

Rhys nodded. 'Might as well. You never know.'

As the search continued, Rhys found his mind wandering.

This search, like so many other inquiries, exemplified the reality of police work—hours of systematic searching, often yielding nothing of value.

'DC Harries,' another officer spoke up, interrupting his thoughts. 'This drawer's locked. Want me to force it?'

Rhys moved over to the desk. 'Hang on.'

He walked back out to the corridor.

Sharon looked up expectantly.

'The locked drawer,' Rhys said. 'Do you have the key, by any chance?'

Sharon's eyes widened in panic and then widened a bit more as something clicked. 'I think there's a spare with the security officer. Hang on.'

She hurried down the corridor.

Rhys stuck his head back around the office door.

'Five minutes,' he said to the Uniform at the desk and got a nod in return.

It took seven, but Sharon came back, dangling some small silver keys.

'Great stuff,' Rhys said, as he took the keys and went to the desk while the Uniform stood by.

The drawer slid open. Inside were a couple of files marked "2025 Strat report". One subtitled "finance", the other "structural". Underneath were several unmarked envelopes.

Rhys, already gloved up, removed an envelope and slid out the contents.

His eyes widened as he pulled out a thin stack of photocopied images. They showed Milburn with a young woman— much younger than him. They weren't explicit, but the intimacy was clear: holding hands, stolen kisses on a tree-lined street.

'Well, well,' Rhys muttered, flipping through the photos.

On the back of one, scrawled in angry red ink, were the words "Cheating bastard".

This was unexpected. Amidst the banality of budget reports and meeting agendas, here was a glimpse into Milburn's personal life, and potential motive for what had happened to him.

Rhys immediately phoned DI Allanby.

'Ma'am? You're going to want to see this,' he said as soon as she picked up. 'I'm sending through some photos now. Looks like our Mr Milburn had a bit on the side.'

As he spoke, a curious Sharon Higgs appeared in the doorway, a puzzled look on her face.

Rhys glanced at the images again. No, definitely not her, though there didn't appear to be much difference in age between the girl in the image and Sharon. Her inquisitiveness had been likely triggered by what she'd overheard in his phone call. But for now, she'd need to be kept out of this loop.

'Be with you in a minute, Sharon,' he said and spread the papers on the desk before taking some snaps.

A little smile of wonder played over his lips as he sent the photos through. One moment, they were cataloguing paperclips, the next uncovering what could be a key piece of the puzzle.

———

At HQ, Jess observed as Gina posted up the images Rhys had found on the Gallery.

'Possibly a dusky equine, then,' Gil observed.

Gina turned a very puzzled look his way.

'He means,' Jess said, arms folded over her chest, 'a dark horse. I presume the originals have gone to CSI?'

'Rhys rang Tannard after he rang us, ma'am,' Gina said.

Jess let out a very long sigh.

'What are you thinking, ma'am?' Gina asked, stepping back to join Jess, scanning the boards.

'I'm thinking there's a lot about Russell Milburn we do not yet know. Such as, was his partner aware of these?'

'You mean the images?' Gil asked.

'The images and the implication of those images.'

'Want me to get her in for a chat?'

Jess nodded.

A grieving partner required careful handling. But Maeve O'Connor had struck her as resilient. The options were to visit her at home again or invite her in for an informal interview.

'No one's taken a statement from her yet?'

The corner of Gil's mouth turned down, and he shook his head.

'Then that's our excuse. Invite her in to give a statement, and we'll show her these—' She nodded at the images. She stayed quiet for a beat and then said, 'Doesn't it always astound you how complicated some people's lives are?'

Gina nodded. 'Like Rhys would say, ma'am, life is like a box of chocolates. You never know what's in there until you take the lid off.'

'Don't tell me Forest Gump is one of Rhys's favourite films?'

'How did you guess, ma'am?' Gina grinned.

'And it doesn't last long for the chronically obese,' Gil added.

'What?' Gina asked.

'Both the box of chocolates, and life,' Gil explained.

'That's so dark, sarge.'

Gil dipped his chin. 'Some call me the sergeant of darkness, some call me the gangster of... I can't remember the rest of it.'

'*The Joker*, Steve Miller band,' Jess said. 'And I think you are paraphrasing. A lot.' She glanced at the wall clock. Almost five.

Warlow's rule was that very little happened after five when relying on other agencies. Though it was a good time to contact people at home. Still looking at the boards, Jess said what was on her mind. 'Last acts for the day. Contact Maeve O'Connor, wait for North Yorkshire police to get back to us regarding Latimer's movements, and where are we with Milburn's phone records?'

'Rhys was chasing those,' Gil replied.

'Be good to see if he'd been receiving any regular calls from someone.'

'You thinking extortion, ma'am?'

'I'm thinking about a box of chocolates with only the orange cream and fudge left.'

'Not your favourite ones, ma'am?' Gina asked.

She received an old-fashioned look in reply. 'No. But sometimes, even I have been known to reach for one in desperation. So, extortion will be the orange cream of this box.'

'Lucky Rhys isn't here, or he'd been drowning in his own saliva by now,' Gil observed.

'Right,' Jess announced. 'Let's plough on for another half hour and then call it a day. Give me enough time to text Evan and find out if he wants to stay offline or be brought up to speed.'

———

THE JOURNEY to and from the hospital, tending to Tom, and chatting made the day disappear. At 3:30, Jodie turned up, having left work early. Warlow witnessed the reconciliation and the way Tom grimaced as Jodie's over-effusive welcome touched tender pressure points. Over a cup of tea, they shared once again the details of the accident, and he heard Jodie warn Tom, in no uncertain terms, that he was not to go back on that road on his bike with the dark nights and mornings looming.

But with her arrival and knowing how capable she was, and how remarkably well Tom seemed, Warlow made the decision that he might as well get back to Wales.

Tom and Jodie's flat was not big, and he felt already like a bit of a gooseberry.

Tom had defaulted to the sofa with an RPG game already playing on the screen. Despite protestations and invitations to stay as long as he wanted, Warlow explained that he ought to get back to work.

'And to Jess and Cadi,' Jodie said.

'Them too,' Warlow conceded.

He was on the Tube when Jess texted:

How is Tom?

> Home. Bruised but OK. I am on the Tube heading home.

Want to catch up?

> Iffy signal. Let me ring you once I'm en route.

By 18.30, he'd travelled back across to Northwick Park, picked up the Jeep from the car park and was on his way to Northolt to join the M4.

By that time, Jess, too, was in her Golf and heading west to Ffau'r Blaidd.

'Good day?' Were the first words Warlow spoke as the connection was made.

'I hope you're sitting comfortably,' Jess replied.

'Sounds ominous.'

'More added wrinkles,' Jess said.

'Right. I'm all ears.'

By the time he reached Nevern, thanks to roadworks on the M4—whenever, had there not been?—and a forced stop for an M&S sandwich and a comfort break at the Leigh Delamere Services, midnight was approaching.

His welcome from Cadi was no less effusive but, so as not to disturb Jess, Warlow opted for his cot in the garden room and a sleeping bag. He'd warned her he might do that, and he felt better for it. No point in the both of them losing sleep.

However, despite struggling with keeping his eyes open for the last forty minutes of the journey, now that he could let sleep come, the bugger stayed away.

Warlow replayed the last twenty-four hours as a reel in his head, with that first and horrifying image of a beaten-up Tom in the Assessment Unit bed stubbornly refusing to get out of his consciousness. He forced his mind around to what Jess had told him of their progress in the case. Milburn having a set of compromising images in his locked drawer had been something Warlow had not seen coming.

Yet, it was ever thus. Rarely did murder not involve people's backgrounds and personalities. Random killings, though they always made the headlines, were mercifully few and far between. Murder, by definition, meant that people were both the victims and the perpetrators, and their actions were driven by motivation, leading to specific causes and effects.

In short, people could be a pain in the arse.

And the more they learned about Milburn, the more complicated things became. But were any of those complications a justification for murder?

Warlow doubted that sincerely.

He had a non-fiction book on the go. A book that had mistakenly found its way into a box of trinkets he'd more or less swept off a desk in his hurry to leave the house when his and Denise's marriage had imploded. Some actor's memoirs where a fading career had rotted into a kiss and tell horror story about how every terrible choice made came directly from the chilliness of her parents. He'd quickly realised that said chilliness had grown out of a desire by those parents to avoid the fallout from a narcissist.

He'd read half, and it quickly became his go-to narcoleptic. And it proved an effective antidote to images of a damaged Tom.

One day, he might drop the actor a line to thank her.

He took that thought to unconsciousness with him.

CHAPTER TWENTY

WARLOW GOT six good hours of sleep but was up early and out with Cadi before Jess made an appearance. When he and the dog arrived back, Jess had showered and changed, looking ridiculously good for 6.45 in the morning.

She grabbed him into a hug and kissed him on a stubbly cheek.

'I didn't hear you come in,' she said.

'Stealth mode,' Warlow replied. 'I'm going to jump in the shower. Keep that coffee machine armed up.'

'We'd better go in separate cars, though. Either of us could be anywhere come 5pm.'

As he stepped into the bathroom, Jess's phone chimed from the kitchen. Early for someone to be texting was his last thought before turning on the hot water.

When he emerged fifteen minutes later, suited and booted, Jess stood ready and held out a cup of coffee, but her brows were forming a vertical furrow, and her lips were thin.

'Is it the aftershave?' Warlow asked.

'Bloody Maeve O'Connor. Texted to say she'd prefer it if we could talk to her at eight-fifteen as she has a Zumba class at nine-thirty at the leisure centre.'

'Hmm.' Warlow sipped the beverage. 'Stamping her authority on the situation.'

'She struck me as pretty hard-nosed when we met her before.'

And someone who dealt with grief by finding comfort in the normal things perhaps, Warlow wondered. The routine things. Warlow had seen too much to question it. And way too much to have an opinion.

'Right, then.' He glanced at his watch and downed the coffee. 'Better get a move on, eh, Cadi?'

The dog looked up on hearing her name and wagged her tail.

'Even more time to spend with your BFF, Bouncer, today,' Jess said.

The frequency of the wag increased exponentially.

After Jess left, Warlow got up from the chair to swill his cup in the sink—only to find himself sitting back down again, sharpish. For the second time in as many days, he felt a dizzy swoop that threatened to upend him, maybe even send him collapsing in a heap. It had happened yesterday too, on the Tube as it reached the station and he stood up to get off.

Swoop—dizzy—sit down. In quick succession. He'd wanted to chalk it up to the shock of seeing Tom injured. Of course he had. But he knew better. It had been happening for a while now, and he always managed to come up with some fiction to explain it away.

Of course, given that he'd been with Tom all day yesterday, alone, he could have broached the subject. Should have asked what Tom thought about it all. But he hadn't. Tom had more than enough on his plate. But was this getting up too quickly even plate-worthy?

Warlow stood up again. This time slowly. No swoop. No dizziness. Nothing except an imploring look from the dog.

He opted for more rationalisation. Put it down to emotional stress—whatever the hell that was.

'Okay Cadi, stop messing about. Let's go. Bouncer will be bouncing.'

———

At 8.18am, Jess sat in an interview room, studying the woman seated across from her. They'd met before, but today, Maeve O'Connor, clad in form-fitting athletic wear, exuded an air of impatience that seemed at odds with her carefully composed expression. She'd arrived precisely on time, a fact that hadn't escaped Jess's notice.

'Thank you for coming in, Ms O'Connor,' Jess began. 'We appreciate you making time for us this morning.'

Maeve's eyes flicked to the clock. 'Of course. As I mentioned, I have a Zumba class at 9:30, so I hope we can wrap this up within the hour.'

Jess exchanged a brief glance with Rhys, who sat silently beside her, before continuing. 'We'll certainly try. We have a few questions about Russell that we hope you can help us with.'

Maeve's posture stiffened almost imperceptibly.

There could have been no doubt in her mind as to why she sat at this table in this room. Still, hearing her partner's name contextualised it abruptly, and despite her best efforts, her reaction proved she was not made of granite.

Jess decided to cut straight to the chase. 'Were you aware of any indiscretions on Russell's part?'

A flicker of confusion crossed Maeve's face. 'Indiscretions? I'm not sure what you mean.'

Rhys cleared his throat, reaching for a manila folder on the table.

'Perhaps these might jog your memory,' he said, sliding several photographs across the table.

As Maeve's eyes fell on the images, Jess expected to see shock, perhaps even horror. Instead, what flashed across the woman's face was unmistakable anger.

'Not again!' Maeve spat, her composure cracking.

Jess barely resisted responding to this unexpected reaction with a similar one of her own. 'Again? Ms O'Connor, has this happened before?'

Maeve's jaw clenched as she pushed the photos away. 'Since we arrived here, there have been several attempts at extortion. Or maybe embarrassment. Hard to tell which.'

'Would you care to explain that?' Rhys, unlike Jess, had failed to hide his surprise.

A deep sigh escaped Maeve's throat. 'I… we assumed it was Latimer, trying to make Russell's life miserable. Again.'

'Latimer?' Rhys asked.

Maeve dropped her chin. 'Jeremy Latimer. Yes. Perhaps I should have mentioned him before, but I presumed you'd be thorough enough to have found out about that idiot.'

Jess ignored the implied criticism because she was too busy connecting this new information with what they already knew. 'We knew about Mr Milburn's previous history with Jeremy Latimer, of course. But if you say this was him, what exactly did he want?'

Maeve shrugged, her earlier anger giving way to weariness. 'I don't know the specifics. Russell didn't like to burden me with the details. But it seemed like they, Latimer, or some other crank, wanted to make his life difficult. It began about three months after we got here. We thought it might be him trying to chase Russ out of another job. So that Russ suffered like he had. Who knows? Latimer is a nut job.'

Jess leaned back in her chair. There seemed to be a sordid logic to what Milburn's partner said. 'How many times did this occur?'

'It's been ongoing since we moved here. At least three or four separate attempts, I'd say. Each time, Russell would receive some sort of threatening message or package.'

'And what form did these threats take?' Rhys asked.

'Mostly text messages,' Maeve replied. 'Sometimes, emails. I mean, he only showed me a few. It was… unsettling, to say the least.'

'And Russell never went to the police about this?' Jess asked.

'He didn't want to make a fuss. Said it would only encourage them if they knew it was getting to him. He thought if he ignored it, eventually he'd give up.'

'Did he have proof of Latimer's involvement?'

'Proof?' She repeated the question as if it were some foreign word. 'Why would there be any doubt?'

'So, we take that as a no?' Rhys asked.

'No,' Maeve confirmed, her voice barely above a whisper. 'Except there were the rats.'

'Rats?' Rhys asked.

'Our dog found two dead ones within the first few days of moving in. Then Russell's mum got ill, so we sent the dog to his dad for company while she was in hospital. He loves that dog—she's such a softy. Could've been a therapy dog without any training.'

'Why are the rats important?' Jess pressed for more detail.

Maeve shook her head. 'I joked once that Latimer had cursed us. Sent a plague of rats.'

'Is there a plague?' Rhys asked.

'There might be because they're still dying. I found one at the bottom of the garden just four days ago. It's strange, isn't it? I mean, why would they be dying? But that's the only strange thing I can think of. The rats.'

'And these photos?' Jess asked. 'Had you seen them before?' 'Not these specific images, no. But there were others… similar. All fake. The texts that came with them were threatening, but not like this. They were more… vague.'

'And you're certain it was Latimer who orchestrated all this?' Jess pressed.

Maeve hesitated for a moment as confusion crept in. 'Russell seemed to think so. He said Latimer had the most to gain from discrediting him. But I suppose… I suppose it could have been someone else.'

Jess and Rhys exchanged a meaningful glance.

'Thank you, Ms O'Connor,' Jess said, gathering up the photos. 'You've been very helpful. One of my colleagues will be in to take a statement now. We should get you out of here by nine. We may need to speak with you again as our investigation progresses. We'll also need Mr Milburn's personal laptop. I'll send someone to retrieve it today. Do you have his password?'

Maeve nodded, hands clasped on the desk now. 'Of course. Whatever I can do to help. But you need to ask Latimer directly if he is behind all this. I'd put money on it.'

'We'll let you know,' Jess assured her. 'Oh, and the last dead rat, did you dispose of it?'

'Yes, it's double wrapped in a black bin bag ready for collection.'

'Perhaps we'll take that off your hands, too,' Jess said.

———

THE TEAM WERE ODDLY quiet when they convened after the interview. Catrin was back, Gina, Gil, and Warlow were studying the boards.

'We thought you'd gone to fetch the rat,' Gil said when Rhys breezed in.

'Am I meant to?'

'Take your pipe with you when you go,' Gil said.

'To stuff it in, you mean?'

'No, to play a bloody tune, man. So that the other buggers can follow you back to HQ.'

'Sorry.' Rhys looked totally nonplussed.

'Pied Piper of Hamlin,' Jess said, walking in behind Rhys.

'Got you.' Rhys nodded and smiled in a way that left Warlow wondering if he truly did, but that was by the by.

'Right, well, that was enlightening,' Warlow said. 'The whole thing might be a rat herring.'

Gil winced. 'Poor.'

'But we should follow it through. We need a look at Milburn's personal computer. That needs to be a priority.'

'Said I'd meet her back at her house after Zumba,' Rhys said.

'You don't need it, Rhys. Stick to rugby training,' Gil said.

'Not me, Ms O'Con—' Rhys stopped, realising he'd taken the bait.

Warlow got down to business. 'Catrin and I need a bit of a catch-up, so let's run through where we are, for everyone's sake.'

Jess stayed on her feet. 'You all saw and heard that interview. Why she failed to mention attempted extortion before is beyond me.'

'Sound like she didn't take it all that seriously, ma'am. The photos didn't faze her one bit,' Gina observed.

'Agreed. And it didn't look as if she was acting there. They did not come as a surprise to her at all. She's telling the truth, on that score.'

'That would be my impression, too,' Warlow said. He turned to Rhys. 'Did we find any evidence of how Milburn got the photographs? Envelopes with postage details?'

Rhys shook his head. 'They were in plain envelopes. Maybe he'd got rid of the original packaging.'

'Pity,' Warlow muttered.

Gina's phone rang. She held a hand up in apology and answered it in hushed tones.

'Is Latimer capable of this kind of thing?' Warlow asked.

Jess and Gil exchanged glances. 'Hard to judge. From the brief encounter by video we had, there's no way of telling.'

'You said he had a high opinion of himself,' Gil added.

'O'Connor certainly thinks he's capable. Perhaps we should have another chat,' Warlow said. 'Shame he's so far away.'

Behind him, Gina, with one hand over the mouthpiece of her desk phone, called out, 'Uh, excuse me, sir, but you might want to hold on to that thought for a moment. It's reception. They have a Jeremy Latimer downstairs wanting to speak to DI Allanby.'

Several sets of eyebrows went ceiling wards.

Gil eventually broke the tension by humming a few bars of the theme from The Twilight Zone.

CHAPTER TWENTY-ONE

THE SAME INFORMAL interview room at Dyfed Powys HQ where Jess had spoken with Maeve O'Connor now accommodated DCI Evan Warlow and DS Gil Jones and their unexpected visitor.

Jeremy Latimer sat across from them, his leather motorcycle gear creaking as he shifted in his chair.

Warlow leaned back, arms folded, wearing an expression of calm curiosity. 'Mr Latimer.'

Latimer beamed. 'Glad to see you have the correct honorific there, DCI Warlow. So many people call me doctor, and I find it irritating.'

Warlow could have explained how he knew. That his own son was a surgeon. That the tradition harked back to the Middle Ages when surgeons got their training in barber shops as apprentices with no degrees. How reverting to Mr from Dr, despite all surgeons being doctors, became a badge of honour to distinguish them from physicians. Instead, he said, 'You've travelled quite a distance. Can you tell us why you felt the need?'

Latimer's eyes gleamed with an unsettling intensity. 'I felt... compelled, Detective Chief Inspector. My previous conversation with DI Allanby left me restless. There's so much more to explain, to make you understand.'

'Well, you have our undivided attention now,' Warlow replied, gesturing for Latimer to proceed.

The man took a deep breath, his words tumbling out in a rush. 'My role in the NHS has always been, some might say… unconventional. I'm not bound by the stifling constraints of tradition. My methods may seem unorthodox to some, but they are revolutionary.'

Gil raised an eyebrow, catching Warlow's eye.

The DCI gave an almost imperceptible nod, encouraging Latimer to continue.

'I've been chosen, you understand? To lead medicine into a new era. My colleagues, they're trapped in outdated thinking, but I see beyond. I can heal in ways they can't even comprehend.'

Warlow listened, his face impassive, but his mind, as Latimer expounded on his "visionary" approach to patient care, writhed with disquiet.

The doctor's words flowed like a sermon, peppered with grandiose claims and thinly veiled self-aggrandisement, emphasising the holistic approach that was so lacking in today's seven-minute society, referencing the average time a GP had to assess a patient.

The he finally drew a breath, Warlow took the moment to re-jig the conversation. 'Mr Latimer, your passion for your work is clear,' he said, 'but I'm curious about how this unconventional approach affected your relationship with your colleagues, particularly Mr Milburn?'

Both men knew that Warlow's question was loaded, but the DCI pressed on. 'We are well aware of how much friction developed between yourself and Russell Milburn. I have a more direct question for you. Did you ever send texts or images intending to embarrass or threaten him?'

Latimer's self-assured demeanour faltered. It lasted only seconds before his smile crept back. 'It would be foolish of me to deny that I have had one or two lapses of judgement in that regard. So, yes, I did. But that was two years ago. A moment of weakness, you understand. Milburn couldn't see the bigger picture, and I was frustrated. I sent some texts.'

Gil shifted weight, and with a voice as dry as sawdust, said, 'Ah, yes. Nothing says, "bigger picture" quite like threatening texts, does it?'

Latimer shot him a look of disdain before turning back to Warlow. 'You must understand, I will be vindicated. The Royal College will accept the vision of my methods. I'll be held up as an exemplar of modern medicine.'

Warlow's doubt showed in the set of his jaw. 'So far, the colleagues we've spoken to don't share your optimism. Your ideas seem... well, let's say they're outside the realm of conventional practice.'

'Conventional?' Latimer scoffed. 'Conventionality is the enemy of progress, Detective Chief Inspector. My techniques may seem unusual to you, but they're the future of healthcare.'

Gil couldn't resist. 'And I thought the future of healthcare was robots, plenty of veg, and AI, not... whatever it is you're selling.'

Latimer's face flushed with anger. 'You mock what you don't understand. I've saved lives with my techniques. Patients flock to me because they know I can help them when others have failed.'

As Latimer continued to extol his own virtues, and with a distinct absence of detail, Warlow's mind was working overtime. The doctor's impromptu journey from York to Carmarthen was telling. Five hours on a motorcycle, driven by some internal compulsion to explain himself. It spoke volumes about Latimer's state of mind.

'Mr Latimer,' Warlow said. 'I think we've heard enough for now. However, I'd like you to stay a while longer. There are a few more questions that must be addressed.'

Latimer's brow furrowed. 'I don't understand. I've told you I'm not involved in Milburn's death. I've come here to help you understand the differences that caused the University Health Board to wrongly suspend me in the first instance—'

'And we appreciate that you came here voluntarily. Nevertheless,' Warlow continued, his tone firm, 'at the present time, you are not free to leave. I'm arresting you on suspicion of involvement in the death of Russell Milburn. You do not have to say anything, but it may harm your defence if you do not mention when questioned something which you later rely on in court. Anything you say may be given in evidence.'

Latimer's face contorted with indignation. 'This is preposterous! I came here of my own free will to clear things up!'

'We are grateful,' Gil chimed in. 'So much so that we'd appreciate the opportunity to discuss the situation further. Our hospitality is legendary. And of course, you are at liberty to contact a solicitor, or, if you like, we can provide one.'

'I don't need a solicitor,' Latimer declared, his chin jutting out. 'I have nothing to hide.'

'Even so, it might be an idea—'

'I do not need anyone else.'

'Marvellous,' Gil said. 'Do you take sugar in your tea?'

'I only drink Rooibos.'

'Then we'll get you a bottle of water.' Gil grinned. 'For your journey to our holding facility in Llanelli. Lovely place.'

'What about my bike?'

'We'll get that taken over for you.'

They left the man to his own devices.

'I noticed he didn't actually explain what one of his individual and special techniques were,' Gil said as they headed back to the Incident Room.

'That's because there aren't any. He probably believes there are, but he's deluded.'

'Messiah complex with a side of narcissism,' Gil mused. 'That's a cocktail and a half in a surgeon.'

'Indeed,' Warlow agreed. 'And now we need to figure out if that cocktail was potent enough to lead to murder.'

By now, elevenses were both on the cards, and very much needed.

'Tannard has the images of Milburn and the woman?' Warlow asked, a mug of tea gently steaming on the desk close at hand.

Rhys, on the verge of dunking a digestive, looked up with the biscuit three inches above the liquid.

'Good save,' Gil muttered.

'Yes, sir,' Rhys replied to Warlow's original question, side-eyeing Gil in the process. 'Though they were printed on some A4 paper, so not exactly high-quality.'

'We'll let the techs do their thing,' Jess said. 'Let Latimer stew. We'll access Milburn's laptop and get his phone records.'

'I'm on that today, ma'am,' said Rhys.

'Who is collecting the rat, then?' Gil asked.

'We could send a Uniform,' Rhys suggested.

'You won't get any of them to go.'

'Why not?' Gina asked.

'They'll think it's a trap.'

'Good one, sarge.' Rhys grinned. They could almost hear his mind whirring, working on a rejoinder. 'I hope she's wrapped it well, like that body the woman kept in her bedroom in Beddau. You know, the one that had gone missing for twenty years.'

'You mean the body next-door?' Gina asked.

'Yeah, we watched the documentary, remember. Wrapped so well it didn't even smell. If O'Connor hasn't wrapped the rat, it'll stink… and I rodent wish that on anyone.'

The groans that followed told him he'd overstretched badly with that tortuous play on words.

'Gina has filled you all in about our chat with the GP?' Warlow asked, re-centring the chat.

'She did,' Jess said. 'And Gil did the same regarding his interview with Leyshon. Both very concerned about plans for the community hospital, but I struggle to pin either of them as our bogeyman.'

'Speaking of which,' Catrin intervened, with a finger up in the air.

'No one said anything about a witch,' Gil said. 'And I dislike the way you're holding up that finger. Please don't turn Rhys into anything amphibious. He's too big to crawl under any rocks.'

'Ivy,' Catrin said, sending her fellow sergeant one of her best disparaging glances.

'As in the Holly and the?' Gil continued. 'If we're talking

favourite Christmas carols, mine is definitely, Shark, The Hairy Angels Thing, as misinterpreted by my eight-year-old granddaughter who belts it out on her karaoke microphone with no qualms. I'm seriously thinking of starting a petition on Change.org to get the title officially changed. Hark, The Herald Angels Sing my ar—'

'As in Ivy Pugh.' Catrin enunciated the words with slow and subdued irritation to cut Gil off. 'Eighty-three years old, known as a regular caller to the control room. Craig mentioned her yesterday in passing because one of his colleagues had been ordered out to visit. Apparently, she lives not far from the old hospital where all this started and keeps reporting strange noises and lights. She called again the night before last.'

'And why is this relevant?' Jess queried.

'Probably nothing, ma'am, but given where Milburn was last seen alive, it might be worth looking into. Craig said she's been fixated on the hospital for years, but what if she saw or heard something unusual that afternoon?'

Warlow nodded slowly.

'Fair enough. It's a good shout. We trace, investigate, and evaluate. Identify, interview…' Warlow let it dangle and looked at Gina pointedly.

'Eliminate or pursue. I can talk to her,' Gina volunteered.

'I'll come with you,' Warlow said. 'We'll feed two birds with one scone.' He side-eyed Rhys.

The DC, his mouth full of biscuit, put down his tea and clapped silently.

Gil sent Warlow a piercing glare and shook his head slowly.

'It's the new non-triggering me,' Warlow said. 'Gina and I can check on Ivy and have a look around the old hospital while we're there.'

'It's worth it, sir,' Rhys said with a mouthful of soggy biscuit. 'I've seen quite a few urban explorer videos on the place.'

'You mean trespassers who've broken in and fed the haunted house nonsense?' Catrin said.

'It's spook city, sarge,' Rhys replied.

'How is Tom, Evan?' Gil asked, moving swiftly on.

'I spoke to him earlier. Already bored at home. Looks a lot worse than it is. But thanks for asking.'

'Cycling in London is a bugger,' Gil said.

Everyone either nodded or muttered their agreement.

'There are some horrifying videos on YouTube,' Rhys said. 'Of people coming off their bikes and that.'

Gil glanced at Gina. 'You need to put some parental controls on that internet of yours.'

In the brief silence that followed, Gil followed up with a slight boast. 'My grandmother started cycling when she was eighty-five.'

'Really?' Gina asked. 'How far did she use to go?'

'Only a couple of miles. Every day, though… We think she's somewhere on the Russian Steppes by now.'

Warlow hung his head before looking up. 'That joke's as old as you are. Catrin, can you get me Mrs Pugh's details? Gina and I will pop over there this afternoon. In the meantime, bums on seats, scut work it is.'

Gil stood up. 'I'm popping down to Financial Crimes for ten minutes. Just had a heads-up from them.'

'Financial Crimes,' Rhys murmured. 'I can't think of anything more boring.'

Jess narrowed her eyes. 'Many a murky deed has come to light by looking at how people spend their money, or even earn it, Rhys.'

'I know, ma'am, but the thought of looking at numbers all day…' Rhys shuddered.

'When I find the secret code that leads us to the Holy Grail, you'll be eating your words,' Gil said.

CHAPTER TWENTY-TWO

AN HOUR LATER, with the team knee-deep in the humdrum of phone calls and screen-staring, Warlow was sitting in the SIO office, when Jess's very attractive head appeared.

'The custody sergeant at the Hub just called. They've processed Latimer and put him in a cell.'

Warlow looked pleased. 'Good. As you say, we'll let him stew while Tannard's lot go through Milburn's laptop. Did he say anything else when they booked him?'

'He hasn't shut up. Insisting it was all a misunderstanding. Said Milburn had it out for him from the start...' She paused, before asking, 'And why are you smiling?'

'Because now I can. Before, it would have been creepy. Lecherous male DCI ogling the younger female DI. Now... it's guilt free.'

'Ogling?'

'Okay, how about looking admiringly?'

'Better.' She grinned. Her phone buzzed. She glanced at the screen and frowned. 'It's Rick.'

'Ooh, buzzkill.'

'I should take this.'

'Use the stairwell if you want some privacy.'

A moment later, Catrin appeared with a printout in her hands.

'Sir, I've got Ivy's address here,' she said, spreading out the sheet on his desk and pointing to a spot on a map. 'It's on an unnamed lane above the old hospital.'

Warlow studied the location. 'Interesting. That side of the patch is riddled with these out of the way little spots. Do you have a copy for me?'

Catrin hesitated. 'It might be a fruitless pursuit, sir. Ivy's known for her... imaginative reports.'

'Possibly,' Warlow conceded. 'We'll only know if we ask her.'

'Yes, sir.'

A few minutes later, a peeved looking Jess returned, stepped inside the tiny office and closed the door.

'Trouble?' Warlow asked.

'Rick's still pushing for that loan. When I mentioned the previous six grand he borrowed, he went quiet. Still won't tell me what the money's for.'

Warlow frowned. 'That's concerning. Any ideas what he might be mixed up in?'

'Honestly? I don't know,' Jess admitted. 'Gambling debts? Investment opportunity? Or maybe he's just desperate and embarrassed.'

'Might be any of those,' Warlow agreed. 'Or something we haven't thought of. He's putting you in a tough spot, Jess.'

'Tell me about it,' she muttered. 'I want to help him, but...'

'But you're a copper, and your instincts are telling you something's not right,' Warlow finished for her.

Jess nodded.

'Whatever you decide, I've got your back. Just... be careful.'

'Thanks, Evan,' Jess replied with a small smile. 'I appreciate that.'

A knock on the door ended the discussion.

'Come in,' Warlow said.

Gina stood there this time. 'Sir, there's something up on the BBC's local news. Something you might want to see.'

———

GIL STEPPED into the cluttered office of Financial Crimes, his eyes immediately drawn to a desk piled high with papers and files.

Sergeant Sarah Davies looked up from her computer.

'Morning. Come to see our slowly growing For-Gil's-eyes-only pile?'

'Thanks for sorting through all this, Sarah. Everything here related to Can Y Barcud?'

'Yep. Every scrap of paper we could find connected to Moyles or Moyles's cottage. It's a mess, I'll tell you that.'

Gil approached the desk. 'I didn't expect there to be so much.'

Sarah agreed. 'Most of it'll be irrelevant, I expect, but it all needs going through.'

'Sarah, I'll be blunt. Have you found anything… compromising? In relation to any officers?'

Sarah's lips flattened into a wry smile. 'Ah. You've had the call from Drinkwater too, then?'

Gil nodded, and Sarah continued, 'Nothing concrete, if that's what you're asking. There are situations where Napier acted for certain individuals in a completely open and honest way. Could be that Drinkwater simply doesn't want their names tarnished by being linked to Napier's firm at all.'

'Could be,' Gil mused, not entirely convinced.

He wandered over to the pile, his attention caught by a stack of old-fashioned black, A4-sized diaries. He picked one up, hefting the big black book in his hands. 'Hand-written entries? Napier's firm was certainly traditional.'

'Old school to the core. Those diaries go back years.'

Gil flipped through a few pages, his mind already racing with possibilities. But the Milburn case loomed large, demanding his attention. He set the diary back down with a sigh.

'I'll need to come back when I have more time,' he told Sarah. 'We're up to our necks in this cyclist murder.'

'No worries. This lot isn't going anywhere. But… be careful. Whatever's in these files, it's got Drinkwater on edge.'

'When isn't he on edge?' Gil quipped. 'As it were.'

That brought a smile to his colleague's lips. But he took Sarah's warning seriously.

As he left the office, he had the idea that those innocuous-looking diaries might hold the key to something. What exactly, he didn't know.

Yet.

―――

GIL ARRIVED back to see the team clustered around Rhys's computer screen.

'Australian breakdancing, is it?' he asked.

'No,' Catrin replied. 'The Health Board have made a statement. I've got it up on my screen, too.'

She walked across to her desk with Gil in tow and nudged her mouse.

Gil began reading aloud, but in a low voice so as not to irritate the others. 'The Dyfed Health Board regrets to announce the untimely death of our Chief Executive, Russell Milburn. As this is the subject of an ongoing police investigation, we cannot comment further on the circumstances at this time. Mr Milburn was a dedicated and visionary leader who worked tirelessly to improve healthcare services in our region. His loss will be deeply felt by all who knew him and worked alongside him. Our thoughts are with his family and friends during this difficult time.'

Gil's brow furrowed. 'Sounds like standard PR fare so far.'

'Keep going.'

Gil read on. 'Despite this tragic setback, the Health Board remains committed to the strategic vision that Mr Milburn helped shape. The proposed changes driven by his hard work, including the consolidation of services and an announcement confirming the site of a new hospital for the region, will press ahead as planned next week. This significant investment in our healthcare infrastructure represents a once-in-a-generation opportunity to revolutionise the delivery of medical services in West Wales. The new facility will bring cutting-edge technology and specialist care closer to home for many of our residents.

'We understand that not everyone will be pleased with these changes. The shifting of resources and services will undoubtedly cause concern in some communities. However, we believe this is the best path forward to ensure high-quality, sustainable healthcare for all our residents in the coming decades.'

Gil cupped his ear. 'I can hear the sabres rattling across three counties.'

'And the sound of hair being torn out,' she added.

Gil continued, eyes back on the screen. 'The reconfiguration will allow us to address critical staffing shortages, reduce waiting times, and provide more specialised care that is currently only available outside our region. This includes expanded cancer services, a state-of-the-art emergency department, and enhanced mental health facilities. We will be holding a series of final public consultations in the coming months...'

Gil dropped his voice. 'And for that read, you can say what you like, this is what's happening.' He continued reading: '... to gather input from residents, healthcare professionals, and local leaders. Your voices are crucial in shaping the future of healthcare in our region. Rest assured, this is what Mr Milburn wished—to see his vision for a stronger, more resilient health service come to fruition. We owe it to his memory and to the people of West Wales to press forward with these vital improvements, blah de blah.'

Gil stood up, arching his back. 'They're certainly not wasting any time, are they?'

Catrin puffed out her cheeks and exhaled. 'No, they're not. If I was a cynic, I might suggest they're using Milburn's death as a smokescreen to push through these controversial changes.'

'Exactamoondough, as the eight-year-old sage that is my

eldest granddaughter would say,' Gil agreed. 'And notice how they're framing it as "what Milburn would have wanted". Makes it harder for people to object without seeming disrespectful to the dead.'

'Clever PR move,' Catrin mused. 'But I wonder how it'll play with the local communities.'

'I'd say this statement just threw a can of petrol onto the bonfire.'

'What do you think?' Gil asked Warlow.

'I think that there's a timetable for these things driven by the release of money from the Welsh government, and any delays will see everything put on hold until a new budget is sorted. Which could mean years. I suspect they had no choice.'

'In a way, then,' Rhys mused, 'if someone did attack Milburn to try to put a stop to these changes, it's backfired.'

'Or given someone more reason to lash out,' Jess observed.

'Where are they with that rat, Rhys?' Gil asked.

'A Uniform has already picked up the laptop and the vermin from Maeve O'Connor, sarge.'

'It's coming up to lunchtime,' Warlow said with a nod at Gina. 'Why don't you and I grab something quickly and then set off to see Mrs Pugh?'

'I don't think I want very much after all that talk of dead rats.' Gina grimaced.

'Oh, I don't let talk of a dead rodent put me off my food,' Rhys said.

'Dead anything,' Warlow muttered. 'As you have proven many times after the most gruesome of postmortems.'

DC Harries had been known to stop for a burger and chips within fifteen minutes of leaving the pathology suite. Most of the team needed at least a couple of hours before they could even face a biscuit with their tea.

'I'll have word with Huw Leyshon about the old hospital. See if he's heard anything about goings-on,' Gil said.

'I'll send you a link for those urban explorer vids, sarge,' Rhys volunteered. 'Like I say, they're worth a watch.'

'Why don't we all watch?' Warlow suggested.

'I'll bring the popcorn,' Gil added.

But it wasn't worth a bag of popcorn. Nowhere near it.

Rhys brought up a video on his screen.

The shaky camera footage showed the explorers cautiously entering the dilapidated building. As they walked down decaying corridors lined with peeling paint and debris, a vlogger's voice, with an incongruous high-pitched west-country accent, trembled slightly as he narrated, 'Look at this place, guys. It's like time just stopped here.'

In one room, they found abandoned medical equipment covered in a thick layer of dust. The vlogger picked up a rusted instrument, turning it over in his hands.

'How much do you think this was worth when it was working? Probably thousands.' He set it down with exaggerated care, as if it were still valuable.

As they ventured deeper, the vlogger grew audibly more uneasy. They came across old patient rooms with rusted bed frames and torn mattresses.

The vlogger's companion, a woman, nervously joked, 'If ever there was a perfect place to hide bodies, this would be it.'

The laughter that followed this sounded hollow and uneasy as the camera darted jerkily to shadowy corners, then panned across a room full of broken wheelchairs and abandoned baby carriages.

'This is bad karma, guys,' the vlogger whispered, his voice cracking. 'It's like everyone just up and left. Like an alien invasion happened.'

Throughout the video, the commentators speculated about the hospital's history and reasons for closure, mixing facts with dramatic embellishments for their viewers. The scene often paused for dramatic effect, letting the eerie silence of the abandoned halls speak for itself.

The footage ended abruptly as the explorers were startled by an unexpected noise—perhaps a falling piece of debris or a small animal scurrying along. The camera shook violently as they fled the premises, their panicked breathing the last thing heard before the video cut to black.

'Definitely something to look forward to, then, sir,' Gina said in a tiny voice.

Gil reached forward and touched her arm. 'I'll meet you two up there, and you can stay outside as our lookout. How about that?'

Gina's smile was worth seeing.

CHAPTER TWENTY-THREE

WARLOW AND GINA trudged up the overgrown path to Ivy Pugh's cottage, a squat stone building that seemed to have grown organically from the hillside. The pale-blue door, faded by years of Welsh wind and rain, stood out against the weathered grey stonework like a fragment of forgotten sky.

As they approached, a high-pitched yapping erupted from inside, followed by a reedy voice berating the dog to be quiet in welsh. '*Bootsy! Bydd yn dawel.*'

The door creaked open to reveal Ivy, barely five feet tall, with a cloud of white curls and thick glasses dangling from a string around her neck. Behind her, a scrappy terrier eyed the detectives suspiciously.

'Oh, you must be the police!' Ivy exclaimed, her face lighting up with excitement. 'Come in, come in. Mind the step, it's wonky. I should get that fixed, but you know how it is. One day, you're thinking about calling a handyman, and the next thing, it's 1995.'

She slid her glasses on and leaned in to look at Gina's badge on her lanyard. 'DC Mellings. We spoke on the phone, didn't we?'

'We did, and this is DCI Warlow. I said we'd be calling.'

'The man with no lanyard,' Warlow said, as she peered in

vain for his ID, immediately realising as he spoke, it would make a terrific title for his memoir. If he ever wrote one.

'Come in out of the wind,' Ivy insisted.

The officers exchanged amused glances as they carefully navigated the step to follow Ivy inside, the dog's yapping reducing both in volume and frequency until it became a sporadic reminder that they better watch out… it was still there.

The interior was a time capsule from the early '70s: floral wallpaper, doilies on every surface, and a faint smell of lavender and boiled cabbage. But, despite its dated appearance, everything was immaculately clean.

'Sit yourselves down,' Ivy instructed, gesturing to a sagging floral sofa. 'I'll put the kettle on. You take sugar? I always say a bit of sweet helps the medicine go down, though I suppose you're not here to give me medicine, are you?' She chuckled at her own joke, a sound like creaky floorboards.

A sound that led Warlow to wonder if Ivy secretly had the odd smoke now and again, though the house itself gave no hint of being a smoker's den.

As their host bustled about in the kitchen, Gina leaned over to Warlow and whispered, 'I feel like we've stepped out of the Tardis.'

Warlow nodded. 'From when Dr Who was science fiction. Not… whatever the hell it is now.'

Gina took in the surroundings. 'It's like my nan's house, only from photos she showed me of when she was a girl.'

When Ivy returned with a rattling tray of tea and hobnobs, the floodgates of conversation opened. 'Weather is awful, isn't it? That rain yesterday… Bootsy barely went out, poor dab. Only for a number one and two. And then the so and so does his business on the cobbles instead of the lawn. I ask you.' She glanced at the terrier sitting on a rug eyeing the biscuit action, and the dog's little tail moved back and forth in acknowledgement. 'Now, you'll be wanting me to tell you about the shenanigans at the old hospital, I expect.'

Ivy settled into her armchair. A move which gave Bootsy permission to join her on her lap from where she fixed

Warlow with a suspicious glare. 'It's a crying shame, it is. I remember when it was built, you know. All the men working there, singing and swearing. It made my mother blush. And after, we used to watch the new mothers leaving with their little babies. I used to love watching them.'

She launched into a sprawling tale that meandered through her life—caring for her mother, after losing their father young—then her siblings, her brother's struggle with "the dust" from the mines.

Warlow allowed himself a pang of empathy, remembering his own father's battle with pneumoconiosis.

'Reg would come home covered in the gritty black stuff,' Ivy reminisced, her eyes misting over. 'I'd say to him, "Reg, you're bringing half the mountain home with you!" But he'd laugh and say, "Ivy, I hope there's water for a bath." God rest him.'

'He never married, your brother?' Gina asked.

'No, none of us did. Didn't see the need. We were close.'

Warlow smiled, kept his voice gentle. 'My dad was a miner too, Mrs Pugh. I understand how hard it must have been for you.'

Ivy's eyes widened behind her thick lenses. 'It's a special kind of worry, isn't it? Watching them go off every day, never knowing if...' She shook her head as if to dispel the memories. 'But that's all in the past now. Though sometimes, I swear I can still hear the pit whistle on quiet nights.'

Gina, touched by the old woman's vulnerability, reached out and patted Ivy's hand. 'You've been through a lot, Ivy. It's wonderful how you've looked after your family all these years.'

Ivy beamed at the young detective. 'Oh, aren't you sweet? And my name is Ivy. Never Mrs. You remind me of my sister, Morfydd, God rest her soul. She had a kind heart too.' She turned to Bootsy, who was now snoring softly on her lap. 'Just like our Morfydd, eh Bootsy?'

Warlow gently steered the conversation back to the present. 'Ivy, you rang us a few nights ago about some strange goings-on at the hospital?'

Ivy nodded vigorously, her earlier melancholy forgotten. 'It's been like Swansea market. And I don't mean since that man on the bicycle was killed. I mean before that. Lights in the windows, chanting in the night. Sometimes, I see the lights moving off towards the old chapel on the mountain. And I know what you're going to say, but I think some of it is the spirits. Old souls trying to find their way forward. From when it was a TB sanatorium, before the hospital was built.'

That piqued Gina's curiosity. 'Spirits, Mrs Pugh?'

'Oh, yes, *bach*. All those poor people who passed on, they're restless, you see. And who can blame them? Stuck in bed all day, coughing their lives away. It's no wonder they want to wander a bit now.'

The officers let that little thought wallow in its own silence for a few seconds. Finally, Gina probed a little further. 'And you've seen these lights yourself?'

'Clear as day,' Ivy exclaimed. 'Well, clear as night, I suppose, since it's always after dark. Just the other night, I was sitting by my bedroom window—I have a lovely view of the hospital from there—and I saw them. Bobbing about like fire-flies, they were. And the sounds! Some wailing and crying. It was enough to give me the shivers. That's when I rang. They're always so nice when I do.'

'Are you sure it wasn't some local kids messing about?' Warlow asked.

Ivy fixed him with a stern look. 'I may be old, but I'm not senile. I know the difference between hooligans and haunting. This was something else entirely.'

Gina, sensing Ivy's defensiveness, quickly interjected, 'We're just trying to understand everything we can. You mentioned a specific night when you heard car doors slamming?'

Ivy's face lit up. 'Oh, yes, the same night before the crying and wailing. Doors sliding and slamming in the dark. It gave me the willies because there'd been no lights like you would normally see with cars. All dark, it was, except for the bobbing lights. Bootsy here was in such a state, weren't you, *bach*?'

The terrier, as if on cue, let out a soft whine.

'How do you manage up here all on your own, Ivy?' Warlow asked.

'Ooh, I'm hardly on my own. People call all the time. I fell and cut my leg, and Janice, she's the district nurse, she calls to check. Nick the postman sometimes has a cup of tea, and the two girls from the *cymorth*... umm, home help, come twice a week. Oh no, not alone, there's a lot worse off. All you have to do is turn on the news.'

They stayed a while longer and talked. Or rather, Ivy talked, and Warlow and Gina listened. He couldn't help but feel fond of the garrulous little woman, with her oddly endearing eccentricities. She had a sharp memory, which, despite its flights of fancy, was impressive.

'Thank you for the tea and the chat, Ivy,' Warlow said eventually as they stood to leave. 'You've been very helpful.'

'Have I? Seems like all I've done is rabbit on. Reg used to say I could talk without breathing.' Ivy beamed, escorting them to the door. 'And will you thank Maggie in the call centre? She's very nice, always. And you know where we are now. We enjoy the company, don't we, Boots?'

As they headed back to the car, Gina turned to Warlow. 'That was... interesting.'

'They don't make them like that anymore, sadly.'

'What do you make of the car doors slamming? Boy racers in their souped-up Astras?'

'More than likely. But I don't doubt she heard something. Sharp as a tack in her own way.'

Gina grinned. 'Did you see how spotless everything was? I could have eaten off those tiles in the hallway.'

They shared a pensive silence as they walked down the lane to their car. They'd see soon enough what state the old hospital was in. But their encounter with Ivy Pugh and her little slice of preserved history had at least broken the monotony of the investigation.

Warlow glanced back at the cottage, a strange mix of emotions stirring within him—amusement, concern, and a touch of melancholy for a world that was slowly fading away.

Gina's phone chirped. 'Text from Gil, sir. Say's he'll meet us in ten minutes. He's just finishing chatting to some residents.'

'He'll have had an afternoon's entertainment, then,' Warlow said, and gently rolled his tongue from within his cheek.

———

GIL HAD FAILED in his attempts at reaching Huw Leyshon. Perhaps he'd switched his phone off for a meeting.

Instead of driving up to the man's house unannounced, he'd gone to check out the nearest habitation to the old hospital. And so, he parked up and ambled along the lane from Tirycoed Road, where parked cars on both sides of the road made it a bottleneck.

Gil strolled, hands in pockets, whistling a tune that sounded suspiciously like the Bananaphone song. The tarmac lane wound around to end at a barricade just beyond a small play area.

No children played on the swings today, and Gil wandered to the edge of the grassed area, peering across at the dilapidated red roofs of the old maternity hospital. It was only thirty yards away, but might as well have been on the moon, given the tangle of fencing and overgrown scrub in between. As he meandered back through a maze of houses, garages, and parking spaces, Gil spotted an elderly gent in a garden, attacking fallen leaves with a rake like they'd insulted his mother.

The man eyed Gil suspiciously as he hailed him. Once a warrant card was flashed, however, the man's attitude took a quick U-turn.

'At last,' he said. 'You here about the vandals, then?'

Gil raised an eyebrow and spoke in Welsh to the man. '*Gallwn I fod*. I could be.' He walked up to the back wall of the patch of garden. 'A nuisance, then, are they, uh…'

'Deiniol Griffiths,' the man said. He had two hands on the rake and favoured one leg as he stood. 'Bloody nuisance, yes.

Not so bad now that the nights are drawing in and the rain has come. But every summer, it's the same. Kids traipsing through the park. They can't drive in 'cause the road's blocked. Thank God for small mercies. They light bonfires behind the hospital, play loud music, and the rubbish! Beer cans all over. Probably shooting up drugs and sacrificing goats for all I know.'

Gil shifted his jaw to one side. He liked Deiniol already. 'Sounds like quite the party. Been much activity lately?'

'Not so much,' Deiniol admitted, looking almost disappointed. 'Council, or someone, put up more fencing. Won't last, mind you. Those buggers could get through the fence at Colditz.'

Gil realised that at least 75% of the team would not have understood the reference to a WW2 concentration camp and subsequent TV series of the same name. But he did.

'Well,' Gil said, pocketing his notebook, 'I appreciate the intel. We'll ask around to see if anyone's lost any goats.'

Deiniol nodded sagely, missing Gil's sarcasm entirely. 'Shame you didn't come a few months ago. Bumper runner bean crop this year, there was. I was giving them away by the armful. About the only person not to have tried my runner beans is Keith Starmer.'

Of course he meant Keir Starmer, but somehow, correcting him would have spoiled the moment.

Another colourful witness. At least this one hadn't tried to set his dog on him or offer him a dodgy cup of tea. Minor victories, Gil thought and muttered to no one in particular, 'Tidy.'

CHAPTER TWENTY-FOUR

WARLOW PULLED the Jeep into the empty car park. The abandoned building sat squat and silent before them, boarded-up windows and uncut grass as emblems of dereliction.

Gil's car sat next to theirs. The door opened immediately, and the big sergeant emerged, coat already on.

Warlow opened his door and stepped out into the afternoon, rain-free but gusting with a sharp wind. He turned back and leaned down to speak with Gina. 'Hang on here. We won't be long.'

Gil appeared next to Gina's window. 'If we're not back by November, tell the Lady Anwen the treasure map is in the jar marked rusty nails in the garage.'

Gina compressed her lips into a thin smile. But it was the only answer she gave him.

'Let's start with a sweep. See if anywhere allows access.' Warlow set off towards one corner.

As they approached the building, the stench hit them first —a noxious blend of dampness, mould, and something indefinably rotten.

'*Arglwydd*,' Gil muttered, wrinkling his nose. 'Smells like something died in there.'

Warlow grunted. 'Never a truer word, Gil.'

They circled to the rear, where corrugated-tin sheeting had been partially torn away from a ground-floor window. The exposed edges were jagged and rusty, requiring careful manoeuvring to avoid scratches.

'Your tetanus is up to date, I hope?' Gil commented.

A difficult scramble made complicated by a desire not to rip any clothes or skin led to a small dark room.

Once inside, the stink intensified. The dank atmosphere pressed in on them, heavy with years of neglect and decay.

Their torch beams cut through the gloom, revealing peeling paint and water-stained walls. Light from holes in the roof allowed some view of the damage deeper in.

'Watch your step,' Warlow cautioned as they picked their way down a corridor strewn with debris.

Broken glass crunched underfoot, mixing with the softer sounds of their shoes squelching through puddles of questionable origin.

Gil's torch picked out a section of wall covered in graffiti. Most of it was crude. Anatomically improbable drawings and misspelt profanities. But one piece caught his eye, eliciting a chuckle.

'What?' Warlow asked, turning back.

Gil gestured to the wall. In neat, almost scholarly handwriting, someone had scrawled: "I used to be indecisive. Now I'm not so sure."

'Bit of wit amongst the filth,' Gil remarked.

They carried on along the passageway, their lights exposing further evidence of illegal occupation. A small pile of empty nitrous oxide popper canisters sat in one corner, alongside a scattering of syringes.

'Hippie crack,' Warlow noted, nudging one of the little metal cylinders with his foot.

'Cheaper than proper drugs, I suppose,' Gil replied. 'Though, not exactly harmless.'

The air grew thicker as they progressed, the smell of stale alcohol joining the cocktail of unpleasant odours. Empty cider and lager cans littered the floor, some crushed, others piled like totems.

They walked slowly, inspecting rooms. Though all had been visited, judging by the graffiti, they found no evidence of current occupation. But then, thought Warlow, who the hell would want to stay in a place like this?

At the end of the corridor, their path was blocked. A haphazard barricade of old furniture piled up against a solid-looking breeze-block wall.

'This must be the way to the annexe the hospital manager was on about. Looks relatively new,' he muttered, running his torch along the solid structure behind the furniture.

Gil frowned. 'I suppose it would be the only way to stop the vermin from getting in.'

Warlow huffed out his agreement. 'Ivy's convinced of recent activity. Seen and heard.'

'The woman who keeps calling about strange noises?'

'That's the one. She swears the noise comes from down here. Voices, sometimes. But also…' Warlow paused, his torch beam settling on the barricade, '… car doors slamming.'

Gil responded, 'Car doors? Here?'

'Exactly. It doesn't make sense. There's no vehicle access to the car park other than through the functioning hospital's car park, and that's…'

'At least fifty yards away,' Gil finished. 'And from what Deiniol the wise told me half an hour ago, the local miscreants who use this place as their playground all come on foot.'

Warlow nodded. 'So, what has Ivy's been hearing?'

Gil scratched the back of his neck where something, possibly with several legs, had fallen onto it, his mind working through the puzzle. 'Could she be mistaken? Maybe it's some other noise she's misinterpreting?'

'Possible,' Warlow conceded. 'But Ivy's as sharp as a tack, despite her age. And she was definite about this.'

'Could the sound be coming from somewhere else entirely? Carrying up from the main road? If the wind is in the right direction…'

Warlow directed his beam of light at the sergeant's face. 'That's not some kind of warning from you regarding wind of another kind, is it?'

'*Er mwyn yr arlgwlydd*, what do you take me for?'

'I take you for someone who would not miss an opportunity of relieving colonic pressure if the situation allowed it.' Warlow shook his head. 'And as for the sounds, she was adamant she heard it coming from here. She's lived in that cottage all her life, so I'm inclined to give her the benefit.'

Gil stepped closer to the barricade, shining his torch into the cracks between the breeze blocks. 'What's beyond here, you say?'

'An annexe that the current hospital want to keep. The rest of this place is no longer NHS property. There are plans to hive it off and make the annexe usable.'

They retraced their steps through the dank corridors, accosted by the cloying smell of mould and decay. As they prepared to climb back through the window, Gil paused.

'You know, there's one other possibility we haven't considered.'

Warlow turned, eyebrow raised questioningly.

'What if Ivy isn't hearing any car doors whatsoever?'

'You mean, it's confabulation?'

Gil shrugged. 'She lives alone, you say. And how old?'

'Mid-eighties at least.' Warlow considered this for a moment, then nodded. 'But I hear what you're saying. And there's no hard evidence that this place has anything to do with Milburn's death. I suppose we could get a proper search done, but… I'll think about it. For now, let's get back to Gina and head to HQ. Cup of tea and a catch-up are in order.'

They made their way back to the Jeep, where Gina was waiting, alert and ready.

'All quiet out here, sir,' she reported as they approached.

'We weren't expecting a mob with pitchforks,' Gil said.

Gina ignored him. 'Did you find anything interesting?'

'Nothing useful,' Warlow replied, climbing into the driver's seat. 'I'll brief you on the way back.'

Warlow fired up the Jeep and let the car idle. He cast one last look at the derelict hospital. In the afternoon light, it seemed to loom larger.

'What aren't you telling us?' Warlow mused.

If Gina thought about commenting, she wisely refrained from doing so.

The drive back to Carmarthen was filled with discussion, theories bouncing back and forth as they tried to make sense of what they'd heard from Ivy Pugh and seen in the old hospital. Or rather, hadn't seen.

Gina listened intently, occasionally offering her own insights.

'Therefore, we've got unexplained noises, no proper answer for cars with slamming doors, and no clear explanation for any of it,' she summarised.

'That about sums it up,' Warlow agreed, his mouth tight.

'And the possibility that what Ivy's hearing isn't car doors at all,' Gina added. 'She might be imagining it.'

Warlow threw her a glance. 'Do you really think that's likely? That she's seeing and hearing ghosts?'

Gina took a beat before answering. 'I don't know what to make of it yet, sir.'

'Are you a believer?'

The DC shifted uncomfortably. 'I'm… not sure, sir. My grandmother was. I've seen nothing myself, but I've heard stories that are hard to explain.'

'From your grandmother?'

'Mostly. She was a bit of a spiritualist. I know it's a bit mad, but she was convinced.'

Warlow nodded, his expression thoughtful. 'I've always been a sceptic myself. Never believed in anything I can't see or touch…' He paused, considering his next words carefully. 'But I believe Ivy. The real question is, what exactly is she seeing and hearing?'

'You think there might be an explanation for all this?'

'There usually is,' Warlow replied, though his tone lacked its usual certainty. Sometimes he dreamt of Denise, his dead ex. Sometimes she would speak to him in those dreams. Was that so very far away from Ivy Pugh being convinced of her family communicating with her from a cemetery not far from where she lived?

'Correction. There always is. But sometimes that explanation isn';t always in the handbook. I also have no doubt it's something unpleasant and unusual. Right.' He killed the engine. 'Let's get inside and start piecing this together.'

———

THE INCIDENT ROOM buzzed with activity reflecting the chaos in Jess's mind. She stood before the Gallery, red lines forming a web of connections that seemed to mock her attempts at clarity.

Her phone vibrated. She recognised the name that flashed on the screen.

'Mol,' Jess muttered, answering quickly. 'Hey, sweetheart. Everything okay?'

'Yeah, I guess.' Molly's voice crackled through, tinged with uncertainty. 'Dad called. He was asking if you're alright. Said he's been trying to reach you.'

Jess's jaw clenched, anger flaring hot and quick. She took a deep breath, forcing her voice to remain steady. 'Did he, now?'

'He seemed worried. Are you okay, Mum?'

The concern in Molly's tone twisted Jess's heart before anger sparked. 'I'm fine, love. Your dad's just being...' She paused, choosing her words carefully. 'Awkward.'

'What do you mean?'

Jess sighed, running a hand through her hair. 'It's complicated, Mol. Adult stuff. Nothing for you to worry about.'

'I'm not a kid anymore, Mum.'

'I know, I know. It's just...' Jess trailed off, her mind racing. How could she explain Rick's manipulation without dragging Molly into his mess? 'Your dad and I are sorting some things out. Things left over from the divorce. He shouldn't have involved you.'

A beat of silence. Then, 'Is this about money?'

Jess's breath caught. 'What makes you say that?'

'Just a guess, since it's Rick's favourite subject.'

'Listen, Mol. Whatever's going on between him and me,

you don't need to get involved, and you certainly do not need to worry about it, okay?'

'Okay,' Molly replied, not sounding entirely convinced.

Jess softened her tone. 'How's Uni going? Classes alright?'

'Yeah, great. Bit stressful with my first essay of the year due in, but all good.'

'You'll smash it.' Jess paused, then added casually, 'How's the new boyfriend? Do you have a name I can use yet?'

Molly's reply came a beat too late. 'He's fine, and no, not yet.'

Jess grinned at her daughter's brutal honesty, but didn't push. 'Well, if you need anything…'

'Yes, Mum.'

'That's my girl.'

'Evan, okay?'

'Working a nasty case.'

'You too, then.'

'We're a team, didn't you know?'

Molly laughed. The sound soothed Jess's heart.

She ended the call just as the door swung open and Warlow strode in, his face etched with familiar lines of concern and determination that always appeared during a case.

He took in Jess's tense expression. 'Everything alright?'

Jess waved her phone, forcing a wry smile. 'I've just been Rick-rolled.'

Warlow's brow furrowed, but he didn't press. 'Right. Well, we've got a new lead. You up for vespers?'

'Always,' Jess replied, pushing thoughts of Rick and his underhanded tactics aside.

Dull anger still simmered, but she pushed it down. There'd be time to deal with Rick later. She had a job to do, and right now, that was the only thing she could control.

CHAPTER TWENTY-FIVE

TIM RIGGON LOOKED at the messages on his phone. There had been a flurry since the statement had been issued that morning. Some congratulatory, others not. But best to stick to the plan, and so his mind remained a whirlwind of budget meetings and staffing issues.

The sudden weight of being acting CEO after Milburn's death required some adjustment on his part. But he remained determined to step up to the plate.

He glanced at his watch. Ten more minutes before Amelia's piano lesson finished at seven. The faint sound of scales drifted from the open window of the paint teacher's house where he'd parked outside. Still, it gave him time to do a little work, and the cul-de-sac had no traffic, with high hedges screening him from the other two houses in the close.

A dull thud against the rear car door jolted Tim from his reading.

He frowned, peering out of the window. Nothing. Probably just a... bird or a soccer or tennis ball from someone unseen playing in a garden?

He stepped out, the cool air a welcome relief after the stuffy interior. Strains of Borodin from the Classic FM hall of fame drifted out with him.

'Hello?' he called, scanning the empty street and seeing no ball.

The attack came out of nowhere.

A figure in a black balaclava lunged from behind a hedge, arm raised.

Tim flinched backwards, half stumbling as he ducked. Something sailed past his face, missing him by inches. It struck the car with a sickening splash.

'What the f—' Tim's words died as the masked assailant bolted, trainers squidgy against the pavement.

Breath heaving from the adrenaline surge, Tim got up to give chase, but his ankle tweaked angrily as he stepped forward. 'Shit.'

He hopped onto his good leg and stepped towards the car, one hand out to balance himself, and froze. An acrid smell assaulted his nostrils. His gaze dropped to his arm.

He had the sleeves of his work shirt rolled up, his tie off. The skin of his forearm looked red and blistered.

The pain hit a moment later, searing and relentless.

'Oh, God.' He choked out the word and let his eyes drift to the car.

The back half, behind where he'd been standing, had splashes of liquid that were turning a strange white colour against the blue paintwork.

'Shit,' Tim said for the second time.

He yanked open the driver's door and fumbled for the half bottle of water in the centre console. Without thinking, he poured it on his arm. The pain went from two to ten very quickly. He fell to his knees, heaving in air.

Phone. Where the hell was his phone?

Tim's vision swam as he punched in 999.

'No… don't faint. Don't bloody faint,' he muttered through gritted teeth.

The operator's voice seemed to come from far away. 'Emergency. Which service?'

'Police,' Tim gasped. 'And an ambulance. I've been attacked. Some kind of acid—'

'Sir, are you in a safe location?'

Tim's eyes darted around wildly. 'I... I think so. He's gone.'

'What is your location?'

Tim rattled off the address, his words tumbling out in a panicked rush.

'Stay on the line, sir. Help is on the way. Do you have access to running water?'

The question snapped Tim back to reality. 'Yes, yes. There's a house...'

He staggered up the drive, cradling his injured arm. The cheery notes of the piano lesson continued, oblivious to the chaos outside.

Tim's fist pounded on the door. 'Help! Please, I need water!'

The music halted. Footsteps approached. The door swung open, revealing a startled, middle-aged woman. Lois Gardner's eyes widened as she took in Tim's wild expression and cradled arm.

'Oh, my God, what happened?'

'Acid attack,' Tim choked out. 'I need water. An outside tap.'

'Around the back.'

Tim staggered around the house, Lois watching him until a voice appeared behind her.

'Was that my dad?'

Lois spun around. 'Amelia, lesson's over. Go and wait in the living room.'

Tim heard his daughter's voice, but she was safe. He'd get back to her in a minute. A coiled hose sat under a tap, a spray gun already attached. Tim turned everything on and let his arm have the full force of a jet of water. It was cold, but too forceful, and he stifled a scream, before dialling down the spray into a trickle.

He leaned against the wall, legs shaking, his whole body shivering with shock.

Sirens wailed in the distance, growing steadily closer.

'Daddy?' Amelia's tremulous voice came from the back doorway. 'What's going on?'

Tim met his daughter's frightened gaze, his throat tight.

How could he explain this? How could he make sense of senseless violence?

'Bit of an accident, love. Daddy's okay, but we might need to go to the hospital, okay? Will you ring your mum and tell her to come and pick you up?' He put down the hose and took his phone from his pocket and handed it to his daughter.

'Your arm's all red, Daddy,' Amelia said.

'Just phone your mum, okay?'

Amelia nodded, her big eyes wide with fright.

But as he got back to the sprinkler, he heard his daughter make contact. 'Mum, it's Amelia. Dad's had an accident…'

————

THE CUL-DE-SAC IN CAPEL DEWI, just five miles from Carmarthen, rumbled with activity, blue lights painting the houses in an eerie, intermittent glow.

Jess ducked under the police tape, her eyes scanning the scene. Rhys and Gina approached, grim faced.

'Anything from the neighbours?' Jess asked.

Rhys shook his head. 'Not a peep.' He gestured towards the high laurel hedges. 'Everyone was either out or claims they didn't see a thing.'

'Nor hear anything. Not until Riggon started yelling,' Gina added.

'Convenient,' Jess muttered. 'What about CCTV?'

'Doorbell cameras only,' Gina offered with a wrinkled nose. 'We're pulling the footage, but these hedges are high.' She waved a hand at the laurels in an echo of Rhys's gesture.

Jess's gaze fell on a small evidence marker near Riggon's car. 'What's that?'

Rhys crouched down, pointing to a mangled piece of plastic. 'Looks like part of a water bottle. It's been sliced vertically.'

A technician in a white suit approached, clipboard in hand. 'We've got preliminary results on the substance.'

'Go on,' Jess urged.

'It's concentrated sulphuric acid, ma'am. Nasty stuff. Probably drain cleaner or car battery acid.'

Jess's jaw tightened. 'He's lucky it only hit his arm.'

She turned to Rhys and Gina. 'It's a quiet road. The attacker must have got here somehow. Let's expand the house to house.'

'On it.' Rhys nodded.

'And get those response vehicles to turn their blues off. It's like a sodding disco for the undead here.'

Jess made her way to a nervous-looking woman standing in the doorway of the house where Amelia had her lesson. 'Mrs Gardner? I'm Detective Inspector Allanby. Can you tell me what you saw?'

'Nothing. I was in the middle of Amelia's lesson when we heard banging on the door. Poor Mr Riggon was in such a state…'

'Did you notice anyone suspicious hanging around earlier?'

Lois shook her head. 'It's usually so quiet here. I can't believe something like this could happen.'

'Thank you, Mrs Gardner. Someone will be along to get a statement from you, and we'll be in touch if we need anything else.'

'I hope Amelia's okay. And Mr Riggon, of course.'

'We understand his injuries are not life-threatening,' Jess said. But didn't add what she was thinking. Thank the Lord for small mercies.

———

EAU DE A&E assailed Warlow's nostrils as he made his way to Tim Riggon's cubicle. The acting CEO sat on the edge of the bed, his arm swathed in bandages. Pale of face, haunted of eye.

'Mr Riggon? DCI Warlow, Dyfed Powys Police. How are you feeling?'

Riggon managed a weak smile. 'Like I've been to hell and back. The pain's better now, though.'

Warlow pulled up a chair. 'You up to telling me what happened?'

Riggon recounted the attack, his voice shaking slightly, matching the non-bandaged hand. 'It was so fast. One minute, I'm waiting for Amelia, the next...' He trailed off, swallowing hard. 'A noise. Like something hitting the body of the car. I thought it might be a kid's ball or a stone. I got out and then... He must have been waiting for me to do exactly that.'

'Did you get a good look at the attacker?'

'Black clothes, balaclava. Could've been anyone.'

'Male or female?'

'I'd say male. Not tall, but too broad to be female.'

Warlow leaned forward. 'Mr Riggon, I have to ask. Is there any reason for someone to want to do this? Any disputes? Nasty neighbours? Have you had any altercations while driving?'

'No. Nothing like that.'

Warlow did not let his gaze drop. 'Could this be related to anything personal? Are you seeing someone outside your marriage?'

'God, no.' Riggon looked genuinely offended.

Warlow nodded. 'Then, is it related to your position at the Health Board?'

Riggon's eyes widened. 'First Milburn, now me. Is someone targeting us?'

'You sound surprised,' Warlow said.

'Of course I'm bloody surprised. Wouldn't you be?'

A long list of criminals who might have harboured thoughts of vengeance where Warlow was concerned flickered briefly in his head. Not the time to be pedantic.

'Then what do you put down as the reason for having acid thrown at you?'

Riggon blinked. The question had clearly caught him off balance. 'I don't know. A mugging...'

'Muggers do not throw acid at their victims. This is an act of malicious intent. So, it goes back to either your work or something outside of that. And given what happened to

Russell Milburn, it's a possibility we have to consider work as high on the list as a possible link. Has there been any unusual activity at work? And I mean, before Milburn was killed. Threats, disgruntled employees?'

Riggon let his eyes drop. His breathing got deeper as he contemplated the implications of Warlow's words. 'Nothing specific. But the changes Russell was pushing through… they weren't popular. Changes never are. Centralising services, potential job losses. People are angry. I get that.'

'And yet, you felt it wise to announce today that the proposed changes would push ahead? I saw the article.'

'That was the Board's decision. They reasoned it would be a fitting way to honour Russell. It fell to me to announce it. I didn't think… Okay, they might be unpopular, but enough to make someone kill or maim?'

The question hung in the air.

Tim's shoulders slumped. 'God, what a mess.'

A nurse poked her head around the curtain. 'Mr Riggon? One of the surgeons is on his way down to have a look. They'll probably want to do a plastics referral just in case.'

Riggon nodded with a grateful little smile tagged on.

'Your daughter okay?' Warlow asked. 'Must have been an ordeal for her, too, seeing her dad injured.'

Riggon's expression softened. 'She's a good kid. Strong, like her mum.'

Warlow stood. 'I'll let you rest. We'll have an officer posted outside.'

As he left the cubicle, Warlow's mind let the tumblers roll.

Two attacks on Health Board executives in four days did not merit even the mention of the "C" word. Someone had declared war on the NHS leadership in West Wales, and he needed to figure out why before anyone else got hurt.

Outside, darkness had come to call, though the hospital lights kept it at bay. Warlow pulled out his phone to update Jess. They had a long night ahead of them.

CHAPTER TWENTY-SIX

'Murder and now assault,' Warlow wrote in a space made for him by Catrin on the Gallery in red letters, with an exclamation mark at the end.

For once, a genuine sense of bewilderment pervaded the entire team as they stood and stared at Warlow's pronouncement early the following morning. He left some space underneath for ideas.

Turning around, he addressed them all. 'Thoughts?'

Gina spoke first, not cowed by the situation, despite being the youngest member of the team. Warlow approved. 'Why assault, sir? Why not attempted murder? Don't you classify the acid attack as life-threatening?'

Warlow scribbled "acid" up next. 'Very good point and one that I have pondered.'

Jess chimed in, 'Knives kill more people than acid, Gina. It's possible the assailant used acid hoping to incapacitate Riggon, and then attack with a knife or something else. But he missed. And of course, acid attacks are used in spite, or as the worst kind of messages.'

'What messages?' Gina inquired.

Jess replied. 'I know more than I need to because Molly had a lecture on this for her degree. It upset her, and I had a hard thirty-minute phone call to let her vent. In places like India, Bangladesh, and Colombia, acid attacks are often misogynistic—men attacking women.'

Gina's brow furrowed. 'Why would they do that?'

'There's a strong cultural element, though it pains me to say so. For example, if a woman rejected a marriage proposal, or turned down a man's advances.'

'But is the MO different here in the UK?' Gina asked.

'Very different,' Jess confirmed. 'Apart from random hate crimes, and that, too, can be misogynistic, here, it's mostly male-on-male violence. Acid has become a weapon in street crimes. Gangs might use it to enforce drug debts, or criminals in robberies. It's easy to hide—easily hidden in a water bottle.'

'That's terrifying,' Gina said, shaking her head. 'But why acid? Why not just use a knife?'

Jess's expression darkened. 'All about reputation, Gina. Using acid can enhance a criminal's street cred. It's seen as more brutal, more intimidating.'

'And in Riggon's case…' Gina trailed off.

'In Riggon's case,' Jess said, 'it's important to consider all angles. Is there a more personal motive? That's what we need to find out.'

Gina nodded. 'Thank you, ma'am.'

Warlow listened to the discussion, his mind churning with possibilities. He offered his two penneth. 'I think this attack was aimed at damaging Riggon. Rendering him or stopping him from functioning. And it's done that to an extent. The question is why.'

'Do we need a closer look at him too, then?' Catrin queried. 'See if he's had any photos through the post, too?'

'Won't do any harm,' Warlow said.

Rhys piped up, 'Tannard has some information on the dead rodents, sir.'

'I smell a rat,' Gil muttered. He deflected the pained looks he received by adding, 'Oh, come on, you were all dying to say it.'

Rhys continued, 'She's asked if one of us wants to go over to Milburn's property with her. She has a theory—'

'What kind of theory?'

A look of perplexed resignation crossed Rhys's face. 'The kind that she won't speak about until she knows it's true.'

Warlow gave a little shrug. 'Fair enough. What time?'

'Around ten.'

'Okay. That's on you. What about Milburn's laptop?'

'I'll chase that up today, sir,' Catrin volunteered. 'That they haven't come back to us yet suggests there isn't much to find. And the same thing appears to be true about the phone records. Can't find any unusual patterns there. But I've asked for more from the period when he left his last job.'

'What's your reasoning there?' Warlow asked.

'Latimer?' Gil guessed. 'Our man with the Messiah complex?'

He got a nod from Catrin in reply.

Warlow turned back to the boards. 'Nothing is adding up here.' He held out a hand without turning around. 'Rhys, laser pointer.'

Rhys took two strides across to his desk with his long legs and returned with the pointer. A present from his mother, it had proved useful in briefings. But nowhere near as useful as it had been when it had fooled a serial killer into believing he was being lined up by a sniper, and in the process, saving a woman's life.

Pointer in hand, Warlow took a step back and circled a photograph on the boards with a red light.

'Milburn gets knocked off his bike and killed. Asphyxiated by a plastic bag.'

This wasn't news, but Gina winced hearing it. 'That still sounds so awful,' she whispered.

'Cold,' Jess said. 'Almost professional.'

Warlow nodded. 'That would've been my thinking, too. But these days, what with the internet and every conceivable form of murder shown every night on bloody TV, it's not inconceivable someone might want to use that knowledge and see if it works.'

He paused, considering the implications of his own disturbing thoughts; that someone might treat murder like a science experiment.

He turned and held up a hand, redirecting the pointer towards Riggon's corporate headshot, taken from the Health Board's website. 'Now Riggon is attacked in broad daylight, with acid, outside his daughter's piano teacher's house.'

'Clearly, the attacker knew his movements,' Jess observed.

'Or followed him,' Warlow suggested.

'And yet, no report of cars at the scene or leaving, and it's a pretty quiet road,' Catrin pointed out.

'Cyclist?' Gil suggested. 'Electric bikes can get you from A to B pdq.'

'But what links these two cases together?'

Catrin pointed to her timeline. 'The obvious answer is the hospital link. Milburn got killed after he'd been at the meeting in the community hospital about proposed closures and reconfiguration of services.'

'And the evening Riggon is attacked,' Rhys said, 'his name is featured all over official reports confirming that the changes are going to go ahead.'

'Did we tell you he made the BBC lunchtime news, too?' Catrin added.

The furrow in Warlow's brow deepened. Something wasn't sitting right with him.

'What don't you like?' Jess asked, noticing his expression.

'I can't put my finger on it. All I know it is irritates.'

'Speaking of Rhys,' Gil said.

'What have I done?' The young officer took umbrage.

'Who knows? The day is young. Still, carpet diem, as they say.'

'As who says?' Warlow glowered.

'Carpet fitters who want to be contacted by direct messaging,' Gil said.

'What the hell was in that tea you gave him, Rhys?' Warlow asked.

'One too many sugars by the sound of it.'

He threw Gil an appraising glance. 'Have you had some news on your Napier case?'

'Lots of files for me to go through. So, I'll be glad to get this Milburn murder put to bed.'

'What about Ivy, sir? Do you genuinely think what she is reporting has anything to do with this case?' Gina asked.

Warlow didn't answer immediately.

If it hadn't been for the constant low hum of activity from the indexers and secretaries behind them in the office and Incident Room, they might've heard the cogs of his brain meshing.

'It's the "C" word, Gina,' Jess said. 'Mr Warlow does not believe in coincidences.'

'I do not,' Warlow agreed. He breathed in and then let it out slowly. 'With that in mind, let's get moving. You're off to meet Leyshon, right, Gil?'

'Correct. I want to ask him about vandalism in the old hospital. He's the community lead for the Black Mountain Hospital and a councillor, after all. This falls squarely under Community Impact Assessment.'

'CIA. I like it, sarge.' Rhys grinned.

'Jess?' Warlow asked.

'Once Catrin gets the older phone records, I thought Gina and I could have a chat with Latimer again. He's out of the picture for Riggon. But he's still a possible for Milburn. I'll chase ANPR for his movements on the day Milburn was attacked.'

'Right,' Warlow said in a way that told them all there was still something on his mind.

'What about you?' Jess asked. 'Having a spa day?'

Warlow clamped his lips together. 'Bit of rumination. I'm heading back to the starting point. Back to the Black Mountain Community Hospital and the spooky spectre of the maternity hospital nearby.'

His mind was already racing ahead, piecing together the puzzle. There was a connection here, he was sure of it. The abandoned maternity ward, Ivy's reports, the attacks—they were all threads in a larger tapestry. He just needed, as always, to know which one to pull for the thing to unravel.

'We meet again at vespers.'

———

RHYS AND GIL walked out of the Incident Room together. Outside, a bright morning beckoned.

'Is it true you've finally got the files from Napier's office, sarge?' Rhys asked.

Gil nodded solemnly, as if he'd been entrusted with the Holy Grail. 'It is.'

'If you need any help, just give me a shout.'

Gil affected an expression of mock surprise. 'That's good of you…' He paused, eyeing the younger detective suspiciously. 'What's the catch?'

Rhys shrugged. 'No catch. Just curious…' He hesitated, then asked, 'Any idea what you're looking for?'

'No.'

'But you'll know it when you see it, right?' Rhys pressed.

'You've got it. The pick it up and look at it approach.' His nose wrinkled. 'But if you're going to be handling dead rats, I'm not so sure I'd want you in the same confined space as me.'

'The rat's in Tannard's lab, sarge. I don't know what it is she wants to show me at Milburn's place. I'm keeping an open mind.'

Gil's eyes lit up. 'To accommodate all the windmills.'

'What?' Rhys's face scrunched up in confusion.

'*Windmills of Your Mind,*' Gil explained, as if it were the most obvious thing in the world. 'A classic from a classic film. The Thomas Crown Affair.'

'Not seen that one.'

'I'm talking about the sixties original. Not the rubbish remake.'

Rhys remained perplexed.

'Spotify it,' Gil suggested, waving his hand dismissively.

'The Windmills of Your Mine,' Rhys repeated. 'Unusual.'

'Mind,' Gil corrected, then tilted his head thoughtfully. 'Though "mine" sounds marginally better. Plus, it's a good game to play. Change one letter of a film title. Or leave one letter out. You ever tried that?'

Rhys shook his head, a grin spreading across his face. 'Can't say I have, sarge.'

'Hours of fun,' Gil assured him. 'Apocalypse Cow. Bark to the Future, The Beer Hunter. That kind of thing.'

'Star Trek: The Lotion Picture,' Rhys responded, looking rather pleased with himself.

Gil lifted an eyebrow. 'You've nailed it. And the lewd versions are always the best.' He pointed a finger at Rhys. 'I'll expect at least ten by tomorrow morning in your best handwriting.'

They left through the exit together, Gil turning right, Rhys left. The latter was already muttering film titles under his breath, his brow furrowed in concentration.

After fifteen yards, Gil turned back and shouted, his voice loud across the car park, 'And be very, very careful with The Count of Monty Cristo!'

CHAPTER TWENTY-SEVEN

TANNARD and her CSI team were already at Milburn's rented property, lined up and ready, their white crime scene suits contrasting with the autumnal backdrop.

Rhys nodded to Maeve O'Connor, who stood in the doorway, arms crossed tightly over her chest. Once again, she wore athletic gear, but with slides on her feet instead of trainers. She watched silently as the team prepared to search the grounds.

'Right, then,' Tannard said, snapping on her gloves. 'Let's see what else this place is hiding.'

The team dispersed, combing through flowerbeds and shrubs with meticulous precision.

Rhys fell into step beside Tannard as they circled the house.

'So, what's the deal with the dead rat?' he asked.

Tannard's eyes narrowed behind her protective goggles. 'Nasty cocktail. Warfarin and crushed slug pellets. Whoever mixed it knew what they were doing.'

'Blimey,' Rhys muttered. 'Not your average garden pest control.'

'Too right,' Tannard muttered. 'That's my way of thinking, too.'

They rounded the corner to the back garden.

A tech called out, waving them over to a cluster of bushes. Two more rat carcasses lay partially hidden beneath the foliage, their bodies already beginning to bloat.

'Bloody hell,' Rhys breathed, hand over his mouth. 'It's a rat graveyard back here.'

Tannard crouched down, examining the scene. 'Recent, too. Can't have been here more than a day or two. Which means the poison is still here.'

The search continued.

Rhys saw O'Connor appear at the corner of the house, watching proceedings with what appeared to be disapproval. He turned towards her, offering what he hoped was a reassuring smile. She didn't return it.

'Got something!' Tannard's voice cut through the air. She stood by a raised flower bed, pointing at a dark lump nestled between the plants.

Rhys walked over, his Tyvek suit crinkling with each step. He approached warily, expecting more dead rodents, but what Tannard showed him now was nothing like that.

At first glance, the object looked like nothing more than animal droppings. Admittedly, from a big animal given the size of the thing. But as Tannard carefully extracted it, dropped it into an evidence bag, and sniffed, much to Rhys's distaste, the sickly-sweet aroma of peanut butter wafted up.

'Bingo,' she said, holding up the bait. 'Peanut butter laced with our poison cocktail. I'd put money on it.'

Rhys walked back to O'Connor, who had drifted a little closer through curiosity.

'You said you and Mr Milburn didn't put down any poison for the rats. Did the owner, or the letting agency, ever mention anything about it?'

O'Connor's face contorted in disgust. 'God, no,' she spat. 'We've got a dog. He's with Russ's parents for now, but… we'd never risk it with Dusty around.'

'You're sure? No pest control companies called in?'

'I said no,' O'Connor snapped. Her voice cracked slightly. 'We wouldn't… Russ wouldn't…'

Tannard had joined them, holding an evidence bag. 'It's

not typical pest control bait. But someone put this here, and recently.'

'Can you think of anyone who might have had access to the garden?' Rhys asked.

O'Connor shook her head, her eyes welling up. 'I don't... I can't...' She took a shuddering breath. 'I mean, there are periods during the day that we would both not be here...'

Rhys resisted the urge to say Zumba.

'This is mad,' O'Connor continued. 'All of it. But what has it got to do with what happened to Russ?'

That was an excellent question. The bait was a new piece of the puzzle, but it only seemed to raise more questions.

They reassured O'Connor again that they'd sweep the garden to collect what they could find, but it might be worth getting a pest control expert in, too.

They came across five more dollops of peanut butter and two additional expired rodents.

'We'll get all this back to the lab,' Tannard said when they'd completed the sweep and as she stripped off her suit near to the CSI van. 'Another rat autopsy might be in order, but I am more interested in the bait. We should get something back on that quickly, and I think that a forensic strategy meeting is in order. I'll text DCI Warlow.'

'Good idea,' Rhys said and looked around at the surrounding houses.

Perhaps it was time he knocked on some doors.

———

A SUPERMARKET CAFé would not have been Gil's first choice of a meeting place, but he spotted Huw Leyshon easily, his weathered face a familiar landmark in this sea of Tesco shoppers.

At the next table, Ian Leyshon hunched over an emptying plate, shovelling in the last of his full English with mechanical efficiency. He barely paused for breath. Grease-stained overalls testified to a morning's hard graft.

Huw nodded as Gil approached. '*Bore da*, Gil. Fancy meeting you here.'

Gil slid into a seat. He nodded at Ian. 'Morning."

Ian grunted in response, his eyes never leaving his plate.

'We've just dropped off a topper mower over in Saron,' Huw explained. 'Had to do some welding on the frame. Ian did a good job, too.'

Ian scraped the last of his beans onto his fork.

'Right,' he muttered, standing abruptly. 'Got some shopping to do.' He strode away, leaving his dirty plate behind.

Huw sighed, watching his son's retreating form. 'He's not been himself lately,' he murmured. 'Be nice if he met someone. But he doesn't go out much. Rugby club on weekends and that's about it. But we're not here to discuss Ian, are we?'

'No, It's about the old hospital, Huw. Heard anything lately? Any more trouble up there?'

'Not lately. It dies down in winter. Too bloody cold for the kids to be arsing about up there.'

'But before that?'

'The usual. Graffiti, broken windows. That damn internet's got a lot to answer for, if you ask me.' Huw shook his head. 'All these ghost-hunting idiots, posting their videos online. Makes the place out to be some kind of portal to hell. It's no bloody help when local kids post stories of ghostly funeral processions up the mountain, and some claim to have seen a shadowy figure in a top hat lingering by the chapel gates and organ music echoing from Hên Fethel at night, though the place doesn't even have an organ.'

'You haven't heard of anything more recent? No flare-ups?'

'Should I have?'

'I chatted with someone near the play area off Tirycoed Road and someone higher on the hill behind, and both claim they've seen some activity. Heard noises.'

'News to me.'

Gil looked at the inch of tea left in Huw's mug. 'What's the tea like?'

'Like tea.'

'Tidy.'

'This all to do with the Milburn business?'

Gil didn't reply. He had expected no revelations here, and Leyshon's response merely confirmed what he'd suspected. The old hospital was a draw for the bored kids. Instead, conversation drifted away to other things and after ten minutes, Ian reappeared, a bag of shopping dangling from one hand. He hovered at the edge of the table, shifting his weight from foot to foot.

Huw attempted a smile. 'All done? Gil here was just asking about—'

'Have you found who killed Milburn yet?' Ian cut in, his voice sharp.

Gil raised an eyebrow. 'We're working on it.'

'When you do, let me know. I'd like to shake the bugger's hand.'

'Ian,' Huw chided, but his son was already turning away.

'I'll be in the van.'

Huw's face reddened, his hands clenched on the table. 'I'm sorry about that, Gil. He doesn't mean—'

'It's alright,' Gil said quietly. 'Grief does funny things to a person.'

Huw nodded, not meeting Gil's eyes. 'That it does.'

They wrapped up the conversation quickly after that, neither man quite able to recapture the easy rapport they'd had before.

In the car park, Gil's eyes spotted Ian's battered pickup truck. He made a mental note of the number plate.

Gil clasped Huw's hand. 'Thanks for chatting.'

'Don't know how much help I've been.'

'You've confirmed what we thought,' Gil assured him.

He watched from his own car as the Leyshons drove away, Ian's truck leaving a trail of blue exhaust in its wake. Ian's bitterness, Huw's unease, the spectre of the community being squeezed still more. It was a potent brew, and one that left a sour taste in Gil's mouth. Still, he was here now, and he might as well text the Lady Anwen to see if they needed anything from Tesco.

He got a text back.

> What are you doing in Tesco?

>> I'm here all the time. You know me. Liddle and often.

He waited two minutes for a reply. When it came, it made him smile.

>> I'm sending you a list. Lean to the left.

That was the thing about marriage. You picked up each other's bad habits.

———

ON THE DRIVE across to the Amman Valley, Warlow called Tom with the phone on speaker.

'How're you feeling?'

Tom's voice came through, still a bit groggy. 'Like I've gone ten rounds. But the painkillers are doing their job.'

'Good. You're taking it easy, I hope?'

'Yes, Dad,' Tom responded, a suggestion of irritation creeping in. 'Jodie's making sure of that.'

'Excellent. I need to pick your brain.'

'Just about the only thing that isn't aching. Fire away.'

'I've got some questions about medical training.'

'Okay,' Tom said, a hint of amusement in his tone. 'But remember, patient confidentiality applies.'

'Of course,' Warlow agreed. 'I'm curious about training failures. You ever come across surgeons who just don't make the grade?'

There was a pause on the other end of the line. 'It happens,' Tom admitted. 'Not often, but it does. We have pretty rigorous assessment mechanisms in place.'

'Such as?'

'Regular evaluations, practical exams, peer reviews. It's a

constant process. You don't just pass med school and get handed a scalpel. But you already know that.'

He did. He'd been on the journey with Tom. 'And what about those who slip through the cracks? Anyone you've known who shouldn't have made it?'

Tom's sigh was audible. 'Dad, you know I can't.'

'I'm not asking for names. Hypothetically speaking, how would someone like that cope?'

Another pause. 'It's tough. The pressure is immense. Some people crack under it. Others… they compensate. Not always in healthy ways.'

'And the system? The checks and balances. Does it work?'

'Most of the time,' Tom replied. 'But it's not perfect. There's always room for improvement.'

Warlow could hear the curiosity in his son's voice now. 'Dad, what's this really about? You investigating a dodgy surgeon or something?'

'Or something,' Warlow said, doing his best not to sound too evasive. 'Just exploring all angles.'

'When I was a kid, I used to think it was cool having a detective for a dad. Now I'm not so sure. I feel like I'm being interrogated.'

'Sorry. Occupational hazard.'

'Yeah, yeah,' Tom said, but there was warmth in his voice. 'Just don't go poking around any of my colleagues, alright? I've got to work with these people.'

'Wouldn't dream of it. Like I say, all hypothetical.'

They chatted for a few more minutes about Tom's recovery before saying their goodbyes.

When Warlow ended the call, he couldn't help but smile. Even with a concussion, his son was still wise to his wiles.

CHAPTER TWENTY-EIGHT

Rumination.

In Warlow's mind, a highly underrated method which ranked up there with walkabouts.

He drove and pondered. He headed for a road he'd never been on and eased the Jeep up the narrow lane behind the old hospital. The track wound ever upwards through fields before the hedgerows stopped near Hên Fethel Chapel, with its cemetery close to the road.

Warlow reversed into the turnoff with the boot against the closed chapel gate and unfolded a map, studying the lie of the land. He'd circled the chapel, Ivy Pugh's cottage, and the old hospital.

This wasn't where Milburn had met his end, but it could be the source of the noises that had Ivy Pugh so rattled.

His attention was drawn to a senior citizen cleaning a grave in the cemetery next to the chapel. Warlow walked through a kissing gate and ambled over, offering a friendly nod.

'Morning,' he called. 'Quiet spot up here.'

The man straightened up, leaning on his rake. 'Yes, it is.'

'How old is the chapel?'

'Been here since the 1700s. But there was something else here before that. A church.'

'You have someone here?'

'Parents and a brother,' the man said. 'And proud of it.'

They chatted for a few minutes, Warlow gleaning titbits about the chapel's history.

'It's not used much now,' the man explained. 'Just at Christmas for the Plygain. We used to get up to one hundred people here before Covid. Now…' The man sighed.

'Plygain.' Warlow nodded. 'That's the all-night carol service, right?'

The man nodded. 'Starts at three in the morning. Unaccompanied carols, some passed down for generations. Tradition. Sadly, dying out.'

Wales had become one of the most secular of countries. But these isolated chapels and churches were a testament to the religious fervour that gripped these communities of old. And, as so often was the case, they were found in the most out of the way places. As if getting there were an act of pilgrimage in itself.

'Mind if I have a look around?'

'Feel free,' the man said. 'I'm here to see to the family. And you might think it's remote up here but at one time, the main road from Llanelli to Neath ran past here. Next to the chapel there was a stable block for horses to feed and that.'

Suitably schooled on his ignorance, Warlow walked down towards the chapel.

Whitewashed walls for the building itself and arched windows with plain glass, iron fencing, and gates. Beyond it, a little further down the hill, stood the second building, with holes in the stone walls where there had been windows and doors and a red corrugated roof.

The place did not look safe, but Warlow had a quick peek inside from the open doorway on the side of the building into the old stable block. Nothing but rubble and collapsed walls now.

He retraced his steps back to the chapel and glanced again at the map. Dotted lines led from where the stoned road ended, leading across a field to a woodland that spread all the way downhill to the edge of the scrubland in one corner of the old maternity hospital's footprint.

In effect, you might get from here to there without getting back to the road, though the way looked untravelled, apart from sheep tracks.

Still, sheep tracks were tracks.

On his way back to the car, Warlow raised a hand to the man in the cemetery, his mind already shifting gears. He drove the short distance to the community hospital, where he sought out Deena Barton again. He found her in her office, and she greeted him with a puzzled expression.

'Back so soon, DCI Warlow?'

'Just following up on a few things,' he replied. 'Can you show me where Milburn changed for his bike ride?'

Deena led him to a small locker room. 'It's a sluice room, but the nurses use it to gown up for changing dressings. It's not much, but it serves its purpose.'

Warlow inspected the area, noting the worn benches and chipped paint. He saw nothing of interest. He straightened and changed tack. 'Any issues with vandalism here? I know the old hospital is within a stone's throw.'

Deena swung her head. 'None. The lights keep them away. We're lucky, I suppose. That old place attracts trouble, but it never seems to spill over to us.'

'And, uh, the van driver, Gary. Is he around? I'd like another word. See if he'd ask if any of the other drivers had seen anything unusual."

'Not here. Could be in transit if he's in work today.'

Warlow saw an opportunity for lightning the mood. 'You mean the verb not the noun, right. Transit?'

He received a half smile in response, which on reflection was probably what his poor effort at a joke deserved.

'Do you have a number for him?'

'I do.'

Warlow thanked Deena before heading out, wondering if he was any the wiser after his trip. The honest answer would be no.

Before he could turn on the engine in the Jeep, his phone

buzzed with a text from Tannard. A strategy meeting? It sounded promising. Which was more than could be said for Gary, who did not answer his phone when Warlow rang him.

But not everyone worked full-time these days. And if Gary worked shifts he'd switch his phone off when not woking if he had any sense.

Warlow decided to try again later.

———

THE INCIDENT ROOM sounded like a hive before smoke was blown onto it. Various specialists, at the last count at least twenty, gathered for the strat meeting.

They were part and parcel of any Major Crimes Investigation. Even so, they were a bit of a gong show as far as he was concerned. Too many people.

He took his seat at the head of the table, surveying the assembled team.

Tannard, the crime scene manager, sat to his right, her face determined and confident. Next to her the forensic specialist adviser. They all had labels in this meeting. Even Jess, as deputy SIO. All she needed was a tin star and a Colt 45.

'Right, let's get started,' Warlow said, his voice cutting through the chatter. 'Jo, what have you got for us?'

Tannard cleared her throat. 'We've made some interesting discoveries at Milburn's residence. Having analysed the cause of death of the rats Ms O'Connor told us about, we investigated and found bait scattered in the garden, but it's not consistent with typical pest control practises.'

'How so?' Warlow asked..

'The distribution pattern and quantity suggest it was deliberately placed to target certain areas. Out in the open on the grass and in flower beds. Our working theory is that someone may have planted it to harm Milburn's dog, possibly as a form of psychological warfare.'

Murmurs rippled through the room. Warlow's jaw tightened.

Targeting dogs was a hanging crime in his book.

'Any evidence the dog was affected?'

'Thankfully, no,' Tannard replied. 'But it's a concerning development. DC Harries is still at Milburn's address, carrying out some house-to-house enquiries.'

Warlow nodded grimly before turning to the CCTV coordinator. 'Anything useful?'

The coordinator shook his head. 'I'm afraid not, sir. No usable footage from either Milburn's scene or the Riggon attack.'

'It's safe to conclude that this was a planned tactic. Whoever is responsible is smart.'

He turned to the digital media investigator. 'What about Milburn's computer?'

'We've found email traces linking back to Latimer's IP address,' the investigator reported. 'But they're from months ago. Nothing recent that stands out.'

'Is Jeremy Latimer still in custody, Jess?'

'He is but no further interview today, as ANPR reveals the motorcycle he uses in York at the time of Milburn's attack. Of course, we're establishing a timeline for him and will hopefully get North Yorkshire police to trace his movements and corroborate all that.'

'Gil? What have you got?'

'We have expanded our investigation to include reports of activity in the abandoned maternity unit next to the Black Mountain Community Hospital. The question is, do we involve PolSA in this?'

The PolSA spoke up. 'What are you thinking?'

Warlow gathered his thoughts. 'Someone may have been hiding there when Milburn left. His car and cycle would have been visible from the old maternity hospital. But it is in a terrible state, and we are looking for trace evidence. Perhaps for now it's something to note but not to act upon. Anything else?'

The digital media investigator spoke for the second time. 'We've had a member of the public come forward with dash cam footage, sir. It shows a cyclist heading away from the attack area about five minutes after the estimated time of the acid attack on Mr Riggon. Dark clothing, masked.'

Warlow's eyes lit up. 'That's something. Is it in the database?'

'Just uploading as we came to the meeting. We'll get it clipped straight away.'

'Good. I want to review that footage as soon as we're done here.' Warlow looked around the room. 'Anything else?'

As the meeting wound down, Warlow's mind was already racing. If they had footage of the cyclist, he needed to get Uniforms back out there, trace the cyclist's potential route, see if they could pick up any more footage along the way. He said as much to the house-to-house coordinator, who made a note the old-fashioned way, with pen on paper.

When the meeting ended, they gathered around Catrin's screen to review the video of the cyclist in Capel Dewi.

'He looks in a hurry,' Gil commented.

A voice from behind made them all look around. 'And it pretty much goes with what Milburn's neighbours said.'

'Rhys,' Catrin greeted the DC. 'What did you find out?'

'That they had seen someone turn up on a cycle with a backpack while Milburn and O'Connor were out. Shortly after they moved in, this was. Two people saw him. But they thought he was some kind of delivery person. He walked in and was only there for five minutes, then walked back out again and got on his bike. They thought it was an electric bike because he did little peddling.'

Jess shook her head. 'It must be the same bloke. Tries to poison Milburn's dog, then attacks Riggon.'

'Someone with a nasty grudge, I'd say.'

'Latimer would do for Milburn, but not for Riggon. He's never met the man,' Jess said.

'Agreed,' Warlow muttered. 'We know the time of the Riggon attack. We should get some bodies on that road to flag down regular users. Check if anyone saw something. If we can get an idea of where this cyclist was headed, we could get more CCTV.'

Doorbell security footage could be useful, though owners

were under no obligation to turn this over to the police. It meant a lot of legwork.

'I'm going to sweet talk CID into getting some help on this.'

'We'd better get over to the Hub at Llanelli and let Latimer go. We can't justify another extension.'

Warlow nodded.

'Cup of tea before you go? And we ought to dip into the HTFT box. I feel the need for baked goods.'

Gil and Rhys made their way to the little kitchen where the kettle was kept. Gil had a spot for the HTFT box. So far, no other staff had the temerity to open it… just in case.

As Rhys filled the kettle, he began whistling. Never a good sign. 'Sarge, you'll never guess what I saw online last night.'

Gil, checking the box, looked up. 'Do I really want to know?'

'It's this thread where people add 'ing' to film and book titles,' Rhys explained, barely containing his excitement. 'It's funny stuff. Like "Jurassic Park-ing".'

Gil groaned. 'Let me guess, you've come up with your own?'

Rhys nodded enthusiastically. 'Reservoir Dogging.'

Gil was quiet for a dangerous thirty seconds. 'Still, I suppose it depends where you add the "ing".'

'Does it?'

'It does. Just thinking of the Spy Who Loved Me and fitting in that 'ing' between the m and the e.'

Rhys's mouth moved as he concentrated and repeated the words in a low murmur. 'The Spy who loved mi—' He cut the word short and sent Gil a look of horror mixed with a barely stifled guffaw.

'You started it,' Gil countered with a very straight face. 'And that kettle will not boil until you press the on button, unless you've suddenly developed telekinesis.'

CHAPTER TWENTY-NINE

It was 10pm at Ffau'r Blaidd. Warlow and Jess were settled on the sofa, engrossed in an episode of Slow Horses. As the credits rolled, they shared a look of satisfaction, and Jess stretched out her legs and stifled a yawn.

'Wonderful stuff, that,' Warlow said, reaching for his bedtime tea. No wine this evening, as it was a school night.

Jess nodded, a sly smile playing on her lips. 'It is. I know why you like it so much.'

'Oh? Let's have it, then.'

'You identify with Lamb, that's obvious' Jess said. 'The swearing, the farting, and the general misanthropy.'

Warlow scoffed, but there was a hint of amusement in his voice. 'I'd like to think I'm a bit more refined than that. Besides, I do not have holes in my socks. But it's the writing, isn't it? Sharp, witty dialogue, complex characters…'

'Maybe,' Jess conceded, her smile widening.

'You've got to admit, there's something appealing about his no-nonsense approach.'

Cadi, sensing the playful mood, trotted over with her stuffed bear, Arthur, offering it first to Warlow, then to Jess. They both gave her an affectionate pat after pretending to take the toy from her, which she was having no truck with.

The dog's presence, as always, provided a soothing balm to the lingering stress of their day.

'Did Latimer give anything away?' Warlow asked, his tone shifting to something more serious.

He'd been curious about the outcome of Jess's meeting all evening. They'd placed a moratorium on work discussions over supper and the TV programme. But now Warlow felt the urge to deconstruct the day a little.

Jess sighed, absently stroking Cadi's head. 'Same old story. He's convinced he'll be vindicated. Keeps insisting it's only a matter of time before everyone recognises his brilliance.' She paused, frustration creeping into her voice. 'I had to listen to him tell me, yet again, how he will be proven right and how everyone else were mediocre arseholes. It's like talking to a brick wall.'

'Delusional, then?' Warlow asked.

'Frustratingly so,' Jess confirmed. 'Did you catch up with Tom?'

'Much better than expected, all things considered. He's in good spirits…' He paused, a thoughtful expression crossing his face. 'Funnily enough, I picked his brain on the Latimers of this world. He says that occasionally, one or two people find out too late that they're not up to the job. Though in Latimer's case, I suspect an underlining personality disorder lurks. As Gil says, mental illness is no respecter of job or status.'

They fell into a contemplative silence, broken only by Cadi's contented sighs as she settled between them, stretched out on a rug.

'How about Rick?' Warlow asked.

Jess tensed slightly, her hand still on Cadi's fur.

'I'd rather not. At least not tonight. I've compartmentalised him, and that drawer stays shut. He is for another day.' Her tone was firm but not unkind, and Warlow nodded, understanding.

'I'd suggest another episode, but our friends of the fruity network have regressed to the old way of serialisation. No new episode until next week, unfortunately.'

'Shame.'

'There is a new Scandi on Channel 4.'

'If it's more than six episodes, I'm out. Those twelve-part marathons are just filler and lingering stares.'

Warlow flicked through. 'It's an eight-parter.'

She shrugged. 'Okay. Are we Danes, Swedes, Norwegian, or Finnish?'

'Swedish,' Warlow said as he navigated to the first episode.

'What's it called?' Jess asked.

'The Bridge over the Arctic Forest Killings.'

Jess threw a cushion at him.

Warlow caught it.

Cadi looked very interested.

The opening sequence was painfully predictable: a slow, brooding montage of an icy, desolate landscape. Snow-covered forests, frost-bitten lakes, and darkened skies stretched out under a drone with a melancholic filter, all set to the obligatory moody soundtrack. Some haunting Scandinavian ballad murmured in the background, heavy on the minor chords and cryptic lyrics, as if the scenery itself was holding its breath for something grim to happen.

'I wonder what Slow Horses is in Swedish.'

Warlow played with his phone and said two words which probably bore no relation to how they should have sounded. *'Långsamma hästar.'*

'Of course it is. Silly me.'

A quiet ease settled between them. A shared comfort from surviving the dealing with the worst of human nature. But the drama didn't captivate the imagination quite like Mick Herron's gritty, character-driven tales, with their cynical take on bureaucratic infighting, flawed characters, and the personal toll of espionage.

Had either of them known what was in store for them in a few hours' time, they might have got some rest a bit earlier. As it was, both were asleep by eleven.

But the night, as it turned out, was yet young.

———

Ivy Pugh jolted awake, her heart hammering in her chest. The darkness of her bedroom was oppressive, but it was the sounds that truly terrified her. Shouts echoed through the night, followed by what she could have sworn was a blood-curdling scream.

No digital clock in the Pugh house. Ivy flicked on the little bedside lamp to peer at her alarm clock. 2.22am. A time when the rational so often yields to the irrational, where sleep eroded the barriers between reality and imagination. Where dreams and nightmares held sway.

Yet, the night held few terrors for Ivy Pugh, usually. Though her belief in the link between life and death was not one shared by many, it gave her succour in the dark watches.

Her family were all close by, buried in Yr Hên Fethel, a few hundred yards up the hill. They watched over her, she believed.

No, Ivy's fears were firmly anchored in the real world. A terror that her own mind might be slipping towards the nether-world that her poor sister had inhabited, cursed by Alzheimer's. Hence, when she heard the voices in the night, she had to verify that this was not some trick played by an ageing brain.

Trembling, Ivy got up and reached for the little flashlight she kept in a bedside drawer. She went to the bedroom door and unhooked a candlewick dressing gown with her stick-thin arms, then shuffled back to the bed to switch off the bedside lamp before crossing to the window, using only the flashlight beam to guide her.

With the curtains opened, her eyes widened with relief as she saw a flickering light on the hill above. But others flick-ered too, closer to her and nearer the hospital grounds. And even as she looked, a deafening explosion rocked the night, and a huge, orange fireball erupted into the sky.

The inferno was mesmerising and terrifying in equal measure. The decrepit building, nothing more than a dark regular shadow on most nights, was now lit up in the dancing orange and yellow nova of an inferno, sending plumes of acrid smoke billowing up to disappear into the starless night. The fire roared, shattering the few glass windows that remained with loud pops.

More shouts pierced the air now, desperate, frantic.

Ivy's hands shook as she clutched her dressing gown tighter.

It's them, she thought, her mind racing. *The spirits are angry. They're reclaiming their territory.*

A sharp knock nearly stopped Ivy's heart. She froze, terror paralysing her limbs.

The knocking grew more insistent, and Ivy moved towards the stairs where she stood at the head, looking down into the dark stairwell and the front door at the end of the stubby hall.

Another knock. A dozen insistent bangs.

No spirit this, Ivy thought.

She took the stairs, one hand, as always, on the wooden rail her father had put in so many years before. One step at a time. Ahead of her, the door shuddered as if something large was pushing against it. Or had fallen against it?

Ivy stood in the hall, shuffling slowly forwards. She flicked on the hall light, and the banging came again, not so urgent this time, as if the light had signalled to it. As if its strength was fading.

With trembling fingers, Ivy turned the lock and opened the door a crack on a chain installed by a nice community policeman who'd called the year before.

What she saw made her gasp.

An apparition stood before her. A young woman, dark-skinned and wide-eyed with fear, swayed on the threshold, swathed in layers of clothing. She spoke rapidly in a language Ivy couldn't understand, her words tumbling over each other in desperation.

'Are you… are you real?' Ivy whispered, her mind struggling to comprehend the sight before her. 'Or are you a spirit?'

The woman's eyes rolled back, and she collapsed, half-sprawled against the door.

Ivy had no choice but to undo the latch. Once undone, the door fell open, allowing the woman to fold across her threshold.

Somewhere in Ivy's head, some old warnings reverberated.

Whatever you do, do not invite these spirits in.

But she'd had no choice, and this bundle of rags and clothes did not look much like a spirit under the pendant ceiling light. But nor did she look like someone from *Cwm Amman*. Ivy knelt, tried to shift the body, but the girl—because now that Ivy saw her face, she saw she was nothing but a girl—was dead weight.

Ivy used her hand against the passage wall to stand upright.

Cold, dank night air pushed in from the outside. No good. She had to pull this girl in and shut the door. Her desperation on the threshold had transcended the meaning of her words.

Perhaps there were pursuers.

Slowly, and with great effort, a couple of inches at a time, the octogenarian woman dragged the girl into her hall and finally, short of breath and red of face, closed the door on the night and all its terror outside.

With badly shaking hands, Ivy reached for the phone—still a landline but at least a wireless handpiece—and dialled the three digits she'd dialled so many times before.

Few people would consider themselves lucky this night, but Ivy cornered what little luck there was and got through to a familiar voice after three rings.

'Maggie?' she said when the call connected. 'It's Ivy. Ivy Pugh. The hospital… it's on fire. And there's a girl… I think she might be a spirit, but she's a solid one. She's collapsed at my door. I don't know what to do…'

As Ivy spoke, the fire down the hill raged on.

Maggie, momentarily toying with ignore this call, saw the lights on her colleagues' boards light up as other calls in.

A fire.

Just as Ivy was describing.

'Maggie?' The old woman's voice sounded strained.

'Ivy, I can hear you, darling. I can hear you. You say someone is in the house?'

'Passed out. She was at the door. The hospital exploded.'

'Is she breathing?'

'Let me…' Ivy leaned over, put her hand under the girl's nose. It took a while for her to straighten. 'Yes.'

'Okay. Other people have called in about the fire. Help is on the way. I'll send an ambulance to your place.'

'What shall I do?' Ivy asked.

'Keep the girl warm. And well done for phoning in, Ivy. We'll get to you as soon as we can.'

CHAPTER THIRTY

WARLOW AND JESS received the call at 5:03am from a CID sergeant who had been dispatched to the hospital as part of the emergency response team. Arson was suspected. The fire service had arrived ninety minutes before and brought the blaze in the annexe at one end of the abandoned maternity hospital under control within sixty minutes. The CID sergeant called to relay the grim news that the Fire Investigator had just discovered a body.

Coffee at Ffau'r Blaidd that morning was accompanied by minimal conversation. Being up so early confused Cadi, even more so when Warlow took her breakfast with her to the Dawes at 5:45, accompanied by profuse gratitude and apologies.

Jess went ahead in her Golf and was already at the scene when Warlow pulled up just before seven.

Warlow hated fires. He had almost lost Jess and Catrin to one deliberately set in a lock-up garage during a recent case. He'd lost crucial evidence in the Bowman case to flames as well.

Fires had a certain finality about them, at least in the arsonist's mind. But there were always clues that a skilled investigator could uncover. The body always had something to tell them, too.

Darkness still ruled as Warlow pulled up. The clocks would all go back shortly to ease the morning's gloom, but it had not happened yet.

The acrid scent of smouldering wood and something much less palatable hung in the chilly morning air. The sky had cleared overnight, and arc lights lit up what was left of the annexe, which had clearly been the source of the blaze. Half its roof had collapsed, blackened walls still oozed smoke. Miraculously, the rest of the old maternity hospital had survived, thanks to the connecting corridor acting as a fire-break when it crumbled.

Warlow found the Fire Investigator at the side of the burnt-out shell. Two CSI vans were already parked nearby, but as always with fires, they needed the investigators' go-ahead before entering the scene.

'Evan,' a familiar voice called out.

Warlow turned to see Chalmers, the fire service investigator, striding towards him in his red helmet. They'd known each other for years, having worked together on many cases in the past.

'Morning, Brian,' Warlow greeted him. 'What have we got?'

Chalmers's face was grim as he replied, 'I know you're keen to get in there, and CSI are like dogs at my heels, but it'll be a while yet. We're still assessing structural integrity and checking for any risk of further explosions.'

'Explosions?'

'There were oxygen cylinders in there. Still are some, so we're cooling those down. Lucky they didn't all go off, or we'd have a much worse situation.'

'Where's the body?' Warlow asked, his voice low.

Chalmers strode around the outside to the rear where the roof had caved in.

Fire officers were already shifting debris, opening a path to the grotesque shape lying in the rubble. Water dripped from the beams above, and even under the harsh arc lights, the view a dozen feet in was poor—cluttered with wreckage and scorched furniture.

'Unfortunately, I've been in and I already have some snaps.' Chalmers pulled out a tablet in a hardened protective case and flicked to some images.

The corpse wore a sickening, leathery grin where the flesh had shrivelled. Where it had not, it remained blackened, with limbs contorted in a final agonised pose. What remained of the clothing clung to the body in charred tatters. And even though the images could not have given off an odour, the acrid stench of burnt flesh assaulted Warlow's nostrils from feet away, making him grateful for the cool morning air.

Chalmers flicked through the carousel. 'We found some keys nearby,' he explained. 'You can just make out a Nissan logo. There's also what looks like the remains of a lanyard trapped under the neck.'

Warlow stared, following Chalmers's gloved finger as he pointed out the still intact ribbon visible and the metallic clasp connecting it to what looked like an ID tag.

'The body is supine,' Warlow said.

Chalmers nodded. 'Probably lying down when overcome by smoke,' he mused. 'Most of the fire damage seems to have come from falling debris onto the body.'

Warlow stared at the blackened tape extending from the burnt and distorted plastic of the lanyard.

'Could be staff,' he muttered.

Chalmers shrugged. 'Strong chance, I'd say.'

Warlow made his way back to the staff car park of the Black Mountain Community Hospital just a few yards away, his gut twisting.

The rear car park was still half-empty at this early hour. The day staff had not yet arrived. His eyes were drawn to the designated areas where a blue Nissan Juke was parked.

Jess joined him. She'd already seen Chalmers's snaps.

'Who called it in?'

'The night manager,' Jess said. 'Someone raised the alarm at around half two.'

'We need to talk to them,' Warlow said, his voice tight with urgency.

Jess looked pale in the strengthening dawn light. 'We can get in through the rear entrance.'

Warlow had been in the ward manager's office before. But the person who sat behind the desk this time, he had not met.

Kofi Akoto had worked four nights a week for the last three years. He was a big man. An imposing figure standing as they walked in, his Ghanaian heritage evident. Despite the early hour and the stress of the situation, he stood ramrod straight.

'Let's sit down, shall we?' Jess suggested.

Akoto nodded, his face drawn with fatigue and concern.

'Mr Akoto,' Warlow began, 'can you tell us what happened this morning?'

'One of our ward staff went out to her car around half two and saw the flames. Not much then, but enough. She rushed back in, and I immediately raised the alarm.'

Jess made a note. 'Did you see anything suspicious before that?'

'No, nothing out of the ordinary.' Akoto shook his head. 'There's usually nothing to see around here. We are always very quiet.'

Warlow's gaze was steady as he asked, 'Where do you park, Mr Akoto?'

A flicker of understanding crossed Akoto's face. 'I think I know where you're going with this,' he said. 'Deena Barton's car is still in her spot. But I don't know why. She might have gone out somewhere. She lives in Llangennech, near Llanelli, but perhaps she has friends here or in Ammanford.'

It was the obvious assumption to make. The kind he might have done under the circumstances.

'And you didn't see or hear anything strange last night?' Jess pressed.

Akoto spread his hands. 'You mean apart from the explosions?'

'We think they were oxygen cylinders,' Warlow explained.

'Then no, nothing. We have no dealings with the old maternity hospital. It's been abandoned for years. I have no idea why the fire broke out.'

Suddenly, Akoto's eyes widened. He looked from Warlow to Jess and back again. 'Wait… I've heard rumours. They say a body was found.' His voice trembled slightly. 'Is that why you are here? Is that why you are asking about Deena's car?'

The implications of his words sank in like an alligator under swamp water. 'Oh God,' he whispered. 'You don't think…'

'We know nothing at this stage,' Warlow said. 'And it won't help anyone if we jump to conclusions.'

'Day staff are coming in. The Health Care Assistant who raised the alarm has already spoken to one of your officers. Are the night staff free to go home? We still have a hospital to run.'

Warlow glanced at Jess.

'CID have a list of everyone on duty last night,' she said.

Warlow turned back to Akoto. 'Of course.'

'I will need to hand over. Should I talk to the staff nurse on duty?'

'Is that what you would do if Deena Barton wasn't here?'

Akoto nodded.

'Then if she doesn't turn up, that's what you should do.'

Warlow and Jess walked outside.

'You're not going to scotch these rumours. Not with her car parked in front of everyone.'

She was right.

'Okay. Let's get Akoto to move his car and get this area screened off. Might stop the day staff from getting antsy. Is Gil on the way?'

'He's already here.'

Warlow looked around. 'I haven't seen him.'

'Ah.' she said in a way that told Warlow he didn't quite have the complete picture yet. 'I got a call on the way here. I told CID they should speak to you directly. Obviously, they forgot.'

Warlow waited.

'Gil's gone up to see our friend, Ivy Pugh. She called in on seeing the fire, too.'

'No surprises there.'

'No. But only after someone knocked on her door and collapsed in her hallway.'

'What?' The word rushed out like a greyhound from a starting box. He hurried towards the Jeep.

'If you're quick, the tea might still be warm,' Jess said.

———

In Ivy Pugh's house on the hill, Gil sat in an overstuffed armchair, a half-empty mug in his hand.

Warlow perched on the edge of a floral sofa, armed with a mug also.

'Now Ivy, tell Mr Warlow exactly what you've told me except leave the premonitions and the fact that you'd seen two crows and a magpie on that sycamore earlier on for now. Just what you saw last night, okay?'

Ivy looked animated, eyes bright, her voice quavering with excitement. 'Well, as I was saying to the sergeant here, I heard the noises again last night. From the old hospital. And then the bang and the fire and—'

'Tell him about your visitor, Ivy.'

Ivy nodded. 'I was already up, looking at the fire when someone knocked on the door.'

'And you answered it,' Warlow said.

He tried to keep the disappointment out of his voice but couldn't. He wanted to tell her she should not have answered a knock in the early hours, but it was far too late for that.

'Of course.' She paused, drawing a deep breath. 'When I opened it, there was a woman there. Jabbering. She looked... well, not right.'

Warlow's brow furrowed. 'What did she look like, Ivy?'

'Like she wasn't from around here, that's for certain,' Ivy replied, her eyes wide. 'You could tell just by looking at her. And when she spoke... well, I think she was speaking in tongues.'

'Speaking in tongues?' Warlow prompted gently.

Ivy nodded vigorously. 'Yes, yes. It wasn't Welsh, and it certainly wasn't English. It was... something else entirely.' She lowered her voice conspiratorially. 'I think she might be a messenger from them.'

'Them?'

'The other side.'

'And she doesn't mean the England rugby team,' Gil muttered.

Warlow threw him a look.

Gil returned it with mock innocence.

'And where is this woman now?'

Gil set down his mug. 'Glangwili. As far as I know, she's still unconscious. I've asked them to alert us when she wakes up.'

'I hope she'll be alright,' Ivy said. 'I want to know what she was trying to tell me.'

'Believe me, we all want that,' Warlow said.

'Did I do the right thing by letting her in?'

For a moment, Warlow was torn between telling her that under no circumstances should she ever open the door in the wee hours without knowing who was there. On the other hand, she'd acted promptly and reacted with the kind of unbridled hospitality that simply didn't exist anymore. Except perhaps in houses halfway up mountains.

'You did, Ivy. But you need to promise me to be careful. Have you thought of getting an intercom fitted?'

Ivy blinked, and Warlow got that sinking feeling he got sometimes when one of the boys started talking tech to him.

'You can get battery-operated peephole-cameras. Probably better off with one of those,' Gil said.

Ivy looked from one officer to the other like a slightly inquisitive sparrow.

Warlow let it go. 'You did well, Ivy. But no more opening the door in the dark at night, okay?'

'Whatever you say, *bach*. Now, can I get you more tea?'

CHAPTER THIRTY-ONE

MIDDAY ARRIVED ON AN EXPRESS TRAIN. The corpse had gone directly to Cardiff. Its fire-damaged state made any kind of normal identification impossible. Its effects, or rather her effects—because it had been female—rings, watch, necklace, plus car keys, all pointed towards Deena Barton. Plus the ID badge attached to the lanyard under the corpse with Barton's name and a twisted and damaged photograph.

Until dental records could be confirmed, however, the identification remained likely rather than proven.

Warlow's mind raced.

Sometimes, such identifying objects were deliberately placed with a burnt corpse to obfuscate. People, he knew all too well, could be devious sods.

They were all back in the Incident Room, awaiting another major debrief. Another episode of the gong show. But Warlow wanted just the investigation team present for now.

'So, we assume it's her, then?' Gina asked, her voice tense.

'Working hypothesis,' Warlow replied grimly.

'If it is, why was she in there?' Jess interjected. 'My understanding was it had been sealed off and locked.'

'That's what Deena Barton told us,' Warlow said.

'Could she have gone in to get something?' Gil suggested. 'Maybe she saw or heard something. Perhaps she was one of the first on scene when it blew up.'

'That's a possibility,' Warlow said.

'But I can tell it's not one that you like,' Gil contended.

'She, like Milburn and Riggon, is an NHS employee. Okay, she was clinical staff, not management. Though she had a managerial role at the community hospital. That's a bloody strong link.'

'Agreed,' Jess said. 'It's the strongest link.'

'What about the woman who knocked on Ivy's door in the middle of the night?' Gina asked. 'What do we know about her?'

Warlow glanced towards Catrin. She obliged.

'Not much. No ID. Hardly any money. She was dressed in old clothes and none of them fitted properly. Dehydrated, significant cuts and bruises. And...' Catrin paused, her expression solemn. 'The latest information is that the doctors found some shotgun pellets embedded in her scalp and clothes. The cuts and bruises probably came from stumbling around on the side of a mountain covered in gorse bushes.'

For a moment, no one spoke.

The clack of keyboards from the support staff in the room behind the gathered team sounded overloud as they stared at Catrin in shock.

'She's been shot at?' Warlow said eventually, his voice low and dangerous.

Catrin shrugged. 'It looks like it. But they were superficial, the pellets.'

'The Fire Investigator rang me,' Jess said. 'They've found some evidence of occupation in the annexe. A burnt-out mattress, some cans, and a stove.'

'Squatters?' Rhys asked.

'Could Barton have disturbed them?' Gil suggested.

'If the woman got shot from behind, it means she was running away,' Gina said, but quietly.

It conjured up an image that they all struggled to imagine.

'We should get something back from Cardiff soon,' Gil said.

He was right. Since they had a high level of suspicion for the corpse being that of Deena Barton, Sengupta or the forensic odontologist should have obtained Barton's records for dental comparison.

'We should.' Warlow pulled on the flesh of his lower lip, letting it slip back through his fingers repetitively. 'But, for now, we have to work on the concrete. Jess, can you chase up the Digital Media Investigators? See if they're getting anywhere by tracing the cyclist from the Riggon attack.'

'No one's going to the postmortem, then?' Rhys asked.

'Don't sound so bloody disappointed,' Warlow snapped, harsher than he'd intended.

The stress was clearly getting to him. He took a deep breath before continuing. 'Sengupta said she was doing it late morning. We would never have made it. Besides, burn victims are never pleasant. But someone needs to go to Glangwili and talk to this woman who pitched up at Ivy Pugh's. We don't even have a name yet, do we?'

'I'll go,' Gil said, standing up. 'I'll take Gina with me. We'll try to get back for the meeting.'

As the team dispersed, Warlow retreated to the SIO office. He had enough paperwork on this case already to keep him occupied, but his mind kept wandering to the shocking revelations. He needed to update his strategy document and his policy log. His investigation plans and lines of inquiry would need a red bloody pen and an extra sheet at this rate. In all probability, he ought to get out his ringmaster uniform from the dressing-up trunk.

Another death meant more resources, so they'd now need to co-opt a finance manager and an analyst to coordinate the intel and develop a strategy. And the Press Officer would definitely need to be on board.

Half an hour later, his phone rang, shattering his concentration.

'DCI Warlow?' Sengupta's voice, calm as always.

'What can you tell me?' he asked, his heart racing.

'Deena Barton. That's definite.'

Warlow didn't speak, but he used four fingers of his right hand to massage the skin of his forehead. 'Smoke inhalation?'

'That didn't help, but it didn't kill her, either. She died from a displaced fracture of her skull caused by blunt trauma. Early indications suggest something hard with a small diameter. Perhaps a hammer.'

'God,' Warlow muttered. 'What else is this case going to throw at us?'

'Thought you'd want to know as soon as possible.'

'Thanks. Full report to follow, I take it?'

'Yes, toxicology and any other findings. But the skull fracture showed up on the CT, and I've just confirmed it.'

'Thanks,' Warlow said, ending the call.

The team needed to know this.

Deena Barton was dead before the annexe was set on fire. Murdered. The fire perhaps set to destroy the evidence. That spoke of a lack of sophistication. Of urgency. Perhaps even panic.

He got up from his desk and walked out to talk to his team.

———

GIL AND GINA strode down the hospital corridor, passing the busy staff in scrubs.

'That's the thing about hospitals,' Gil muttered. 'You see no one walking slowly.'

They took some stairs to a surgical ward and, as they approached the room, Gil nodded to the uniformed officer standing guard.

'Morning, sunshine,' Gil quipped. 'Exciting shift?'

The young officer rolled his eyes. 'Like watching paint dry, sarge. Are we guarding her or making sure she doesn't do a bunk?'

'Bit of both. Tell you what, we're going to be a good half

hour. Why don't you grab yourself some breakfast? We'll monitor things and let you know when we leave.'

'Cheers, sarge, I'm starving.'

'Tried the canteen? They always like to see a man in uniform up there. You'll probably get an extra helping of sausages.'

'I know one of the cooks.' The Uniform, about the same age as Gina, grinned. 'Want me to bring you back anything?' He had a close-cropped beard and blue eyes that lingered a little longer on Gina than they had on Gil.

'No need. But ask for a drop of bromide in your tea.'

'What's that, sarge?'

'An old joke. Go on. You're on the clock.'

The Uniform hurried away.

'Bromide?'

Gil nodded. 'Bit of an urban myth. Used to be said that the army put bromide in squaddies' tea to quell their libidinous urges. All a load of tosh, of course, but it's still out there in the ether as a bit of a trope for people of a certain generation.'

'Was he being libidinous?'

'You forget I have two daughters who, fortunately, followed their mother in the looks department, and I have seen the way young men sometimes look at young women. My paternalistic instinct is to slap down any such urges before they become too… big.'

'I can't tell now if you're being rude or not,' Gina said.

'Let's keep it that way. Ah, there is a lesser-spotted staff nurse. Excuse me?'

The nurse in scrubs, gloves, and a white plastic apron swivelled and looked at Gil's proffered ID.

'How's our mystery guest?' he asked.

The nurse sighed. 'Physically, she's not too bad, considering. The doctors removed eight shotgun pellets from her scalp under local, bless her. She's underweight and has various cuts and bruises, but nothing life-threatening.'

'And mentally?' Gina inquired, her voice soft with concern.

'Hard to say.' The nurse shrugged. 'She hasn't said much. What she has said we don't understand. Seems scared, mostly.'

Gil nodded. 'Right, let's see what we can find out.'

They entered the room to find a slight woman, olive skinned, wisps of dark hair under a loose scarf, sitting up in bed. Her features were aquiline, and her eyes were remarkably a light grey-green, brim full of wariness as they approached. She wore a standard-issue hospital gown, and it looked as if one of the staff had given her a blue scrub cardigan against the cold.

'Good morning,' Gil said cheerfully. 'I'm Detective Sergeant Jones, and this is Detective Constable Mellings. We'd like to ask you a few questions if that's alright.'

The woman stared at them blankly, her brow furrowed in confusion.

Gina stepped forward, her voice gentle. 'Do you speak any English?'

That elicited a slow headshake, her gaze darting between them.

Gil scratched his chin. 'Any English at all?'

The woman managed a stuttered, 'Water,' with a rolling of the final letter r.

Gina shot Gil a look before turning back to the woman with a warm smile. 'It's okay,' she said, miming eating. 'Are you hungry? Thirsty?'

The woman shook her head again.

Gil pulled out his phone and opened up a map app. 'Let's try this,' he muttered, showing the screen to the woman. 'Where are you from?'

The woman's eyes lit up with recognition. She ignored the phone but pointed to herself. 'Afghan. Pashtun.'

'Afghanistan. Right, well, we're going to need a translator.'

Gina nodded. She poured water into a plastic beaker and handed it to the woman. 'Let's see if we can at least get her name.'

Gina pointed to herself. 'Gina,' she said clearly, then pointed to Gil. 'Gil.'

Finally, she pointed to the woman, raising her eyebrows in question.

The woman seemed to understand.

'Maryam,' she whispered.

'Maryam,' Gina repeated with a smile. 'It's nice to meet you, Maryam.'

Gil's phone rang. He stepped out into the hallway to take the call.

'Gil, it's Jess,' came the reply. 'We've got the postmortem results on Barton. Blunt force trauma to the skull. And there's something else…'

As Jess filled him in, Gil's expression hardened.

When he ended the call and returned to the room, Gina was sitting by Maryam's bed, speaking softly and miming to communicate.

'Everything alright?' Gina asked, noticing Gil's expression.

'We need to talk,' he said, gesturing for Gina to join him in the corridor.

Once outside, Gil lowered his voice. 'The postmortem on Barton threw up blunt force trauma to the head as a cause of death, but they also found traces of an accelerant on her clothes. The same type used in the hospital fire.'

Gina's eyes widened. 'You don't think…'

Gil nodded grimly. 'I hate to say it, but right now, Maryam in there is our prime suspect for both arson and murder.'

Gina glanced back at the room, her face a mix of disbelief and concern. 'But she's… she's so vulnerable.'

'I know.' Gil sighed. 'But people do many things when they're threatened or panicking. She might have been hiding out in the annexe.'

'What?'

'There's more to this story, I'm sure of it. We'll get to the bottom of it, one way or another. Now, let's see about getting that translator.'

Gina walked back into the room.

Through the open door, Maryam looked over towards Gil.

'What aren't you telling us, young lady?' he murmured.

Gina paused at the door, her hand resting on the frame. 'Whatever it is,' she replied, 'we need to find out fast.'

CHAPTER THIRTY-TWO

As Jess waited for the CCTV coordinator's call, her phone buzzed. She glanced at the screen, and her heart sank.

Ricky.

She inhaled deeply, steeling herself before answering.

'Ricky.' Her voice was carefully neutral.

'Jess, hi!' His forced cheer grated on her nerves. 'How's it going? Feet up in the rural idyll, is it?'

Jess's gaze drifted to the mess of reports and photos strewn across her desk—the wreckage of a case that was anything but idyllic.

'Of course,' she said flatly. 'You?'

'In the middle of some suit's idea of a crackdown on bike crime. It's non-bloody-stop. I can't stay long.'

She could have pointed out that he had called her, but she wouldn't waste her breath.

It didn't take him long to get to the point.

'Have you, um… thought about what we discussed?'

Jess rolled her eyes. Here we go. 'So, we're skipping the small talk, then?'

'Oh, come on, Jess,' Ricky whined, his voice taking on that familiar, insufferable pleading tone. 'Do I have to beg?'

'What do you mean, beg?' she snapped, her patience fraying. 'You're asking me for another six thousand quid. Of course you're going to have to beg.'

'Don't be like that.'

'Like what, Rick? Like someone who's sick of being treated like a bloody ATM?' She forced a breath in, grounding herself. 'You still haven't told me why you need this money.'

'I told you. Business opportunity. One-off. So—'

'Business opportunity,' Jess interrupted, sarcasm dripping from every syllable. 'In the Caribbean?'

A heavy silence.

When Ricky finally spoke, his voice was barely a whisper. 'What?'

'Oh, come on, Ricky. Did you think I wouldn't find out?'

'I don't know what you're talking about,' he stammered, but the guilt bled through his words.

Jess let out a bitter laugh. 'Really? Because your girlfriend has been telling everyone about your romantic Christmas getaway. And believe it or not, I still have contacts in GMP. And your girlfriend can't help herself.'

That girlfriend. The one he'd rolled around with in a seminar room until a startled snatch squad burst in looking for a briefing space. The reason Jess had never spoken the woman's name out loud. Euphemisms had sufficed.

'Ah, shit,' Ricky muttered, his voice thick with defeat. 'Look, Jess, I didn't want to say anything because—'

'Because what?' Jess cut in, her anger rekindling. 'You thought I'd be upset?'

'Well… yeah,' Ricky admitted, sheepish now.

Jess laughed, a hollow, humourless sound. 'Ricky, I'm going to Australia with Evan in a few months. Me and Molly. Why the hell would I care about your holiday plans?'

'You're what?'

Jess tutted. 'Shit, I forgot to ask if it would be okay.'

Another silence. Then, sullenly. 'The both of you?'

'Yes,' Jess said firmly. 'And you can stop that crap right now. You lost the right to object when you and her did the Watusi on night shift.'

'Watusi? That's a new one,' Ricky muttered.

'Whatever.' Jess sighed, suddenly exhausted. 'Look, I'm not giving you six grand. Or five, or anything else.'

'Just a loan, Jess—'

'What about what you already owe me?'

'It's just for a while, to tide me over—'

'That's what you said last time.' Jess ignored his protests. 'So you need to set up a standing order for the other six grand, and I won't tell Molly.'

'What's it got to do with her?'

'You send her the money. Four hundred a month.'

'What? Jess, come on—' Ricky's voice was edging toward panic now.

'Take it or leave it, Ricky,' she said coldly. 'There's no more coming from me until you do and Molly confirms receipt of the first payment. And you'd better tell Molly why you won't be around for Christmas, because I'm not doing your dirty work.'

'For God's sake. You can be a real cow, you know that?'

Jess let out a sharp, humourless laugh before her voice dropped, hard and unforgiving. 'Not that she'll be bothered. But she's your daughter, Ricky. She's not some inconvenience you get to ignore when it suits you.'

Silence. Long and heavy.

Finally, Ricky exhaled. 'Fine. I'll do it.'

'Good,' Jess said, her grip on the phone tightening. 'I'll transfer another 3k as soon as I see proof of that repayment.'

A pause. Then, cautiously: 'How about four and a half—'

'Three.'

'Just hear me out—'

'No, Ricky.'

'Come on, Jess. I wouldn't ask if I wasn't desperate.'

'And I wouldn't say no if I wasn't done.'

Another silence.

'Right,' Ricky muttered, his voice small, defeated. 'Well… bye, then.'

'Enjoy your holiday,' Jess said.

As she hung up, she let out a long, shaky breath and

closed her eyes. Sometimes, it was hard to reconcile some of the choices she'd made when she was young with who she was now. Ricky being one of them. And then she thought of Molly and backtracked. He'd got one thing right.

The conversation had left her feeling drained and slightly nauseous. Still, at least she'd get some of her money back, and Molly would benefit. If she felt even the slightest pang of guilt at using Molly as leverage, she quashed it by reasoning that she was only playing Ricky at his game. And he was far less likely to default on a payment to Molly than he would to her.

She made a mental note to call Molly later. She wouldn't wait for Ricky to tell her. Right now, though, she had a case to deal with. Who would have thought that a murder could be a welcomed distraction from her complicated personal life?

Fifteen minutes later, Jess sat in a dimly lit room, her eyes fixed on the high-resolution monitors before her. Normally, the CCTV coordinator got a desk in the corner of the Incident Room, but this time, she'd been invited to the Digital Forensic's enclave. The coordinator, a Uniform in his late forties called Mike, with salt-and-pepper hair and tired eyes, and a media investigator named Sarah, a sharp-eyed woman in her thirties, flanked her on either side.

'Right,' Mike began, his fingers dancing across the keyboard as he clicked through to the first image. The screen flickered to life, showing a grainy scene. 'Here's our first sighting. Dashcam footage from Capel Dewi.'

Jess leaned in as she studied the pixelated image of the cyclist pedalling furiously down the rain-slicked road. The figure was a blur of motion, barely discernible in the harsh glare of oncoming headlights.

'And the next?' she prompted.

Sarah took over, her manicured nails tapping efficiently on the touchpad as she brought up another clip. 'Five minutes and eighteen seconds later, another dashcam. He's making good time, averaging about fifteen miles per hour, by my calculations.'

'Then we lose him until here,' Mike continued, switching

to a new feed. The image quality improved dramatically as he pulled up footage from a fixed camera. 'Ffairfach Square, caught by a Hikvision DS traffic cam.'

'How can you be sure it's him?' Jess asked.

Sarah leaned forward, using a laser pointer to highlight a bright spot on the cyclist's back as he turned on the Llandybie Road. 'That reflective logo on his backpack. It's quite distinctive—appears to be a Proviz REFLECT 360 model. It's unmistakable, even at this distance and resolution.'

Jess nodded, impressed by the level of detail. 'Good catch. Then what?'

'Nothing for a while,' Mike admitted, a note of frustration in his voice. 'But we pick him up again here, in Glanamman.' He pulled up another feed, this one from a convenience store's external security camera.

'Is this near the hospital?'

'Not far,' Mike admitted. 'About three hundred yards from the river bridge.'

As they watched the cyclist join the B road, the door behind them opened with a soft whoosh. Gil and Gina entered, fresh from their hospital visit.

'What have we got?' Gil asked, his voice gruff as he moved to stand beside Jess, his eyes immediately drawn to the screens.

'Our mystery cyclist,' Jess replied, nodding towards the central monitor.

'We've been tracking his route using a combination of public and private CCTV networks,' Sarah explained. 'Though he or she has done a good job of avoiding most traffic and security cameras.'

They watched in tense silence as the figure on the screen appeared across a stretch of road.

'That was a pharmacy on the Gwaun Cae Gurwen Road.' The grainy image made the movement appear jerky and unnatural. 'And here is where we strike lucky. This was taken from the CCTV camera on the local doctor's surgery. The cyclist takes the exit on the mini roundabout, heading uphill.'

'Hold on,' Gil said, leaning closer, his nose almost touching the screen. 'Run that back, can you?'

He watched it again, eyes locked on the screen. 'That's next to the pub, isn't it?'

'Yeah, The Raven.'

'I know that bloody turnoff. It leads up to the Garnant Golf Club.'

'I didn't have you as a golfer, Gil,' Jess said.

'I am not. But I have been up that road as a part of this investigation. To the Leyshon property.'

For several seconds, the only sound was the soft whirring of computer fans.

'Where does that road come out?' Gina asked.

'It doesn't. It ends on the mountain,' Gil replied.

Jess glanced at her watch. 'If we hurry, we'll catch Evan before the meeting.'

Gil nodded. 'I think we need to have another chat with Ian Leyshon. This is too much of a coincidence.'

'Looks like our suspect list just got shorter,' Gina said.

But something in Jess's gut told her it would not be as straightforward as they hoped. Cases that seemed this clear-cut often held the nastiest surprises.

Jess turned to the tech experts. 'Great work but keep digging. I presume he doesn't come back down?'

'Not in the next twenty-four hours,' Sarah replied. She'd frozen the image with a shot of the cyclist disappearing up the hill at the roundabout.

Jess hurried out. They had no firm evidence that this cyclist had been the attacker. Only that he'd been flagged as fleeing the scene with no other evidence of anyone else in the vicinity. And Gil's revelation that there were persons of interest near where the cyclist was heading meant it all merited further investigation.

A thin enough thread.

But it was a thread worth pulling on.

CHAPTER THIRTY-THREE

RHYS DROVE.

It was the job Audi and Rhys slid into the seat before Gil had reached the car. Gil sat in the passenger seat, glancing occasionally in the wing mirror to make sure the response vehicle containing two Uniforms was keeping up. With Rhys driving, they made good time.

'You realise that we are not in pursuit of anyone,' Gil said.

'Thought you'd want to get there sharpish, sarge,' Rhys replied as he overtook a van on the straight stretch of road between Ammanford and Glanamman.

'Never mind sharpish. One piece-ish will do just fine,' Gil said. He studied the passing countryside and muttered, 'Glynmoch.'

'Pardon?'

'Glynmoch. Valley of the pigs. It's just across the way.' He pointed to a nondescript area of hillside. 'It's the name of an old mine. Two men died there in the seventies. An explosion. Made national news for a while.'

Rhys looked pensive. 'It's funny because I know people talk about the mines and that, but when they do, it seems such a long time ago. For someone my age, I mean.'

Gil sent him an appraising glance. 'It's not for the people who live here. They still have the blue scars under their skin.

And there have been mines here for a lot longer than there haven't been. A century and a half's worth. It runs deep.'

'Mr Warlow comes from a mining family, doesn't he?'

'He does. A valley over but cut from the same cloth.'

Rhys drove on. Gil could tell he was deciding on something to say.

'Did I tell you that Milburn's partner told me, off the record, that he didn't like all this sentimental stuff about the mining?'

Gil turned to look at him. This time with outright wariness. 'I'd hardly call it sentimental. But go on, tell me.'

'She said he'd never been to somewhere so... non-diverse. He said the whole Health Board needed to be shaken up from that point of view.'

'Right,' Gil said, anticipating the worst. 'Like a can of paint?'

'He'd said that mining and tinplating had essentially fuelled the empire and colonialism and had a lot to answer for.'

'So, we should have left it there, then?' Gil asked, his voice remarkably calm. 'The coal.'

'She didn't say that exactly,' Rhys said, seeing the dangerous light in Gil's eyes.

'No. And that's the point with presentism. Viewing the past through a hand-wringing lens gets you nowhere. The stuff they dig out of the ground here did indeed fuel the engine of growth and progress. The whole of the Industrial Revolution, in fact.'

Gil pointed through the windscreen at the buildings. Some of them boarded up. Many of the houses had scaffolding, with another government incentive for insulation and eco-efficiency making the rounds. 'There were half a dozen trains a day to the stations in these villages at the turn of the twentieth century. Hard to believe now, isn't it? The coal here is like a black diamond. It burns hot and clean. Rub a lump on your white T-shirt and you won't see a mark because it's so dense. And yes, I know all about fossil-fuels and climate change, but the miners who dug it out didn't. And they didn't run foreign policy for Queen Victoria either. So, I don't buy into any of that theorising, critical or otherwise. And if you felt the need to tell Mr Warlow about Milburn's ideological bent, make sure you do it from behind a bomb-proof wall.'

'I thought it was over the top, sarge. Makes you wonder why he took the job.'

'Doesn't it? Perhaps he saw himself as an agent of change. I wonder if he'd told anyone else around here how he felt.'

At the mini roundabout a few yards past the surgery in Garnant, they took a right and climbed the hill.

'Was that a sign to a Golf Club, sarge?' Rhys twisted his head to read.

'Indeed. On land reclaimed from the old opencast mine. You can see one or two holes from Huw Leyshon's place.'

'Does he know we're coming?'

'He does not. Thought we'd give his son Ian a surprise.'

'What if he's not there?'

As they pulled into the drive leading in to the old colliery manager's property, Gil pointed to a parked-up flatbed truck up ahead with the words "Leyshon Agri Repairs" written on the door.

'Looks like we might be in luck,' the sergeant murmured.

Their feet crunched on the aggregate underfoot as Gil and Rhys approached the square stone house.

A cool breeze rustled through the nearby trees, carrying the faint scent of manure and wet grass. The when and where of farmers muck spreading was a thing of great mystery to both men. Gil once mentioned that he suspected the agricultural community had set up drones to track his location, filling the air with the scent of farmyard dung as part of some vendetta against him.

After several unanswered knocks, Gil jerked his head towards a large steel-clad shed across the muddy yard.

'Looks like we're heading to the grease pit,' he muttered.

As they neared the workshop, the acrid smell of welding fumes and motor oil assaulted their nostrils.

'Smells like my uncle's garage if it mated with a burning tyre factory.'

Gil pushed open the heavy door with a protesting creak.

Inside the cavernous space was a cluttered maze of half-finished trailers and broken farm equipment. Acetylene tanks stood as sentinels along one wall, while spare welding masks, lines, and tool chests lined another.

A figure emerged from behind a horse box, wiping grease-stained hands on an equally dirty rag. Ian Leyshon's broad shoulders were hunched defensively as he eyed the newcomers.

'Can I help you?' he asked, his voice gruff and suspicious.

'Me again,' Gil said.

'Dad's out.'

'It's you we came to see, Ian.'

The man's eyes darted between the two officers. 'What's this about?'

Rhys stepped forward, his tall frame silhouetted against the daylight through the open door. 'We hear you're a cyclist, Ian. Mind showing us your bike?'

Ian hesitated, his fingers tightening on the rag. 'Who said I was a cyclist?'

'Are you?'

'I've got a couple of bikes, yeah. So?'

'Call it intuition.' Rhys's smile was stiff.

'Any here?' Gil asked.

After a momentary impasse where it looked as if Leyshon might continue to be difficult—part of his sunny disposition, Gil had already concluded—he shrugged with forced nonchalance. 'Yeah. They're in the garage.'

He led them outside to a separate, smaller building with more equipment and where three bicycles hung from wall hooks. The machines gleamed incongruously in the grimy workshop, each different. One a chunky mountain bike, one a road bike with the added blasphemy of an electric battery, and one an older model with taped drop handlebars.

Gil stepped closer and read the slightly faded letters on the old road bike. 'Tommasini. Not a make I know.'

'Dad's old bike. Vintage by now. It's just for show. I use

the mountain bike, mainly. It's good to jump on and get away up here.'

Gil spotted a backpack dangling from one of the bikes. He twisted it so its hidden logo became visible. It matched the one from the CCTV footage.

'Do you cycle to here from your place?' Gil asked casually.

'Sometimes, in the summer. Good exercise.'

'How far is that?'

'I'm in Pontamman. Only four miles.'

Gil sighed and turned to the younger man. 'Where were you at 7pm two nights ago?'

Ian's face darkened, his features twisting into a scowl. 'Why do you want to know that?'

'Just answer the question,' Rhys pressed, taking a step closer.

In a flash, Ian lunged for a nearby wrench, the metal gleaming wickedly in the harsh light.

Rhys reacted instantly, his training and flanker instincts kicking in as he tackled Ian to the ground.

The impact sent tools clattering across the concrete floor.

'Uniforms!' Gil's yell echoed in the expansive space as he joined Rhys to restrain the squirming man.

Two officers rushed in from outside. It took them and the threat of a taser to subdue Leyshon and get him cuffed.

'I've done nothing!' he yelled, his face a dusky red and contorted with rage.

Gil walked outside and used his work phone, speaking calmly but urgently. 'Catrin, it's Gil. We need backup and forensics at the Leyshon property. We've found the bike and the backpack. And warn the custody sergeant at Ammanford that we'll be bringing someone in.'

'I was at home two nights ago. What the hell is this?' Ian yelled.

'You could have said that before lunging for a wrench,' Rhys said, his jacket half off one shoulder. 'Now you are being detained on suspicion of assault.'

'Who the fuck have I assaulted?' Ian bellowed. 'You think

I killed that toe-rag Milburn? I was nowhere near him. I've got witnesses.'

As the Uniforms led a still-protesting Ian Leyshon out into the daylight, Rhys glanced at Gil, adrenaline still coursing through his veins.

'That could have gone smoother,' he said, brushing dust from his jacket.

'Ian's got a temper,' Gil said. 'That's why we brought the cavalry. Now we need to track down his dad. I don't want him hearing this second-hand. And we need forensics up here to look at his truck.'

He stepped across to the vehicle and knelt close to the big front bumper for signs of a collision.

'He could have had the whole shebang fixed, sarge.'

'He could.' Gil peered at the grill. 'But we can ask him that when we question him, right? Now, I wonder if that coffee place across the road from Ammanford nick will be open.'

Rhys checked his phone. 'It is, sarge.'

They walked back to the car.

'Those thumbs of yours move with the speed of light,' Gil observed.

'Only where food is involved. It's like they take on a life of their own. I've been known to order a takeaway in under fifty seconds.'

'A record to be rightly proud of. Now, as soon as another response vehicle arrives, we need to get back to Ammanford. And sharpish.'

In the driver's seat, Rhys grinned.

————

WARLOW SLUMPED INTO HIS CHAIR, loosening his tie with a weary sigh.

Jess and Catrin exchanged looks, noting the lines of fatigue etched on the DCI's face.

'How'd it go upstairs?' Jess asked, sliding a steaming mug of tea towards him.

Warlow grunted. 'About as well as you'd expect. Drinkwater's in full damage control mode. Two deaths and an acid attack don't exactly scream "safe community" to the public.'

Catrin leaned forward, her voice low. 'What about Maryam? Are we keeping that under wraps?'

'For now.' Warlow nodded. 'That's the one silver lining. The press are in the dark about her, and we need to keep it that way. Drinkwater was crystal clear on that point.'

Jess raised an eyebrow. 'He mentioned Geraint Lane by name, didn't he?'

Warlow's grimace was answer enough. 'Said, and I quote, "The last thing we want is that vulture Lane sniffing about. This is just up his street."'

'God, he's changed his tone. Remember when Lane was his and Two-Shoes's flavour of the month?' Jess shook her head.

At the mention of Lane's name, Catrin went noticeably quiet, her gaze fixed on the desk in front of her.

Jess shot her a concerned look. 'Catrin? You alright?'

Catrin flicked her eyes across. 'I heard something about Lane's book. The one he's been threatening to write. It's gone up on preorder on the Zon. He's calling it, *Strangled and Shattered: The Twisted Killings of a Madman.*'

Warlow and Jess sat up. Neither of them intended to comment.

'It's got an actual release date now. February next year.' Catrin's voice was barely above a whisper.

A paralysed quiet descended as everyone considered the implications. They all knew what that meant—Catrin's ordeal at the hands of Roger Hunt would soon be public knowledge, twisted and sensationalised by Lane's particular brand of journalism.

Warlow bared his teeth. 'We'll help you deal with that when the time comes. For now, let's focus on the case at hand.'

Jess added her support, 'Exactly. Lane can wait at a long arm's length for now.'

Catrin managed a weak smile, grateful for their words.

'You're right. Rhys has texted to say that Ian Leyshon has been processed at Ammanford, and they'll be interviewing him in thirty minutes once his solicitor arrives.'

'Then that's where I'm going next.' Warlow straightened up, his fatigue momentarily forgotten. He looked pointedly at Jess. 'You happy to lead on finding out what Deena Barton did that got her killed?'

'Already have her phone records,' Jess said.

'Okay. Hi bloody ho it is, as a certain sergeant might say.'

CHAPTER THIRTY-FOUR

WARLOW STOOD in the dimly lit observation room at Ammanford Station, his eyes fixed on the monitor relaying the video feed. The interrogation room was not as somber as some he'd been in: panel lights in the ceiling, cream walls, green door, grey carpet, pale wooden table. Positively festive compared to some.

Ian Leyshon sat rigid in his chair on one side of the table, arms folded tightly across his chest, his jaw clenched in defiance.

Gil and Rhys sat opposite, their postures a study in contrast. Gil leaned back, the more relaxed one of the pair, while Rhys hunched forward, his long frame coiled with tension.

The duty solicitor, a thin man with wire-rimmed glasses called Howard, completed the tableau, his pen poised over a pad, a phone next to him on the desk.

Everything was being recorded.

'Let's talk about the proposed hospital closures, Ian,' Gil began, his voice deceptively casual. 'You've been quite vocal about your opposition, haven't you?'

Leyshon's eyes narrowed. 'No comment.'

Gil nodded with a toothless smile. He'd been expecting this response. 'It's understandable. I know where you're coming from. These changes affect everyone in the community. Must be frustrating, feeling like your voice isn't being heard.'

Leyshon allowed himself a noisy inhalation and exhalation, but he remained silent.

Rhys spoke next. 'We know about your mother, Ian. How the system let her down.'

For a second, Leyshon's mask slipped. A flicker of pain crossed his features. 'It did,' he said. Then quickly added, 'No comment.'

'Tell us about your cycling, Ian,' Gil said, changing tack. 'Bit hilly for my liking, but you must know the roads around where you live pretty well, right?'

Leyshon didn't move but his lips shaped to answer, 'Yeah, I do.'

'Well enough to anticipate someone's route? If you wanted to follow them up the Betws Mountain to Mynydd y Gwair, for example?'

'No comment.'

Gil pressed on. 'It's not the bike, Ian. Too dark to identify that, but the backpack has a reflective logo. Did you know that?'

'What backpack?'

'The one hanging up on your mountain bike. And the cyclist who attacked Tim Riggon had a backpack just like that. The shape of that road bike fits too. The one with the electric battery. Both hanging in the garage next to your workshop.'

Leyshon's nostrils flared. 'I don't know what you're talking about.'

'Trouble is,' Rhys added, 'we have good CCTV footage of that bike and backpack leaving the scene and heading to your place.'

The muscles between Leyshon's eyes bunched. Was that confusion, or a realisation of how he'd messed up? 'No comment.'

The interrogation continued, a tense dance of probing questions and monosyllabic responses.

From the observation room, Warlow saw the frustration building in his officers, matched by the growing unease in Leyshon's body language. The suspect's leg jiggled under the table, his fingers clenching and unclenching on his biceps.

A knock at the observation room door broke Warlow's concentration. A uniformed sergeant entered, wearing a grimace of apology.

'Sorry about this, sir, but there's someone downstairs insisting on speaking to whoever's in charge. Says it's urgent.'

Warlow frowned. 'Tell them to wait. We're in the middle of an interview.'

The sergeant didn't leave. 'It's Huw Leyshon, sir. The father. He's very agitated, and… sir, I think you're going to want to hear what he has to say.'

Warlow glanced back at the interrogation room, where Gil was now leaning across the table, his voice barely audible through the glass.

'It's not looking good, Ian,' Gil was saying. 'There'll be more evidence. Always is. It's only a matter of time. Cooperation at this stage might go a long way.'

For the first time, genuine emotion flashed across Ian Leyshon's face. Was he frightened, suddenly as he shifted in his seat.

The solicitor, Howard, leaned over to whisper urgently in his ear.

Gil and Rhys waited, patient predators sensing their prey's weakening resolve.

'No comment,' Leyshon said.

'Last night, did you go to the community hospital to meet Deena Barton?'

'Deena Barton?… No comment.'

Sighing, Warlow stepped out of the observation room, his own frustration upping his pulse so that it thrummed in his ears. He was about to meet an angry, protective father. He recalled his own anger at hearing about Tom's injury and of how he could happily have strangled the van driver at that moment.

As he pushed through a door into reception, loud voices reached him.

Warlow took the direct route, walked forward, and held out his hand. 'Mr Leyshon, we haven't met. I'm—'

The older man stared at the offered hand but didn't take it. His own were too busy wringing together in agitation.

'Where's Gil?' Huw demanded, his voice cracking. 'I need to speak to Gil Jones.'

Warlow held up a placating hand. 'Sergeant Jones is occupied, Mr Leyshon. I'm Detective Chief Inspector Warlow. I'm in charge of this case. How can I help you?'

Leyshon's taut jawline augmented his thin bloodless lips. 'You don't understand,' he spluttered. 'It has to be Gil. He knows me.'

'I'm listening, Mr Leyshon,' Warlow said, his voice steady. 'Why don't you tell me what's so urgent?'

Leyshon looked up at something on the ceiling that was visible to no one except him. Something far away from this place and perhaps time. A memory he sought to escape into for just a moment? Or perhaps someone he begged forgiveness from for what he was about to do. When he looked back down, it was with a terrible, set expression. 'You've got the wrong man.'

Warlow tilted his head, trying to dissect the real meaning behind those words. 'If that's true, Mr Leyshon, who is the right man?'

'It was me,' he whispered. 'I did it. All of it.'

Warlow blinked rapidly, but he kept his expression neutral, and his surprise damped down. 'I'm a father too. Two boys. I can sympathise with how you're feeling, but this is a serious matter—'

'It's me. It's all me. And I won't need a bloody solicitor because that will take too long. Ask me what you want. No more delays. Just let Ian go.'

Warlow turned to a nearby officer. 'Tell DS Jones to halt the interview with Ian Leyshon. Tell him we have a new situation.'

———

THEY RECONVENED in the interview room once they had Ian Leyshon back to the custody suite. This time, the older Leyshon sat hunched, a broken man, as Gil and Warlow settled into chairs opposite him.

'Alright, Huw.' Gil was gentle. 'You've made some serious claims here. Why should we believe you?'

Huw's eyes, red-rimmed and weary, looked up at Gil. 'Because it's the truth,' he croaked. 'I tried to scare Milburn off. Thought I could intimidate him.'

'Milburn?' Gil said.

'How?' Warlow asked.

'Photos,' Huw mumbled. 'Fake ones. It's amazing what you can do with AI these days. I don't know who the girl was. You just tell the AI what to do. Prompts they're called. All sorts of courses online. The AI picked the girl.'

'That's a bit—'

'Far-fetched? You should take a look. You can make anyone look like they're doing anything.'

Gil wanted more. 'What kind of photos, Huw?'

Huw's cheeks flushed. 'Compromising ones. Not salacious, not porn, but enough. Him with… with a young woman. I thought if I threatened to expose him…'

'Christ, Huw,' Gil breathed, leaning back in his chair.

'I even…' Huw swallowed hard. 'I tried to poison their dog.'

The room fell silent. Both officers realised this was the kicker.

No one outside of the investigative team knew of the poison. Only the forensic team, Warlow's team, and the person who laced that peanut butter.

'I wish I hadn't. A dog doesn't choose its master.'

'Bit late for that.'

'Is the dog—'

'He's fine. So, why?' Warlow asked. 'Why go to such lengths?'

Huw's hands were shaking. 'Because I hated him and all

the others like him. Swanning in. No respect for our community, for our history. I wanted him scared. Wanted him gone.'

'But you didn't kill him?' Gil probed.

Huw's head jerked upwards, eyes wide. 'No! I didn't want him dead. I wanted him gone.'

'And Riggon?' Warlow asked. 'The acid attack?'

Shame flashed across Huw's face. 'That was me, too,' he whispered. 'I thought… one more incident, and they'd scrap the changes. Pull the plug on the whole restructuring nonsense. I know how it works because we've asked for things over the years. It's all tied to budgets and financial years. There are spending windows, and if you miss that window…'

'But it backfired,' Gil finished.

Huw nodded miserably. 'Everything's backfired.'

'How do you mean?' Warlow pressed.

Huw's composure crumbled. Tears spilled down his cheeks as words poured out. 'They've ruined everything that matters. There's nothing here for the kids—no jobs, just alcohol and drugs. My wife was let down, and even my son's marriage has fallen apart. Why do you think he's living with me?'

Warlow felt a pang of sympathy. He'd seen his own valley stripped and left to fester, gradually wasting away like a corpse in a gibbet.

'Huw,' Gil said. 'I need you to be absolutely clear. Did you kill Russell Milburn?'

Huw's head snapped up, eyes blazing. 'No! I told you! I thought about it, God help me. But I wanted no one dead. Just… just gone.'

'Were you at the community hospital last night?'

'What? No. Why would I be?'

Leyshon's words hung in the cramped room. The only sound was his ragged breathing.

Warlow studied him, seeing not a hardened criminal, but a desperate man drowning in a sea of change he couldn't comprehend, forced to react by the wrong mind of logic. The kind that bordered on psychopathy.

'Alright,' Warlow said finally. 'We'll need to verify everything you've told us. But for now, I'm placing you under arrest for the assault on Tim Riggon and attempted blackmail of Russell Milburn.'

As Gil recited the caution again, Huw seemed to shrink in on himself, all fight spiralling away like dirty water down a drain.

Leyshon looked up through hollow eyes.

'What about Ian?' he asked, his voice barely a whisper.

Gil answered. 'We need a written statement from you. And I would recommend a solicitor. But if what you're saying is true, he won't be facing charges for the attacks.'

Relief washed over Huw's face, followed quickly by shame. 'I've ruined everything, haven't I?'

Neither detective answered and the silence spoke for them.

As a uniformed officer led Huw away, Gil turned to Warlow. 'You believe him?'

Warlow massaged his forehead. At this rate, he'd be through to the bone within days. 'About the attacks, yes. And I believe he didn't kill Milburn either.'

Gil nodded.

'Not quite the full picture, yet, though' Warlow added.

'You still think he's covering for Ian?'

'What wouldn't you do for your kids, Gil?'

'We're in a police station, so I am definitely not going to answer that.'

CHAPTER THIRTY-FIVE

THE AFTERNOON and evening passed in a rush of activity. Warlow met with Tannard at the Leyshon property. They concentrated on the bicycle and Ian Leyshon's truck. But Tannard suggested they look at Huw Leyshon's vehicle, too.

The search warrant included the house. What they needed to find was evidence of one of the Leyshons being on that mountain with Milburn. And being near the hospital the night of the arson attack. They might get that information from the men's mobile phone activity and cell site data, but that might take all take a little time.

After leaving for work that morning at 5.30am, Warlow got back a little before 9pm. Jess, a half hour before him. Once again, they opted not to discuss work. They ate a simple meal, drank water only, and headed for an early night. Yet, no matter how late Warlow got in, he insisted on collecting Cadi.

He'd realised long ago that he needed interaction with the dog as a salve to the day's tribulations. He got support and understanding from Jess, but from the dog, he got something else that nourished his heart and soul. As indeed did Jess, who, up until moving in with Warlow, had never owned a dog, Rick having considered them an expensive and unnecessary extravagance.

Warlow's cut-off point was 11pm. If he got back before

that curfew, he'd made a promise to himself that he'd get the dog from the sitter. And the Dawes, who looked after Cadi while they worked, understood perfectly.

That night, after their meal, with the weather dry since mid-day, Warlow and Jess took Cadi out in the dark, armed with headlamps, to the estuary and let her run. They walked back through the cool but dry-for-once autumn night arm in arm, chatting in low voices about everything but dead cyclists and incinerated ward managers.

Sometimes, it helped to keep life simple—and dogs were the best way to do that.

———

THE CLOCK on Ivy Pugh's bedside table showed two minutes before 3am when she jolted awake, her heart fluttering like a trapped bird. There it was again. An eerie chanting, rising and falling on the night air, punctuated by the odd wail that seized her breath.

Ivy lay rigid in her bed, the patchwork quilt pulled up to her chin as she strained her ears.

How many nights had she heard these sounds now? Too many to count. But tonight was different somehow, charged with an expectation that made the hairs on her arms stand on end.

She waited, hardly daring to breathe, for the knock on her door. Surely, it would come, as it had that fateful night when the strange girl had collapsed on her threshold. But the minutes ticked by, and all remained still, save for those haunting cries drifting on the breeze.

As she listened, a new thought wormed its way into Ivy's mind. A "what if" thought. What if it wasn't strangers making those sounds at all? What if it was her family calling to her from Yr Hên Fethel? Reg, Mam, Dad, even Morfydd, who she'd been closest to. All of them up there in the old cemetery, reaching out across the veil.

The idea took hold, growing roots in her imagination until she could think of nothing else. With trembling hands,

Ivy pushed back the covers and swung her legs over the side of the bed, feeling the worn carpet under her feet.

If her family were calling, she should not ignore them.

Moving with a purpose that belied her years, Ivy dressed quickly; a thermal vest, cardigan, her good walking trousers and shoes, and a woolly hat. Her coat was behind the door downstairs in the hall. She paused only to put a lead on Bootsy before slipping out into the night. Through a gate, across a field to the lane.

It stretched ahead, a narrow strip of pale moonlight leading up to the chapel in one direction and down towards the main road in the other. The dog was some comfort, though his tense body and pricked ears told her he was just as uneasy as she was.

Her breath clouded in the cold air as she forced herself forward, a pull of both curiosity and something deeper driving her on. Faint voices drifted on the breeze, rising and falling, urging her closer.

The wind, sweeping up the valley from the south and west, rattled the trees. Leaves fell around her to skitter like small animals across the hard roadway. The muffled chorus of wails and chants, reached her ears again.

The darkness seemed to press in around her, a three-quarter-moon hidden for now, making the night as thick as treacle. The familiar contours of the lane took on sinister shapes in the gloom. Gnarled trees became grasping claws, shadows pooled like ink in the ditches. Every rustle in the hedgerow, every whisper of wind through the leaves, set Ivy's nerves jangling, and made Bootsy's ears prick up.

The moon emerged again, enough to make the shadows seem darker, more forbidding. Ivy's footsteps scraped against the tarmac, each step aggravating the stiffness in her left hip, always worse at this late hour. She kept glancing over her shoulder, the unsettling sense of being watched growing stronger with every step, though the lane behind her remained empty and silent. The thin beam of her torchlight added little solace.

Halfway up the hill, a fox's bark shattered the silence. A

high-pitched "yap" that might have passed for a person's hoarse shout, so close and loud that Ivy nearly leapt out of her skin. She lost her footing, barely managing to recover and avoid falling. Because a fall wouldn't do at all. Not on her brittle bones.

Bootsy let out a low growl.

Heart pounding, Ivy pressed on, the damp night air clinging to the skin on her face like a shroud. At last, she reached the kissing gate of Yr Hên Fethel.

The old cemetery lay blanketed in shadow, headstones jutting from the earth like broken teeth. Ivy hesitated for just a moment before pushing through, the hinges creaking in protest. A sound that seemed to reverberate through the entire valley.

She made her way carefully between the graves, mindful of loose stones and tufts of grass that might trip her. The Pugh family plot lay near the back, but Ivy found she couldn't bring herself to approach it just yet. Instead, she paused in the centre of the graveyard, tilting her head to listen.

The chanting came and went around her, waxing and waning on the wind. But she realised quickly that it wasn't coming from the graveyard. In the moonlight, she turned off her torch because the better to see in the distance.

Ivy frowned, turning slowly on the spot as she tried to pinpoint the source. There. Halfway down the hill, in the no-man's-land between Yr Hên Fethel and the hulk of the old hospital. From a lightless, featureless patch of nothing.

Ivy's heart sank as she realised her family wasn't calling to her after all. But as disappointment washed over her, it was rapidly replaced by a spark of curiosity.

Who, or what, then, was making those sounds? And why here, of all places?

She hesitated, torn between investigating further and returning to the safety of her cottage. In the end, curiosity won out. With one last glance at the silent Pugh headstones, Ivy set off towards the chapel and the old stable beyond, wonderment overcoming her fear. As she picked her way carefully down the slope, she cocked her head, straining to make out words in the strange, lilting language. Suddenly, a name rang out, faint but coherent.

Had she heard correctly? Had she heard the word, "Marion?"

It came again. But not Marion. Something like it. Was it Maryam?

Ivy stood, looking down towards the dark hillside.

Was she being silly? Was this all in her head?

A sudden bout of coughing wracked her as the chilly night air triggered a reflex. What on earth would Morfydd have said if she could see her? But then, perhaps she could. Perhaps this was all her doing. The family's doing. But staying out here would do no one any good. She'd catch a cold. Pneumonia even, and end up in the hospital she could see the lights of behind the old maternity unit below.

Ivy didn't want that. Her time would come. No need to hasten it. And if the irony of that realisation struck her, standing alone on the edge of a graveyard in the dead of night, it did so gently.

Whatever this was, whatever she was hearing, she would tell the nice policeman. Or she could tell Maggie on the end of the phone. She turned and retraced her steps along the stony road, where tufts of grass grew in the middle, all washed in shades of grey under the moon.

Then, without warning, a figure emerged from the gloom near the gate. A man's silhouette, tall and menacing. He waved a walking stick at her.

'Hello?' she called out in a tremulous voice.

She flicked on the little torch, oblivious as to how ineffectual it would be at that distance. She took a step forward and her foot caught on an inconveniently large stone. Ivy pitched forward, arms windmilling as she lost her balance.

The world tilted crazily around her.

At the same time, a deafening crack split the air.

Heat rushed past Ivy's head as she fell, the gunshot blast missing her by mere inches. But pain exploded in her wrist as it hit the ground hard, the breath knocked from her lungs in a high-pitched warble of fear.

Bootsy's frantic barking pierced the night.

The sound seemed to galvanise the shadowy figure. Without a word, it turned and fled, melting into the darkness as swiftly as it had appeared.

Ivy lay on the damp ground, her hand weak and unresponsive, trying to comprehend what had just happened. The night, which had seemed merely mysterious before, now became infinitely more dangerous. The thought of trying to make it back down the hill to her cottage seemed an insurmountable task. As the adrenaline ebbed, replaced by a bone-deep weariness and fear, Ivy Pugh sat alone in the dark with only Bootsy for company as the pain in her wrist blossomed and spread.

The dog was making a racket, sensing that something was awry.

He was still barking twenty minutes later when blue lights appeared, slowly climbing up the lane towards the old chapel.

CHAPTER THIRTY-SIX

WARLOW AND JESS got the call this time from Gil at 7am. They were both up. But it ended up being a two-coffee working breakfast in the kitchen of Ffau'r Blaidd by the time they'd spoken to all the parties concerned.

'You're with Ivy now?' Warlow asked. He had the phone on speaker on the kitchen table.

'Yep. At Glangwili Hospital.'

'What happened?' Jess asked.

'Someone in the community hospital thought they saw kids around the old place in the early hours.'

'Sure it was kids?' Warlow sipped his coffee.

'No. Not after what happened. Anyway, we sent a car just to check it out. While they were there, they heard a shot being fired on the mountain. At three in the morning. They went up for a shufti and heard Bootsy and saw the light from Ivy's torch at the chapel. She's broken her wrist.'

'How is she?' Jess wanted reassurance.

'Made of stuff they should be using as tank armour. They've set the bone and she wants to go home. The hospital has no reason to keep her in. I said I'd run her back.'

'What's the story?'

'I'm low on details, and the staff here have adopted Ivy, so

I've been kept at arm's length. All I know is she said she'd heard noises and someone had shot at her.'

The silence around the breakfast table went on for a very long six seconds.

'Right, let me know once you leave. I will meet you at Ivy's cottage,' Warlow said.

When Gil rang off, Jess and Warlow sat looking at each other without speaking.

'Do you have any idea what the hell is going on, Evan?' she said, eventually.

'No,' was his blunt and demoralising reply.

'I'm meeting the translator at nine this morning to try to get some sense out of Maryam.'

'She hasn't said much, yet?' Warlow asked.

Jess wrinkled her nose, her coffee cup held in both hands, elbows on the table. 'Whether that's because she can't, or won't, we'll find out this morning.'

Cadi, recently breakfasted, was now thanking Jess and Warlow in turn by stuffing her pet bear into their elbows and thighs as they sat, almost causing a coffee spill.

Warlow reached out and fondled her ears.

'A gunshot, though?' Warlow muttered.

'Well,' Jess said, with a thin smile. 'All we can say for certain is that it isn't either of the Leyshons.'

'That is true,' Warlow agreed. 'What do you think?'

'I think there is more than one ball in play in this particular game.'

'You do?'

Jess nodded. 'I know you prefer all the targets lined up so you can topple them with one slingshot, but sometimes there are just too many ducks to get in a row.'

'I'd better stop you there before you run out of metaphors. Let's just agree to differ.'

'Lets. Toast and marmite?' Jess pushed up from the table.

'The breakfast of champions, eh, Cadi?' Warlow replied.

The dog's eyes followed Jess as she walked to the bread bin.

———

JESS AND GINA convened in the corridor outside Maryam's room. Once again, Jess excused the uniformed officer that stood sentinel. Gina clutched a file to her chest, while Jess shook hands with Benazira, the young Afghani translator.

'Call me Beni.' She had soft, smiling eyes.

'Thanks for coming,' Jess said.

'I have no lectures until this afternoon.' Beni smiled. A big broad smile.

'Where are you studying?'

'Swansea uni.'

Jess's turn to grin. 'My daughter's there. Criminology.'

'The apple fell close to the tree, then,' Beni teased.

Jess acknowledged the sentiment with a tilt of her head. 'You?'

'Communication and journalism.' She had only a trace of an accent, and Jess guessed she was first generation.

When they entered the room, all eyes immediately locked onto Maryam. The woman looked frail and diminished against the crisp hospital sheets.

'How are you feeling?' Jess asked, her voice gentler than she'd intended.

Beni translated.

Maryam's eyes, dark and fearful, settled on the translator, surprise replacing the suspicion. But her mumbled response was barely audible over the ambient hospital noise.

'She says she's in pain, but the doctors are taking good care of her,' Beni relayed.

Jess nodded, pulling up a chair, wincing as the metal legs scraped against the floor, causing Maryam to flinch. Jess instructed Benin to explain who they were. 'We need to ask you some questions, Maryam. It's important.'

Beni translated, and Jess studied Maryam's face.

She drew back into her pillow as if she were retreating from the moment. Years of experience told her this woman was terrified, hiding something significant. Notably, there was no nod of agreement in response.

'Why were you at Ivy Pugh's door, Maryam?' Jess asked, keeping her voice firm but not unkind.

She watched as Maryam's eyes flicked to the window.

'I was lost,' came the whispered response in Pashto.

Beni translated it in a calm, neutral tone, but the terror in the original whisper remained just as palpable and an obvious lie.

'Maryam, were you at the old hospital? Did you stay there?'

Maryam's face flushed. Panic widened her eyes as she denied vehemently, words tumbling out in a frantic stream.

'She says she can't talk. She's afraid for the others,' Beni interpreted, her own brow furrowing.

'What others?' Gina asked.

But Maryam clamped her mouth shut, tears welling in her eyes. The woman turned her head away, grimacing as the movement pulled at her wounds.

Frustration bubbled up inside Jess. Whatever this reluctance was, and she'd seen it a hundred times before where someone was protecting someone else, they needed answers here.

'Ask her if she set fire to the hospital,' Jess instructed Beni.

Maryam's reaction was instant and visceral.

'No! No fire!' she cried in broken English, her voice cracking.

Jess noticed her trying to push herself up, gasping in pain as the sudden movement jarred her injuries. Taking a deep breath, Jess softened her approach. She reached out, her hand hovering near Maryam's, but not quite touching. 'Maryam, are you seeking asylum?'

A flicker of hope crossed Maryam's face as she nodded, tears spilling onto her cheeks.

'Please… no go back,' she pleaded, her English faltering.

'Back where?' Gina prodded. 'Afghanistan?'

Jess watched intently as Maryam shook her head, then whispered something to Benazira. The young translator's eyebrows shot up in surprise.

'She says not Afghanistan… Calais.'

Jess exchanged a bewildered glance with Gina. The pieces weren't fitting together, and Jess's confusion mounted.

Taking another deep breath to centre herself, she tried again. 'Beni, I need you to tell Maryam something very important. She's under suspicion of arson, possibly worse. We need her to be honest with us.'

As the words were translated, Jess watched the colour drain from Maryam's face. The woman's hands flew to her mouth, stifling a sob.

'Please,' Maryam choked out between sobs. 'I did nothing. Safe place.'

Unable to contain her frustration any longer, Jess stood abruptly, tension radiating from her stiffened back. 'Maryam, we can't help you if you don't tell us the truth. Who are these others you're protecting?'

Maryam's sobs intensified, her thin frame shaking with each ragged breath. 'I can't,' she wailed in Pashto. 'They will hurt them. Please, I beg you.'

The desperation in her voice was heart-wrenching, and Jess's resolve wavered. Sighing heavily, she turned to an unhappy Gina. 'Let's give her some time to recover.' She flicked her gaze towards Beni. 'Tell her we'll be back in half an hour, but she needs to think hard about what she wants to tell us.'

As they filed out of the room, the sound of Maryam's muffled weeping followed them.

Outside, Jess turned to Beni again, softening her voice. 'Thank you for your help. I know that wasn't easy.'

Beni nodded. 'She's so scared,' she murmured. 'I've never seen anyone so terrified.'

'Can you hang on for another hour?'

Beni nodded.

'Let's get some coffee. I'm probably going to turn into a bean, but this case is so frustrating. I'm convinced she's the missing piece here.'

Warlow was depending on her to get answers here.

For now, they still had nothing but questions, and a traumatised woman too afraid to give them those answers.

———

Catrin sat in front of her screen, frowning. She barely registered the surrounding activity in the Incident Room, lost in the digital trail of Deena Barton's life.

She'd been combing through the hospital manager's records for hours, a task that might have seemed mundane to some, but Catrin knew the devil was often in these details.

Her eyes scanned rapidly across the screen, absorbing information, searching for anomalies. The Health Board had, for once, not objected to a forensic search of the ward manager's office. All clinical files were put aside because Catrin had only been interested in the personal stuff. Barton had kept it all as paperwork in a file.

Suddenly, she sat up straighter, her fingers freezing over the keyboard.

'That can't be right,' she muttered, leaning in closer.

According to the invoice, Barton had purchased her car, a 2024 Nissan, outright. No finance, no loan. Just a lump sum payment.

Really? On a ward manager's salary, that seemed… unusual.

She dug deeper, her curiosity piqued.

Barton had separated from her partner of ten years, thirty months before. Other staff members had given up that information. She'd been bitter about it. But there had been no children in the mix. As a distraction, she'd thrown herself into her work.

A sad but not unheard-of story in this age of throwaway relationships.

Might happen to me one day, Catrin thought. But Craig better have an iron jock-strap if he ever decided to play away.

Holiday receipts popped up next, photographed by the techs, and uploaded on the database and all paid in instalments. Exotic locations, luxury resorts since the divorce. The Maldives, a villa in Santorini. Again, perhaps not that unusual for someone to decide to pamper themselves and seek solace from a breakup. It wasn't so much the rationale that bothered

Catrin. It was the funding. Again, not impossible on Barton's salary, but certainly eyebrow-raising. The woman would have had not much left to live on.

Then came the clincher: three prepaid cards held together with an elastic band, one a multi-currency card like one that she and Craig used abroad sometimes.

Catrin's pulse quickened.

This wasn't just unusual; it was a red flag.

'Where are you getting this money from, Deena?' Catrin whispered to herself.

She knew Barton didn't have a current partner—that had been established early in their background checks. Catrin leaned back in her chair. She missed being out in the field, the adrenaline rush of active investigation. But this—this meticulous piecing together of a puzzle—this was where she could truly shine.

She pulled up Barton's employment records, cross-referencing dates of large purchases with any changes in her job status. She'd been in post for six years at least. No promotions. No side hustles as far as Catrin could tell. Nothing stood out immediately, but Catrin wasn't deterred. She'd learned long ago that persistence often paid off in cases like these.

Next, she explored Barton's social media presence. It was sparse, but even the lack of content spoke volumes. No flashy posts about expensive purchases or luxurious holidays, even though there was a clear paper trail showing she'd been to such places.

Was Barton intentionally keeping a low profile for the world at large? And doing so despite evidence of her visits to high-end destinations?

The morning ticked by. But Catrin barely noticed, her focus unwavering as she followed the digital breadcrumbs. . Something didn't add up—quite a lot, in fact—and she was determined to uncover the ugly truth at the heart of it. She quickly compiled her findings into a report and found an email and a number for a contact in Financial Crimes, rang, and left a message.

There wasn't a lot here, but they had expertise, and this needed explaining in ways she could understand.

As she hit "send" on the email, and copied it to DCI Warlow and DI Allanby, a small smile played over her lips. She might not be chasing suspects over the mountains and in hospitals, but she'd just opened up a whole new avenue of investigation.

Catrin stood up and stretched again, feeling a satisfying pop in her back. She glanced at the clock, surprised to see how late it was. Lunch beckoned and a call to her mother to find out how Betsi was, while she waited for the bean counters to get back to her.

CHAPTER THIRTY-SEVEN

WARLOW PARKED at the bottom of the going-nowhere lane that led to Ivy Pugh's house, next to the job Audi. He could hear muffled voices, the deep, cheerful tones of Sergeant Gil Jones predominating.

And it was Gil who answered his knock, relief clear on his weary features. 'Evan, glad you're here. It's been... interesting.'

Warlow stepped inside. 'What's that smell?'

'Ah, that's Ivy's Highland Morning pot-pourri. Quite the aroma, right? I know its name because, when my eyes stopped watering, I saw she'd cut out the label and placed it next to the bowl. Whether to remind herself of what it was to reorder, or for some other Ivy reason, I have yet to find out. Perhaps she sleeps better at night dreaming of nights in the Scottish forests, or safe in the certainty that the smell keeps rodents at bay. Both work.'

Since liaising on a case where they'd caught a killer on the run from Scotland, Warlow had kept in touch via the odd, cryptic Facebook message, with DCI Duncan Bone from Police Scotland. It was likely he'd have something choice or inappropriate—likely both—to say about such an unlikely representation of ambient Scottish air.

Rhys stood in the small sitting room, looking somewhat out of place among the floral patterns and doilies.

'How is she?' Warlow asked.

Gil made a face. 'Not making much sense. Keeps talking about voices in the night, and how her dead sister tripped her up to save her from a man with a big stick. It's all a bit…' It looked as if he wanted to twirl a finger near his temple but thought better of it and simply threw his hands up.

'Did she have a concussion?'

'No, sir,' Rhys said. 'A bit of hypothermia, but she's fine now, so the A and E bods said.'

Warlow nodded. 'Where is she? I'm not suggesting she'll say anything different to me, but I'm familiar with the geography, so let's at least find out what the hell she was up to.'

Ivy sat propped in a chair in the living room, supported by a mountain of pillows, her wrist encased in a white cast. Her eyes, magnified by thick glasses, zeroed in on Warlow. She smiled.

'Ivy,' he said gently, pulling up a chair beside her bed. 'It's Evan. Remember me? Can you tell me what happened?'

'Of course, I can. I remember it all. First of all, it was dark. Middle of the night dark. I heard them again, the voices. I think it's only me that hears them because I'm up here. Up above the hill. And they were chanting. I thought it might be the chapel. I thought it might be my lot.'

'Your lot?'

'In the cemetery. So, I got dressed, took Bootsy and a torch, and went to look. To have a word with the dead, you know?'

Warlow didn't. But this was not a time to question anyone's convictions. He knew his eyebrows had crept upwards but was powerless to stop them. 'What time was this, Ivy?'

'Around half past two in the morning. Closer to three by the time I got there.'

Warlow nodded, very slowly. 'You went out up the hill, alone, at three in the morning… in the dark?'

'I crossed the field on the path first. Then up the lane to the chapel,' Ivy corrected him.

'Silly me,' Warlow said. 'Of course. Slippery field first. Then dark lane. What did you see, Ivy?'

'Not so much see as heard. I went to see my lot, but it wasn't them. The voices were coming from down the hill, not the chapel. I could hear them much more clearly from the other side.'

Warlow tried to concentrate.

The other side? Did she mean of the cemetery, or the supernatural divide?

'Okay,' he said, not wanting to interrupt. Not yet.

'But then I got cold and when I turned back, there was a man,' she whispered, her eyes wide. 'By the kissing gate. He had a stick. Hard to see, but the moon was my friend and poked his head out. Except it wasn't a stick, was it? It was something else.'

'Go on,' Warlow prompted.

'I was scared. I turned away... but then Morfydd, my sister, she tripped me up. She was always doing that when we were little.'

Rhys looked like he might be on the point of asking if she meant Morfydd, her dead sister, but Gil's glance stopped the question before it got going.

'I heard the snap when I fell.' Ivy waved her plastered hand with disconcerting cheeriness. 'The sound was awful, but it saved me, don't you see? The stick was a gun. It made an awful noise. Bootsy started to bark, and the man ran away. I heard his feet on the road.'

She smiled at the dog. '*Yr hen Bootsy bach.*'

Good old Bootsy, indeed.

'I have him to thank, as well as Maryam.'

Warlow froze, his mind racing. 'Ivy, did you say Maryam?'

Ivy blinked, confused. 'Maryam? No, Morfydd, my sister. I know she wasn't there, but perhaps it was her who put that stone for me to trip over.'

But Warlow was certain he'd heard correctly the first time.

He turned to Gil and Rhys. 'Have either of you mentioned the name Maryam to Ivy?'

Both men shook their heads, looking puzzled.

Warlow turned back. 'Ivy, it's very important. You mentioned a name just now, not your sister's. You said Maryam. How do you know that name?'

Ivy's face crumpled in confusion. 'I... I don't know. But I heard it. In the dark. One of the voices said it. Wailed it.'

Warlow leaned forward. 'Ivy, can you remember where exactly you were when you heard that name?'

'By the old stable at the chapel. Looking down towards the old hospital. That's where the voices were loudest, see. That wasn't where I fell, mind you.'

Warlow sat back. Outside, he could hear the constant whirr and clank of machines and the warning beeps from reversing vehicles.

'Anyone know what they're doing out there?'

'It's the farm. They're clearing land and building a new barn as far as I know,' Rhys said. 'Fades into the background after a while, though.'

'Does it? It's a constant noise, isn't it? It was like that the other day when I was up at the chapel...' Stating the obvious was not something Warlow liked to do, but at the same time his mind was doing the algebra here, processing the equations thrown up by the implications of Ivy's words.

The cemetery and the noises and Maryam.

He exchanged a significant look with Gil and Rhys. His brain fizzing, trying to fit all this together. He stood up and looked down at Ivy.

'Not a great idea going out at night on your own like that, Ivy.'

'I wasn't alone. I had Bootsy.' Ivy stated this as if it excused everything.

'The fierce attack canine.' Warlow glanced at the little dog flat out at the foot of the bed.

But the milk had already been spilt, and he had no time for tears. 'Right, we'll be back shortly. Is there anyone we can contact for you?'

'No, my carers have phoned, and they'll be along soon. They'll make a fuss, I know they will. But there's no need.'

Warlow exchanged a knowing look with Gil, who simply shook his head.

'I'll be fine,' Ivy said.

Warlow motioned the other two outside. 'You both heard her say Maryam?'

Rhys and Gil nodded, but Rhys seemed less convinced. 'She might have muttered her name when she turned up here the other night.'

'But Ivy's been asking after her, and she didn't know her name then,' Warlow said. He held up a finger. 'What can you hear?'

'Machinery,' Gil answered.

'Exactly. But you would not hear that at night.'

Through a window, Warlow watched two women in matching dark trousers and navy anoraks walk up the hill.

'Proper help,' Warlow said. 'Rhys, get over to that farm and ask them to stop everything for an hour. Politely insist.'

'On it,' Rhys said and headed down the lane to the car, stopping only to talk briefly with the women who, once he passed, exchanged a giggle of delight between them. He had that effect.

Gil took the carers inside and emerged a minute later. 'She'll be fine,' he said. 'As my new friend Pauline just said, Ivy breaking her wrist might actually slow her down a bit.'

'Okay, let's go,' Warlow ordered.

'Where to?'

'We are following in Ivy's footsteps.'

'I have nothing approaching appropriate footwear.' Gil lifted one comfortable brogue. Dare I ask what your thinking is here?'

'You can, but I'd rather wait until we are with the dead.'

'Oh,' Gil said. 'We going to a council meeting, are we?'

'Very funny.'

'Nice to be appreciated.'

A wooden gate directly opposite led through a field. Warlow ploughed ahead.

'Hang on, are we sure there are no cattle in here?'

'It's sheep,' Warlow said and looked down. 'And they've kindly manured the path for us.'

Gil sighed and began humming the funeral march while avoiding the worst of the green ewe-berries on tip toe.

'You auditioning for the Bolshoi?' Warlow asked.

'Go on, mock as much as you like.'

'Thank you. I will.'

When they got to the far side of the field, the sound of engines and construction suddenly died.

'Thank you, Rhys,' Warlow muttered and turned to wait for Gil. 'Right, Nijinsky, you all set?'

'Et tutu, Brute,' Gil replied and stepped out onto the tarmac. 'Aren't you glad Rhys isn't with us? We'd be an hour explaining those last two sentences alone.'

Warlow set off uphill to the kissing gate, pushed through, and walked along the stoned lane towards Yr Hên Fethel Chapel and the ruined stable.

———

CATRIN WAS MAKING GOOD PROGRESS. Her chat with a sergeant in Financial Crimes had been illuminating, even if it had been a tad jargon heavy.

He was the sort of chap who enjoyed the fact that he knew a lot about things other people did not. Still, needs must. He'd explained to her that cash purchases these days were difficult. The Financial Conduct Authority already had checks in place for cash deposits. £20,000 per day was the current limit and would soon be cut to less. A Money Laundering and Terrorist Financing Report wanted a shift away from paying in slips. £10,000 remained a trigger for purchases or payments.

Catrin had confirmed that Barton's car had been paid with cash and was told that some businesses had status as cash dealers, but that was all changing.

The Financial Crimes officer also confirmed that prepaid

credit and gift cards had long been a favourite laundering or payment for services approach for nefarious activity.

Catrin thanked him, now even more convinced that something was amiss. She turned to the reports of the interviews conducted with Barton and, once done, went back out to the Gallery and the Job Centre. Something bothered her. Something which she could not yet grasp.

She looked hard at the images of Barton, the community hospital, and what they'd discussed at their briefings relating to Milburn, who was tied to Barton and the hospital now more than ever.

Was there something here they weren't seeing?

Something left undone.

She found it after a while. A simple, circled name. Someone who had seen Milburn at the community hospital on that last day and who had as yet, not given a formal statement.

But why not, she wondered?

Catrin went back to her desk, found the number of Estates and Logistics at the Health Board, and made the call.

CHAPTER THIRTY-EIGHT

WARLOW AND GIL retraced Ivy's steps, their footfalls muffled by the damp earth. No traffic noise up here, the odd bleat of a sheep, only now that Rhys had halted all work on the building project.

Warlow stopped every few yards to listen intently.

'Are we waiting for a message from the great beyond?' Gil asked between gasps. The hill they'd just climbed had been steep.

Warlow's response was terse. 'Who knows? Hard to tell since you're wheezing like a rusty bellows.'

'Pot, kettle, black. And less of the rusty, please.'

Eventually, they reached the old, ruined stable. Warlow stood still, gazing down towards the old maternity hospital and the site of the fire.

The quiet surrounded them, eased only by the wind's sharper gusts.

Gil shifted his weight, restless. 'All I'm hearing is sheep—'

A sound cut through the air, faint but unmistakable, snuffing out Gil's commentary.

A cry? A shout? Hard to discern, but the desperation in it was palpable, like a wounded animal gasping for its final breath. It came to him on the wind, muffled and distant, but laced with a raw edge of fear, the kind that crawled under your skin.

Warlow strained to listen. Not just noise; this, it was a plea. A soul on the brink, teetering between holding on and slipping into the darkness forever.

Voices from beyond? But beyond what? His eyes raked the landscape and he cupped his hands around his mouth and bellowed, 'Hello! Is anyone there?'

Gil half turned to look at the cemetery. 'I hope to God no one is filming this. And I hope even more that no one answers from the gallery.'

Seconds stretched into an eternity.

Warlow kept his eyes fixed downhill, and he felt rather than saw Gil turn towards him. 'If you want, I can nip home. I think we have a Ouija board in the gar—'

The response came, fragmented and distant, but undeniably human.

Warlow quieted Gil with a raised hand.

'Hear that?'

Gil shifted his gaze to follow Warlow's, his sceptical amusement evaporating in an instant. Both men straining as the breeze wafted about them, shifting their heads to locate what they could hear.

Somewhere on that breeze came the sound of people begging for help.

'What the…' Gil muttered.

'Where's the source?' Warlow growled.

Gil had already moved towards a thin path south of the old stable ruin.

They scrambled through a gap in a tumble-down stone wall, then right, following the border of a field.

The cries grew louder, sharper, sporadic bursts of anguish that drew them on. They pushed forward, adrenaline driving them through the rough scrub, until they stumbled upon a patch of wild, untamed ground surrounded by trees. No fence. No barrier. Just raw, open land—and the sound of suffering, closer now, pulling them into the unknown.

Gil, panting openly, asked, 'Why isn't this part fenced off?'

'Spoil,' Warlow replied, looking down at the black earth under the grass, his breath also coming in short bursts. 'Old mining works. It might be unstable. You can't grow much on this stuff.'

They pushed through thin trees, heading west for two hundred yards. The voices were clearer now, still muffled, but there were words, too, in an unfamiliar tongue.

Suddenly, the ground dipped and rose in uneven, grass-covered trenches, leading to a jagged wound in the earth. A dark, oval-shaped opening, no more than four feet long and three feet high, gaped before them. It was sealed off by a rusted metal plate, held in place by a wooden bar braced across it. Large stones were stacked hastily around the edges, more for disguise than security, Warlow guessed. It was a crude attempt to hide the entrance, but the desperation behind it was clear. Designed to keep something, or someone, out.

Or was it in?

The officers exchanged a horrified look as that same thought entered their heads simultaneously, before frantically attacking the barrier with bare hands.

Rocks tumbled free, scraping their skin, but they didn't stop. Desperation fuelled them as they wrestled the heavy wooden bar loose and dragged the rusted metal plate aside.

What hit them first was the smell; urine, faeces, and stale air, mingling into a thick, nauseating stench. It clung to the back of their throats, nearly unbearable in its foul richness.

As the dim light from outside crept into the suffocating darkness, Warlow saw them. Blinking faces looking out, hollow and haunted. Eight gaunt figures, men and women, their eyes wide with fear. Their clothes, caked with mud and filth, clung to their frail bodies as they huddled together in the cramped space.

Behind them loomed a wall of collapsed rock, a reminder of the fragile grip they had on life in this tomb.

One man held up his arms in pleading. His words came out in broken English, thick with an accent Warlow couldn't place. 'You help... please... you help...'

Warlow reached down, grasping the man's trembling hand, and pulled him up. It wasn't easy. The man was frail and his legs seemed barely able to support his weight.

Had a ladder been used to lower them into this hellish pit?

Straining, Warlow heaved, and with Gil's help, they dragged the man up and out. All the while the sergeant's voice kept steady, offering a stream of quiet reassurances as they worked. 'You're safe now. We've got you. All of you are safe.'

The man's eyes, dull with exhaustion, flickered with the faintest glimmer of hope. With the first one out—and all he could do was sit on the ground, weeping quietly—the two detectives helped the others.

Gil whispered only once to Warlow, 'What the hell is this, Evan?'

But the DCI had no answer yet. Still, he zeroed in on one word in Gil's sentence.

Hell.

These weren't lost workers or misguided urban explorers. These were people who'd been hidden, trapped, locked away. Their very existence a secret until now.

With five people still left, Gil waved a hand for Warlow to pause., he reached for his phone and made a call. They needed backup and medical help.

Warlow knelt beside a young woman, her eyes vacant with shock and dehydration. He draped his coat over her shoulders, feeling her frail form shaking beneath the fabric.

Gil barked instructions, ended the call, and squatted down to reach for another prisoner. His words to Warlow emerged low and urgent. 'This changes everything.'

Warlow nodded.

The dead cyclist, the fire at the hospital, and now this. All pieces of a puzzle forming a picture far darker and more complex than he'd imagined.

When they got everyone out, Gil led the way down. They were closer to the abandoned hospital here than the chapel, and downhill made sense given the state these people were in..

Sirens wailed in the distance as Warlow followed the rag-tag procession. The rescued individuals kept together, murmuring in their native tongue, casting furtive glances at their surroundings as if afraid this freedom might be snatched away at any moment.

Gil took another call and stood away. When it ended, he turned back.

'Ambulances are five minutes out. I've called in everyone we can spare.'

'We'll need translators, social services and we need to keep this quiet for now. I don't want whoever's behind this finding out before we speak to these poor souls.'

A new thought shot through his head.

He turned to the man they'd pulled out first. 'Maryam?'

The effect it had on the man was electrifying.

He grabbed Warlow's arm. 'Maryam?'

Warlow had her photo on his phone; he scrolled to it and saw the man's face light up with unbridled joy.

He turned to the others and pointed to the phone, uttering words to Warlow that had no meaning for him, but the animation within them did. As the first flashing lights appeared on the road, Warlow took a deep breath. A case that had begun with a dead cyclist had just exploded into something far more sinister. Human trafficking, potential slavery, and God knows what else, all happening right under their noses.

He looked at the rescued individuals, their faces a mixture of relief and lingering terror.

Whatever had brought them here, whatever horrors they'd endured, it was up to him and the team to unravel it all. But their joy at seeing the photo of Maryam had been a sight to see. It seemed obvious to him that they'd feared her lost.

That joy deserved to be passed on.

He took a quick photo of the group, stood up, and made the call to Jess.

WARLOW'S PHONE call changed everything at the hospital. Jess, Beni, and Gina crowded around Maryam's bed again, but little seemed to have changed from the desperate look on Maryam's face.

Jess nodded to Beni, who leaned in close to the woman.

'We have something to show you,' she murmured in Pashto.

Maryam's eyes widened anticipating some new horror.

Jess produced her phone, tilting it to show the group photo Warlow had sent. Maryam's gaze locked onto the screen.

The change was instantaneous. A galvanic cattle prod of wonder. Maryam's frail body surged with life, her hands trembling as she reached for the phone. 'Laila!' she cried, her voice cracking. 'Rashid!'

Tears streamed down her face as she clutched the device, her fingers tracing the faces of her loved ones. 'My sister, my husband, my family…'

Beni translated rapidly in a voice thick with emotion.

Jess and Gina exchanged glances, their own surprise obvious.

Maryam's words tumbled out in a torrent, Beni struggling to keep pace. 'I thought they were dead. I thought they'd been taken.'

It took a moment to calm her down, but she would not give the phone back immediately. Eventually, Beni managed to get her to give it up and, for the first time, she smiled and grasped Jess's hand in gratitude for showing her that.

'*Manana, Dera manana.*'

The floodgates opened. Beni translated as Maryam spoke.

'We left Mazar-i-Sharif in the dead of night,' she began, her eyes haunted. 'The Taliban… they are everywhere. We crossed mountains that clawed at our feet with snow and ice, rivers that tried to swallow us.'

She described their perilous journey to Turkey, smuggled across borders like contraband. 'In Calais, we huddled in tents that couldn't keep out the cold. Every day was a battle against hunger, disease.'

Maryam's fingers twisted in the hospital sheets as she recounted their desperate gamble. A small boat that pitched and rolled in the unforgiving Channel. 'The waves were mountains, ready to devour us. Children wailed, men prayed. I thought the sea would claim us all.'

Jess's jaw clenched, imagining the terror of that crossing.

Gina's eyes glistened with unshed tears.

'We landed on a beach,' Maryam continued. 'A man was waiting, with a van. He herded us in. It was as white as a shroud. The windows were blacked out. We drove for hours, nothing to drink or eat.'

Her voice dropped to a whisper. 'Then a prison that was our new hell. Cold concrete, darkness, the stench of fear and unwashed bodies. They fed us scraps, treated us like animals. One toilet for nine. No heating, bare walls, the windows boarded up.'

Maryam's gaze turned inward, reliving the nightmare. 'That night I saw a chance. He came to fetch us again, for the van. Our captor. I did not know where he was taking us. I ran. I hid in the shadows, my heart pounding so loud I was sure it would betray me. But he found me. He was shouting, burning with rage.'

She mimed swinging a hammer, her body flinching at the memory. 'I thought death had come for me. Then she came —the woman. She sometimes brought us food but did not speak. They fought like demons, she and the man, screaming words I couldn't understand.'

Maryam's hands flew to her mouth. 'He struck her, again and again. I saw her fall. Then the flames began to dance, hungry and wild. He was burning the prison.'

Jess leaned forward, every muscle taut. This was it—the missing piece of the puzzle.

'I pushed him,' Maryam whispered. 'I don't know why or how… he stumbled, and I ran through a door into the night. I ran until my lungs burned and my legs wanted to give way.

He shot at me, and I got stung.' Her hand reached up to her neck and scalp.

'Then I saw the house and a light. On its own in the dark. I banged on the door. An old woman answered. Perhaps an angel, I don't know. Then it went dark, and I was here. Can I see them again?'

Jess showed her the image. 'I thought I had left them to die,' she sobbed. 'But they live. They live!'

'They're all safe,' Gina said. 'This photo, the man who took it, he has them now and nothing can happen.'

Beni translated.

The room fell silent save for Maryam's quiet weeping.

Jess felt the pieces clicking into place; the fire, Deena Barton's injuries, Ivy's mysterious visitor. It was all connected, a web of human suffering and cruelty that made her stomach churn.

Gina squeezed Maryam's hand gently.

'You're safe now,' she murmured, though the words felt hollow in the face of such trauma.

Jess straightened, her mind already racing ahead. Another thread to pull.

Our captor.

'Beni,' she said softly. 'Please tell Maryam that her bravery has saved not just her life, but the lives of her family and who knows how many others. We'll need her help to make sure the people responsible for this are brought to justice. No one is going to send them anywhere.'

As Beni translated, Maryam's tears slowed. She nodded, a flicker of steel showing through her fragile exterior. 'Thank you.'

Jess and Gina talked in the corridor. 'It all fits.'

'But what about the shooter?'

'Evan's still in Ammanford. Let's get back to HQ. We can put our heads together there.'

CHAPTER THIRTY-NINE

CATRIN WORE A SLIGHTLY preoccupied expression as Gina and Jess walked into the Incident Room.

'All okay, Catrin?' Jess asked.

'I think so.' Catrin smiled, though it seemed a tad forced, and her eyes flicked back to her screen once or twice before giving her colleagues her full attention.

Gina, still buoyed by the morning's revelations, looked pumped. 'We've had the most amazing morning, Sarge. Have you spoken to DCI Warlow yet?'

Catrin shook her head.

Gina looked at Jess for permission.

'Go on, then, fill your boots,' Jess said.

Gina launched into a blow-by-blow account of what had happened: Maryam's reluctance to speak, then Warlow's find of the trapped asylum seekers, and finally the heart-rending truth of what had brought Maryam to Ivy Pugh's door.

'That's an eventful day,' Catrin said.

But Jess could see she was keeping something back.

'What's happened while we were away?' she asked. 'What aren't you telling us?'

'I think, listening to that story, I may have found who shot at Maryam.'

Warlow, Rhys, and Gil were back at the community hospital. Someone had offered them a cup of tea, gratefully received, with the added wisdom of Gil's mantra, 'Never refuse a cuppa. You never know how long it'll be until the next one.'

Once again, the circus was in town: CSI vehicles, response vehicles, and somehow, the bloody press had pitched up.

Warlow was well aware of how they worked. They might have slipped someone in the functioning hospital nearby a couple of tenners to alert them if anything happened. Consequently, Warlow had hunkered down in the ward manager's office. It was barely big enough for three grown men, two and a bit if you took Rhys into consideration, but it provided, for the moment, a bit of respite.

Gil's phone chirped; Catrin on video call.

Her face appeared.

'Are you sitting comfortably?' she asked.

'As can be,' Warlow said, moving into shot, with Rhys above and behind him, looming. 'Go ahead. The gang's all here.'

'That would make a lovely family photo.' Catrin stifled a grin. 'DI Allanby asked me to call you, sir. I've been running down Deena Barton's finances.'

'Hit the jackpot, did you?' Gil asked.

'You be the judge.' Catrin explained about the money and how her train of thought led to unexplained connections between Barton and the abandoned hospital annexe, and an unticked box on the actions board.

'The van driver, sir. Gary.' Catrin said, addressing Warlow. 'You wanted a statement from him because he was the last person to see Milburn alive in the car park. But he never rang you back.'

'What?' Warlow expelled the word at least half an octave higher than needed.

'Gary Prentice doesn't exist. I've spoken to Estates and Personnel at the Health Board and the hospital. They do have vans running between Glangwili and the community hospital in Ammanford, transporting drugs, laundry, et cetera, but there is no Prentice on their books. Plus, the vans run at set times. I'm afraid Deena Barton led you, and probably the staff at the hospital, up the garden path.'

'Deena Barton and Prentice working together?' Rhys sounded confused. 'What exactly were they working on?'

'Trafficking, is my guess,' Catrin said. 'Deena Barton has been spending a lot of cash, and she's spending it all on holidays and cars. Always careful not to hand over too much to trigger suspicion. I think they were using the annexe as a staging post for people, sir. Maryam, the woman at the hospital, tells a horrible story of getting here via Turkey and Calais and a boat—'

'Trafficked to where, though?' Gil asked.

'Does it matter?' Warlow muttered. His voice sounded low and angry. He felt the heat rising in his face.

Catrin had more of the harrowing story to tell. 'I think Barton fooled the community hospital into thinking Gary was kosher. An NHS delivery driver using the annexe for storage. Maybe storing gas cylinders out of the way of thieves, other equipment, who knows. She had an ID made up for him so that no one would question his presence. It would probably give him carte blanche to come and go. IDs need photographs. Like the one Tannard found in Barton's files and on her laptop. That photograph has been positively identified by Maryam as the man who brought them from wherever their small boat landed to the hospital annexe in his van.'

'You've been a busy bee, Catrin,' Gil said with a hint of admiration.

'I also ran his photo through the facial recognition software from PNC. His real name is Rory McDermot. Irish national. I'm waiting for details to come through from Dublin, where he has history.' She took a breath.

'What else?' Warlow muttered with a vulpine grin. 'I know there's more. I can see it in your eyes.' He was secretly enjoying this. Catrin in this mode was a *tour de force*.

'As McDermot, he was arrested a couple of years ago in

connection with a modern slavery investigation into quick fashion sweatshops in the Midlands. No charges brought. But it doesn't leave much to the imagination, does it?'

'Shit,' Gil said. 'He'll be in the wind by now, then.'

'Not quite,' Catrin said. 'He may be in the wind, but it's blowing against him. APNR cameras picked up the van this morning at 10am on the A48 at the Tenby Road roundabout heading west.'

'Damn,' Warlow muttered. 'Gil, what time is the ferry from Fishguard to Rosslare?'

'Normally, 2pm,' Catrin replied.

'You said that without moving your lips, sarge,' Rhys said to Gil.

Catrin pressed on. 'But that was cancelled because of staffing issues. Next one is at 1.30am.'

Warlow was on his feet. 'Let's get some bloody bodies down to Fishguard. We're on our way. Put Jess on.'

'She told me to tell you to get in touch with her en route. She'll want to tell you what Maryam told her.' Catrin swallowed loudly. 'I'd rather she did, sir.'

'Where the hell is she?' Warlow snapped.

'She and Gina are on their way to Fishguard, sir.'

Warlow couldn't hide the grin. 'Why does that not surprise me? Right, let's going. Catrin, get the coastguard to monitor traffic leaving the coast for Ireland. Though, I doubt McDermot has a boat. He seems keen on his van. If he is, the only way across is by ferry, but you never know.'

'Already done it, sir.'

'Then what the hell are we all waiting for?'

———

THEY FOUND McDermot's van abandoned in a lay-by outside a farm gate two miles from the terminal.

He was now on foot.

He might have opted to lie low, but then again, the ferry was within walking distance. He'd want to leave the country if he could.

Warlow had two options. Flood the terminal with Uniforms or take a softly, softly approach with plain clothes officers.

He opted for the latter.

———

By the time they found the van and got organised for surveillance, it was near 11pm, and the ferry had not yet begun boarding.

The cacophony of disgruntled passengers and squalling infants ricocheted off the terminal's vaulted ceiling. Gil, his eyes stinging from hours of vigilant scrutiny, almost missed the flicker of movement. But there it was again. A furtive glance, a too-casual adjustment of a baseball cap from a figure trying very hard to be unobtrusive on a seat near the dark window facing the train station in the waiting area.

Gil side-stepped someone with a suitcase to keep his target in view.

'Possible sighting,' he murmured into his radio, edging closer through the sea of bodies.

It would have been less obvious if he'd had one of those tiny cuff mics the FBI always seemed to have in films. But instead, he had a radio in his hand that screamed law enforcement from thirty yards. That might have been what gave the game away.

The suspect's head snapped up, eyes locking with Gil's.

Time slowed, stretched taut like an elastic band, then snapped.

McDermot bolted, shoving aside a bewildered family, their cool box clattering to the floor.

Gil gave chase, dodging irate travellers and wayward luggage.

'Suspect on the move!' he bellowed into his radio. 'Heading towards the passenger check-in!'

———

OUTSIDE, at the vehicle check-in, Jess's hand flew to her earpiece.

'Gina, with me!' she barked, already in motion.

Gina fell in step as they sprinted towards the commotion inside in time to see McDermot barrelling towards the passenger boarding gate and the covered walkway that led to the ship some two hundred yards away.

But this was now an international border, and steel shutters guarded the way.

McDermot crashed into them shoulder first, but they didn't yield. Cursing, he ran outside through a door towards the cargo area, vaulting over a barrier to disappear into a labyrinth of lorries and containers.

Jess skidded to a halt at the passenger checkpoint.

'Which way?' she demanded.

A wide-eyed security guard, alerted by the activity, gestured in the direction of the cargo zone.

'Gina, take the left flank. I'll go right. Box him in. I'll let Evan know.'

They split up, Gina going on towards the ferry end of the parked-up vehicles, weaving between panelled vans and towering steel behemoths. Even though engines were off, some of the refrigerated lorries still idled, and the stench of diesel fumes caught in Jess's throat as she scanned for movement, her hand hovering near her baton.

A flash of movement caught her eye. A shape scrambling up the side of an articulated lorry, silhouetted against the arc light on the loading bays, hauling himself onto the roof.

'I've got eyes on the suspect!' Jess whispered into her radio. 'He's on top of a vehicle!'

McDermot moved, leaping from one lorry roof to the next with reckless abandon. Jess pursued on the ground, keeping pace as best she could while navigating the maze below. A sudden thump and clatter followed by a yelp of pain brought her to a halt next to a wagon.

Had he fallen?

Gina, alerted by the noise, appeared opposite Jess, and the women circled the truck.

Both heard the metallic clang.

Jess mimed a movement underneath the lorry.

Gina nodded.

It sounded as though McDermot had climbed up into the undercarriage of the trailer.

Jess quickly scanned the area. Her eyes landed on a coiled hose pipe attached to a nearby standpipe. She dashed towards it and wrestled with the hose: red, thick-walled, and heavy. She turned the water on, and the hose began to inflate, then signalled to Gina to speak.

'Come on out, McDermot. You're only making this worse for yourself.'

A muffled curse was the only response.

Jess returned, dragging the hose.

'Right,' she said. 'Let's see if we can flush him out.'

She turned the valve, sending a powerful jet of water surging forward.

Kneeling, both hands on the hose, Jess directed the stream underneath the trailer.

The effect was immediate A startled yelp echoed from within, followed by the sound of clattering metal.

'Bit chilly in there, is it?' Gina called out.

Suddenly, McDermot appeared, spluttering and dripping, hands up to fend off the jet of water Jess was playing up and down his chest, face, and, occasionally, below the belt. A move that caused him to double up with surprise and pain, judging from the groan.

Not exactly protocol, but she did it anyway.

Gina appeared behind him, shorter than him but armed with a baton. 'On the ground,' she ordered. 'Hands behind your head.'

Jess shifted the jet away but kept it on.

'Hands behind your head,' Gina yelled as McDermot fell face down.

Jess dropped the hose and joined Gina in an instant, kicking at the knife McDermot held in one hand and helping to subdue the waterlogged suspect.

'Move your hands down to behind your back,' Gina

ordered, producing her handcuffs to secure the coughing suspect.

'Piss off,' McDermot grunted and, in one movement, attempted to get up.

He'd got onto one knee when Rhys arrived and, with one long leg, stamped on his back to get him prone once more.

McDermot let out a grunt of air.

'Move again, and we will taser you,' Rhys said

Gina used her handcuffs.

Jess delivered the caution just as Warlow and Gil arrived with more backup.

'Rory McDermot, I'm arresting you on suspicion of the murder of Russell Milburn and Deena Barton. You do not have to say anything, but it may harm your defence if you do not mention when questioned something which you later rely on in court. Anything you say may be given in evidence.'

Warlow took in the scene of the dripping suspect and the puddles forming around the trailer.

'Well,' he said, eyebrows raised. 'Remind me not to have a water fight with you two.'

Gina couldn't suppress a grin. 'Thought he could use a bit of a cooldown, sir.'

Flashing blue lights were approaching at speed.

'Anything to say?' Gil asked as they got McDermot to his feet.

In response, the man spat at Gil's feet.

'Custody suite in Haverfordwest it is, then,' Gil said. 'They do a nice line in anti-spit masks, though I think the boys will have one in the van for you.'

As they drove him away a few moments later, Warlow stood with his team under the ferry terminal lights, the huge ship forming a backdrop.

'Too late for the pub to celebrate this one, but we will.' Warlow raised an imaginary glass. 'To a job well done. All of you.'

'Catrin needs a special mention,' Jess said.

'She does. Our secret weapon in the bowels of HQ.'

'Like Brains in Thunderbirds,' Rhys said.

'You hit the nail on the head there,' Gil replied. 'Except, she isn't a puppet, and doesn't wear glasses.'

'You know what I mean, sarge,' Rhys said.

'I do. Did I tell you I once went out with a marionette, but it didn't work out. I wanted an open relationship, but she fell to pieces when I said no strings attached.'

'Come on,' Warlow said, turning towards the waiting area and the warmth. 'I'm declaring this a banter-free zone. I need my bed.'

CHAPTER FORTY

'RIGHT, let's sum up where we are,' Buchannan said, his voice filling the seminar room. It was ten hours after they'd arrested McDermot.

Warlow stood, hands braced on the table.

'He's refusing to talk. No surprise there.'

Jess chimed in, 'I've been liaising with the Garda. Detective Inspector O'Brien says they've been investigating a food processing plant near the Northern Ireland border. Apparently, they've uncovered evidence of refugees being kept in squalid conditions, half starved and threatened with deportation if they complain. The place is owned by McDermot's uncle.'

'Christ,' Gil muttered.

'It gets worse,' Jess continued. 'Looks like our friend McDermot is a trader in people.'

Modern Slavery.

The room fell silent as the implications sank in.

Warlow, seeing the horror in the eyes of his team, felt a surge of pride. There could be no mitigation here. They'd caught a monster.

'And we think McDermot killed Milburn?'

'Tannard has his van, sir,' Rhys explained. 'There is some

evidence of damage to the passenger side bumper and wing. It'll take a while for forensics to do their thing, but he is the best fit.'

'It's likely Milburn's request for a site visit to the old building the day after the meeting at the community hospital triggered McDermot to act,' Jess added. 'He couldn't afford to let anyone inspect the place before he got the people they were holding in there away, plus any evidence.'

'And how does the second murder victim, Barton, fit into all this?' Buchannan asked.

'Social media records,' Gina piped up. 'She and McDermot connected through a dating app about six months ago.'

'Catfishing?' Buchannan asked.

Gina shrugged.

Warlow's face darkened.

'So, he's used the old hospital as a likely spot to hold people before he got them across to Ireland. Then co-opted Barton to get access to the annexe?' Buchannan asked.

'Looks that way, sir.' Gina nodded.

'From Maryam's statement, it appears it all went south when Barton had a pang of conscience,' Warlow explained. 'My guess is she suspected what McDermot was going to do with them. As it was, he'd found the old mine halfway up the hill.'

The room went quiet.

They'd all visited that spot. A squalid hole in the ground with no daylight. The calls for help only audible to an old lady who heard them cry out at night when the machines that drowned out their noises during daylight hours shut off.

How easy would it have been to dismiss Ivy Pugh's reports as nothing but the ramblings of a confused old woman? But, as Gil had already said, they did not make them like Ivy anymore.

Buchannan cleared his throat. 'The Irish want McDermot extradited.'

McDermot had made a run for it. Callously abandoning his prisoners who may never have been found.

'No,' Warlow said firmly. 'He's ours. We've got him on a murder charge.'

'I agree.' Buchannan nodded. 'The CPS will have to weigh in, but it's like a sick case of top trumps. My recommendation, and it will be the Chief Constable's too, is that the Irish can have him after we've finished with him.'

'He'll never get parole,' Gil muttered.

'Then they'll be waiting a long time, won't they?' Jess said with a dangerous smile. 'What about the Leyshons?'

'We've released Ian,' Warlow said. 'As for Huw, it's up to the CPS whether there's enough for an extortion charge. No actual demands were made, so it's murky. But he's admitted to the acid attack. He'll be charged with that.'

'And the asylum seekers?' Gina asked.

A question that brought a much-needed smile to Warlow's lips.

'Being processed,' Buchannan replied. 'They're all Afghans. Genuine refugees. We found some of their paperwork in McDermot's van. They've been found accommodation.'

'Not exactly the promised land, is it?' Gina said. 'Like my dad says, the country is in a mess.'

Buchannan flicked his eyebrows up and flattened his mouth before replying, 'That, detective constable, is all relative.'

———

LATE MORNING AT THE HOSPITAL, three days after Ivy Pugh fractured her wrist and had it set, she went for a check-up X-ray. DC Gina Mellings willingly provided transport. Catrin met her there.

With her X-ray done and with a green flag from the orthopaedic surgeons and strict instructions on dos and don'ts, Gina and Catrin leant against a cream-coloured wall as Ivy approached Maryam's bed.

The patient looked a lot better.

Noises in the corridor outside faded to a background buzz.

Maryam's eyes, dark and expressive, widened as she recognised Ivy. Her voice, weak but filled with wonder, broke the silence in her broken English. 'You… you help me…'

Ivy nodded, her plastered arm in a sling, her eyes magnified behind thick glasses, bunched in a smile.

'I'm so glad you're alright, love,' she said, grinning.

Without warning, Maryam sat forward and pulled Ivy into a tight embrace. 'Thank you,' she whispered, her voice choked with emotion. 'You saved us. You saved my family.'

Ivy, initially startled by the sudden movement, softened into the hug, her good, un-plastered arm snaking across the shoulders of the woman in the bed.

She patted Maryam's back gently as the woman's tears fell freely, leaving damp spots on her hospital gown.

'No need to cry,' Ivy murmured. 'I just did what anyone would do.'

From their spot by the wall, Catrin and Gina exchanged a glance, both trying to think of anyone they knew who would have done what Ivy had done, and failing. And both fighting to hold back tears as they watched the deeply moving scene unfold before them.

In that moment, the barriers of age, culture, and circumstance melted, leaving only the raw, powerful connection of two human beings bound by a random act of kindness.

Ivy could have easily not answered that knock on the door. Even on answering it, no one would have blamed her for instantly slamming it shut. But she had done neither of those things. She had done the exact opposite and helped a total stranger without hesitation.

Gina turned to Catrin and whispered, 'Got a spare tissue, sarge?'

'Beginnings of a cold, Gina?'

'Something like that,' Gina replied.

'Must be catching.' Catrin blinked quickly and reached into her bag to fetch one for each of them.

As the day wound down at HQ, Gil approached Rhys's desk. The job Audi's keys jingled in his hand.

'Fancy a drive up to the Amman Valley?' he asked.

Rhys looked up from his computer screen in surprise. 'What have we forgotten to do?'

'Thought I'd check in on young Megan. Our drone girl.'

Understanding dawned. Rhys's eyes lit up. 'Ah, right.' He nodded, pushing back his chair and reaching for his jacket. 'I'll come along.'

'You'll have the Audi to yourself first because we can go via Llandeilo, and I'll drop my car off there. Then you can chauffeur me across to Cwmgors.'

Gil dropped the car off at his, and they travelled the last eleven miles together, as they had done what seemed like a lifetime ago when they'd interviewed the Llewellyns the very first time.

'I'm beginning to think you're a bit of a softie, sarge.' Rhys grinned as Gil changed the radio channels.

'Watch it,' he growled. 'I've got a reputation to maintain.'

Gil settled on a channel. A Welsh channel playing Welsh songs. But these were with some laid back soft Latin beats.

'Carwyn Ellis,' Gil said. '*Ar Ol Y Glaw.*'

'It's not raining, sarge,' Rhys said.

'That's the song's name. After the rain. Suitable metaphor for this bloody case.'

And it was music to ease the soul.

As they headed east to keep a promise they'd made to a traumatised child, the tension of the day slowly evaporated, replaced by a sense of purpose and camaraderie. They spoke little because it had all been said.Neither man objected to this small act. Fulfilling a promise made to a traumatised child.

Sometimes the small things were as important as the big gestures.

LATER, Warlow sat in the dark, ensconced in the room at Ffau'r Blaidd that doubled as his office. The only illumination came from the laptop screen on the coffee table in front of him and a few lights dotting the blanketing darkness along the estuary, mirroring the stars above. He nursed a glass of red wine, its berry aroma mingling with the scent of wood smoke from the lit burner.

The laptop showed Tom's face, now mostly healed but still bearing faint traces of his accident. His arm, visible in the sling, a painful reminder of how close they'd come to tragedy.

'I'll be off for another few days, but then I can go in and help in out-patients at least.'

'You're sure?'

'Ask Jodie. I am driving her mad.'

'The woman is a saint.'

'Don't you start. Right, I'm off. I've got some reading to do for a seminar.'

'I thought you said another few days?' Warlow protested.

'It's a seminar, Dad. At least I can bulk up my CPD.'

'Fair enough,' Warlow agreed.

Tom narrowed his eyes. 'You don't know what that is, do you?'

'What do you reckon?'

Tom snorted. 'Continuing professional development.'

'Right. Off you go, then. I'll speak to you soon.'

The screen changed to his screensaver, and Warlow sighed deeply, his mind wandering to the darker corners of his career. The horrors he'd witnessed, the burden of responsibility that came with every case and that threatened to overwhelm him occasionally.

Threatened but never succeeded.

He pondered the fine line between success and failure, how a single misstep could mean the difference between justice served and a killer walking free.

And still he hadn't told Tom. About the dizzy spells, the swoops. Nor Jess either. Just sat on it, as if that made it noble. As if silence was strength. It didn't do to dwell on these things, he knew, and yet being human meant inevitably replaying those moments of doubt and uncertainty occasionally.

'Stop right there with the sighing,' Jess interjected, entering the room with her own glass of red.

He turned to look at her. 'I can't help thinking that if I had not gone to London, perhaps I'd have chased up McDermot's missing statement—'

'Tom needed you. That's not a weakness, Evan.'

'But we could have missed McDermot completely...' Warlow began, his voice trailing off as he stared into the depths of his wineglass.

'Excuse me? We caught the sod thanks to the team you've built,' Jess said, settling onto the arm of Warlow's chair. She placed a hand on his shoulder. 'It's not a crime to care about your kids. Nor to care about the murdered victims and the people that are left behind. That's what makes you good at your job, DCI Warlow. It's not a flaw, it's your strength.'

Warlow looked up at her.

Cadi lifted her head up from her bed, wondering what the fuss was about.

'Your team solved this case because you've instilled those values in them. They're not just following orders, they're following your example.'

Warlow set down his glass and arched his back. 'I suppose you're right.'

'I know I'm right,' Jess said.

'You're a good cheerleader. Do you have the uniform to go with it?'

That earned him a very blank look.

'But cases like this, they get under your skin,' Warlow said.

'Of course, they do,' Jess replied. 'They're bound to. Remember what you said to Rhys the day you came back for the coastal path case, and I quote. "The day you stop feeling affected by these things is the day you should hand in your badge."'

A tiny smile played over Warlow's lips. 'Using my own words against me. Below the belt.'

'Compassion is in short supply these days. But it's what

makes you good at your job, Evan. It's what makes you a good dad, too. Tom and Alun know that. I do, too. Even Molly.'

'Molly? Now that's an acid test if ever there was one.' Warlow grinned.

Cadi, once again drawn by some canine brand of emotional intelligence, appeared at Warlow's elbow and nudged his hand. For a moment, the warmth in the room seemed to come from more than just the fire. It radiated from the connection between these sentient beings. A dog and two people, bound by respect and shared values, and something else that neither of the two humans, at least, had thought they'd ever find again.

Warlow reached out, one hand on the dog's head, the other covering Jess's hand.

'But thank you,' he said. 'I think I needed to hear that.'

'The builders want me call in to chat about flooring. Will you come with me tomorrow? We could grab a bite at the pub afterwards?'

An image rose in Warlow's mind: Jess's half-built cottage in the village of Rosebush, a walk in the old quarry with Cadi bounding ahead on a muddy trail, her tail wagging with unbridled joy. The promise of a good meal at a zinc-roofed pub at the end of the walk and a cool pint to wash away the day's troubles.

It was in these simple pleasures that Warlow found his anchor, his respite from the complexities of his work. Life didn't need to be a constant battle against the darkness. Sometimes, the best remedy was the most straightforward: fresh air, good company, and the comfort of familiar surroundings.

A small smile tugged at the corners of Warlow's mouth.

'Now you're talking my kind of language,' he replied, feeling the tension in his shoulders ease at the prospect of a new day and what it might hold.

———

THANK you for reading this book. If you've enjoyed this trip to the Hipposync universe, the adventure continues with **DRUID'S MOOR:**

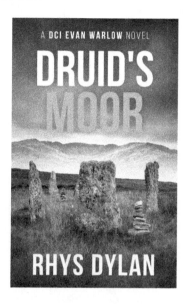

DRUID's MOOR

A girl vanishes. A farmer stumbles upon her, wandering near ancient standing stones, whispering of "the other ones." A detective, weary and unwell, is drawn into a case that feels far too familiar.

As Evan Warlow and his team dig deeper, they uncover hints of ritualistic crimes, hidden graves, and a network of the powerful and the corrupt—all of whom are willing to kill to protect their secrets.

As the fog rolls in and the case grows darker, one thing is certain—the past is never truly gone.

CAN YOU HELP?

WITH THAT IN MIND, and if you enjoyed it, I do have a favour to ask. Could you spare a moment to **leave a review or a rating**? A few words will do, but it's really the only way to help others like you discover the books. Probably the best way to help authors you like. Just visit my page on Amazon and leave a few words.

AUTHOR'S NOTE

This story is, in many ways, a return.

A Word With the Dead is set in a part of Wales I know intimately—towns shaped by coal, chapel, and community, and by a history that's often as bruised as it is proud. I grew up among people like those you'll meet in these pages. People who carry their humour close and their hurts closer. People who, like the places they inhabit, are caught between the tug of the past and the push of the present.

At its core, this book reflects communities grappling with the slow erosion of services, the quiet dismantling of institutions that once held them together. The Russell Milburn storyline—centred around NHS restructuring—echoes real conversations I've heard time and again. About fairness, about loss, about how easy it is for decisions made far away to rip through people's lives close to home.

There's a thread of anger here, yes—but also care, humour, and resilience. The kind I've witnessed all my life.

This isn't just a murder mystery. It's about what happens when old loyalties are tested by new realities. When the past isn't quite the sanctuary it's made out to be.

And while Warlow and his team may be fictional, the truths they encounter are anything but.

All the best,

Rhys

P.S. For those interested, there is a glossary on the website to help with any tricky pronunciations.

Only one thing is for certain; Warlow will not rest until he finds out.

———

By joining the club, you will also be the first to hear about new releases via the few but fun emails I'll send you. This includes a no spam promise from me, and you can unsubscribe at any time.

ACKNOWLEDGEMENTS

As with all writing endeavours, the existence of this novel depends upon me, the author, and a small army of 'others' who turn an idea into a reality. My wife, Eleri, who gives me the space to indulge my imagination and picks out my stupid mistakes. Tim Barber designs the covers, Sian Phillips edits, and other proofers and ARC readers sort out the gaffes. Thank you all for your help. Special mention goes to Ela the dog who drags me away from the writing cave and the computer for walks, rain or shine. Actually, she's a bit of a princess so the rain is a no-no. Good dog!

But my biggest thanks goes to you, lovely reader, for being there and actually reading this. It's great to have you along and I do appreciate you spending your time in joining me on this roller-coster ride with Evan and the rest of the team.